THE CHATAINE'S GUARDIAN

THE CHATAINE'S GUARDIAN

A NOVEL BY
ROBIN HARDY

WORD BOOKS
PUBLISHER
WACO, TEXAS

A DIVISION OF
WORD, INCORPORATED

THE CHATAINE'S GUARDIAN
A Novel by Robin Hardy

Scripture quotation on page 9 is from the Revised Standard
Version of the Bible (RSV), copyright 1946, 1952, © 1971 and 1973
by the Division of Christian Education of the National Council of
the Churches of Christ in the U.S.A. Scriptures quoted within
the body of this book are the author's own paraphrase.

Library of Congress Cataloguing in Publication Data:

Hardy, Robin, 1955–
   The chataine's guardian.

   I. Title.
PS3558.A62387C48   1984   813'.54   84-7311
ISBN 0-8499-0383-1
ISBN 0-8499-2990-3   (pbk.)

Printed in the United States of America

to Steve and Stephanie

ACKNOWLEDGMENTS

There are many gracious people who must be mentioned here. . . .

To Ernie Owen, Al Bryant, Pat Wienandt, and the many at Word Books who carried out the publication of this book;

To my friend and editor Anne Christian Buchanan, whose skillful help made a good manuscript better;

To O. Stanley Miller and Dennis Hill, who created the beautiful cover;

To Beverly Phillips and Dr. Phil Van Auken, whose unreasonable enthusiasm over an early draft gave me the audacity to go on;

To Dr. and Mrs. Thomas L. Moore—my brother Tom and his wife, Cyndie—whose incisive criticism forced me to do yet another rewrite;

To my family, especially my parents John and Joyce Moore, my Waco pastor Dr. Charles Dixon, John and Denise Harlan, and friends at Western Heights Baptist Church who were encouragers and prayer warriors;

To Rev. Gerald Tidwell and the members of First Baptist Church of Durant, Oklahoma, who welcomed us into their fellowship—

To all these people I owe a great debt of gratitude.

And to the Father of lights, from whose unbounded imagination came creativity beyond my ability and insights beyond my wisdom, I owe a debt beyond repayment.

He who dwells in the shelter of the Most High,
   who abides in the shadow of the Almighty,
will say to the Lord, "My refuge and my fortress;
   my God, in whom I trust."
For he will deliver you from the snare of the fowler
   and from the deadly pestilence;
He will cover you with his pinions,
   and under his wings you will find refuge;
   his faithfulness is a shield and buckler.
You will not fear the terror of the night,
   nor the arrow that flies by day,
nor the pestilence that stalks in darkness,
   nor the destruction that wastes at noonday.

A thousand may fall at your side,
   ten thousand at your right hand;
   but it will not come near you.
You will only look with your eyes
   and see the recompense of the wicked.

Because you have made the Lord your refuge,
   the Most High your habitation,
no evil shall befall you,
   no scourge come near your tent.

For he will give his angels charge of you
   to guard you in all your ways.
On their hands they will bear you up,
   lest you dash your foot against a stone.
You will tread on the lion and the adder,
   the young lion and the serpent you will trample under foot.

"Because he cleaves to me in love, I will deliver him;
   I will protect him, because he knows my name.
When he calls to me, I will answer him;
   I will be with him in trouble,
   I will rescue him and honor him.
With long life I will satisfy him,
   and show him my salvation."

Psalm 91 (RSV)

1

I am Penuel. This is my account to you of what I have witnessed and done in accordance with your instructions regarding Deirdre of Lystra.

As you know, Deirdre was heir and Chataine to Surchatain Karel, ruler of Lystra. At that time the Continent was fractured into many small, independent states, each with its own lord, laws, and army. Before they were united under the great Ruler, each jealously defended its own borders and rule.

I will commence this narrative with the day during Deirdre's tenth year that her father Karel assigned a guardian, Roman, to ward her. . . .

The nursemaid sighed as if to fortify herself and opened the door separating her room from the Chataine's sleeping room. She sighed again as she saw what she expected to see: total disarray in the elegant room that had been perfect when she had put the Chataine to bed the night before. She bent to pick up a velvet overrobe and little brocade slippers. "I must speak to the guard about not letting her out of her room at night," she muttered. She gathered other items that obscured the thick-woven rug: dresses tried on and discarded; gold jewelry laid out in the semblance of a face; a platter with pastry crumbs on it, purloined from the kitchen.

Clearing this litter uncovered something else—a crude stick doll, like those the village children played with. "Ugh!" The nursemaid lifted it with two fingers and tossed it into the faintly glowing embers of the fireplace.

Turning to the windows in the far wall, she drew apart the heavy velvet draperies and opened the shutters. Early morning air and light filled the close chamber. "Chataine, dear, wake up," she said to the massive canopy bed. There was a child-sized lump under piles of downy quilts, but it did not move.

She crossed over to the bed and pulled back the quilts to look down on her charge. Slender little form and delicate little features; fair, creamy skin and thick wheat-colored tresses—who could be angry at such a child? Then the nursemaid saw her own missing necklace, her one piece of jewelry, wrapped around the little wrist. Sighing again in exasperation, she unwound it, urging, "Chataine, wake up."

"Go away, Nanna," the child mumbled, pulling up the quilts.

"You must get up now, dear," the nursemaid insisted, throwing the covers back.

Deirdre shrieked, "Nanna! What are you doing? I said leave me alone!" She yanked the quilts back over herself.

Nanna said, "Chataine, today is a special day. Your father has summoned you to an open audience this morning. I must get you dressed."

"An open audience?" repeated Deirdre, alarmed. "Why?" Usually, whenever her father wanted to see her other than at table, he merely summoned her to his chambers. An open audience meant that he had something to tell her from his throne in the audience hall, and all of the court would be gathered to hear it. It was a scary prospect for a child of ten.

"Your father is assigning you to the care of a guardian today." Nanna's round face seemed to go taut—wrinkles and all—and Deirdre discerned that she disapproved.

"But Nanna, why? You are my guardian."

The nursemaid raised her eyebrows. "Your father has evidently decided you need more protection than an old woman can give."

"Nanna . . . does this mean I will never see you again?" Deirdre's eyes misted.

"No, dear, of course not. I will still be here to dress you and attend you. You will need the sol—uh, the guard only when you leave the palace grounds."

Deirdre caught the slip and wrinkled her nose in disgust. "Father is giving me over to a *soldier?*" Soldiers were different from the palace guards. The Cohort—the guards—were selected from the standing army or from the town at large to serve inside the palace as a special unit. They were picked on the basis of youth, a pleasing appearance, and refined manners, and they dressed in much finer clothes than the common soldiers. Appointment to the Cohort required no special skill in warfare or service. Rather, Deirdre's father often used it to repay favors owed to prominent townspeople. All Deirdre had observed of the soldiers, however, was that they were big and sweaty and usually covered with dust.

Nanna patted her hand reassuringly and sat on the bed. The shifting mattress tilted Deirdre into her plump side. "Your father has hand-picked this one for you. I am sure he has selected the best to be found. He will take good care of you, dear. I know it."

Deirdre peered into Nanna's face to see if she believed what she had just said, but the nurse had already turned briskly to the business at hand: "Now up and let me dress you, Chataine." As Nanna helped her don lacy linen underclothes and a rose-colored dress with many folds, Deirdre's round blue eyes widened in apprehension. She envisioned her father handing her over to a great hairy brute and ordering, "Now teach her to mind!"

She began to whine. "I promise to be good, Nanna, if you'll let me stay with you."

"Poor dear," murmured Nanna, tying on the Chataine's little cap. "Don't worry. I will see to it that this—this soldier understands how to treat you." The nursemaid took her hand to lead her quickly down the cool stone corridor to the great stairway. Descending, Deirdre could see people crowding from the foyer to get into

13

the audience hall. They parted like a furrow to let her into the hall. It was an ornate room, with oaken paneling and bronze sconces. Costly needleworks in brilliant colors hung centered in each oak panel. As they passed one needlework, Deirdre glanced at it and took comfort. It was a large tapestry depicting herself in the garden with a white horse and hound. It reassured her she was someone of position.

Leaving Nanna in the crowd, she advanced with trepidation up the deep purple runner to the black marble dais supporting a massive bronze throne. This was the Surchatain's judgment seat, from which he pronounced sentences and appointments.

Announcement of an open audience always drew a large crowd of courtiers, palace officials, and wealthy notables from the town of Westford, which was clustered around the palace. One never knew—the Surchatain at one time would single out a deserving person for praise and reward; more often, however, he pronounced judgments of death by hanging.

They waited. Deirdre took her position near the front, shifting from one foot to the other. Then the murmur of the crowd hushed as the crimson-robed Counselor, Eudymon, entered and stood before the dais. Always straight, poised, and correct, the Counselor was the perfect statesman. His black hair, tinged with grey, was smoothed back to show a high, fine forehead. Deirdre did not like him. He was always thinking.

Eudymon announced: "The High Lord and reigning Superiority of the independent state of Lystra, the gracious and beneficent Surchatain Karel." In one wave the crowd dropped to their knees. The Surchatain entered in a swirling purple mantle, the symbol of highest authority, and sat on the bronze throne. The audience stood.

Karel at forty was slight of build but quick and tough. His movements were emphatic and his eyes habitually angry. Now those eyes went straight to his daughter. "Deirdre." She stepped up and bowed low before him, as instructed. He looked her over for a moment. "Deirdre, you are my Chataine and my only heir" (he paused and tightened his lips) "and I cannot risk losing you by accident or design in this perilous country. You are no longer a baby, and I cannot hope to keep you shut up safe in the palace

14

forever. Therefore, I am assigning a guardian to you. He shall watch over you every moment that you are outside the grounds. *However*, he is not your servant; he answers to me alone. And this is he." Karel gestured through the crowd. A young man in common soldier's garb stepped up before the dais. "He is called Roman."

Deirdre looked. He was tall and solid. He looked middle-aged to her eyes, but actually had turned twenty-two a few months before. He had thick, straight black hair and brown skin. His face was, she thought, incredibly ugly—craggy and lined, with a broad nose and heavy brow. He stood silently, regarding her also.

Then Deirdre realized her father was addressing the soldier: "Here is your charge. And here is your vow: Do you, Roman, swear to guard and protect the Chataine Deirdre with your life whenever she is out of the palace, until she is married or until such time as you are relieved of your duty?"

"I do, High Lord." The voice that came out of that rough face was soft and very deep.

The Surchatain continued, "And do you swear to obey all my instructions and prohibitions to you regarding her?"

"Yes, High Lord."

"So be it. I have but a few last words of warning to you. If she is injured while in your care, you will be flogged. If she is injured severely, or kidnapped, or killed, you will be executed. And if there is any impropriety in your manner toward her—if you so much as touch her wrongly—you will be executed by torture. Do you understand?"

"I understand, High Lord."

"Then this audience is ended." Karel rose to leave, and the spectators fell on their knees again. "Counselor, to my chambers." The two strode out without a glance behind.

The crowd melted away, some glancing curiously at the Chataine and the soldier. Deirdre stood evaluating Roman. He stood looking at her. "I want to go out and play," she said.

The Chataine kicked her pony, urging him past Roman's mount. She could not possibly hope to outrun him, but at least she wanted to let him know who was in the lead. Then an inspiration struck her.

"I want to go down and play with the village children." The villagers—the poorest element of Westford—lived in huts clustered on the branch of the river. Those children welcomed her in their games, while the town children inexplicably shunned her.

"No, Chataine; your father has expressly forbidden that."

"He need not know." She directed her pony toward the valley, but Roman's charger cut her off. "I cannot let you do what your father has forbidden. You know that."

She eyed him petulantly, then shook her long hair. "If you do not let me go, I will tell him I fell from my pony and hurt myself." She had heard her father's warning to him, and thought it might prove useful.

"If he believes you, he will have me flogged," Roman replied. "But I still will not allow you to play in the village, so it will have gained you nothing. Besides, I do not believe you are a liar."

She stared at him. Was he mocking her? But his face was unreadable. He glanced at her, then turned his horse toward the high crest of the hill on their right, up and away from the valley. He led up the long, winding path to the crest and she followed. Looking down over the bluff, Deirdre reveled in the panorama spread before them. Her father's orchards and fields connected in a brilliant patchwork that met with the forest on one hand and the west fork of the river on the other. The Passage, many called it, for it was the only river emptying on the southern coast large enough to navigate. The Passage divided itself north of Westford and formed a lake on the eastern branch before trickling its way to the Sea through high rocky cliffs in eastern Lystra. The west fork was stronger, forming a large delta of rich farmlands and natural ports. For that river, and the trade it spawned, Lystra was highly envied by her neighbors.

Surrounding a branch of the river Deirdre saw mushrooms—no, the thatched houses of the villagers. Smoke curled up in wisps from cooking fires, around which moved little people and animals. The forest was also beyond the village, stretching out to infinity. It strained her eyes to try to take it all in.

Roman pointed down to the village. "You see how many of the villagers use the fast water upstream for bathing and toileting. Then downstream, in the gentler waters, is where the children often play, and where they have of late been drawing water. It is no coincidence that many have become ill and died. We have repeatedly warned them about fouling their water, but many will not listen. It is not safe for you to play there.''

Deirdre listened as he talked, watching him gesture. In all the times that she had been refused permission to go to the valley, this was the first time any explanation had been given. She had always assumed it was because the Chataine was too exalted to run with villagers. "Why has no one ever told me that?" she demanded. Roman only shrugged. She studied him thoughtfully.

In his chambers, the Surchatain rubbed his hand through his wooly brown hair and dropped onto a couch. Eudymon stood before the fire, watching him out of the corner of his eye. He seemed to be debating whether to speak or wait for the Surchatain to open. Finally, the Counselor offered, "You have made a wise decision in appointing her a guardian. That is sufficient action to take on the basis of a mere rumor.''

"Rumors such as this are too dangerous to treat lightly," Karel answered. "If Corneus *has* hired an assassin, and if he succeeds in killing my heir, upon my death the whole province will be spoil for the highest bidder. And even though his country is small, Corneus controls much wealth. A coup such as this would be child's play for him.''

"True." Eudymon looked concerned. "And you cannot appoint another successor while Deirdre yet lives. Which will be for many years," he added quickly at Karel's look.

The Surchatain nodded slowly and murmured, "But . . . have I done enough?" He did not seem to address the question to Eudymon.

"Perhaps you should remove her to safety for a while," the Counselor suggested.

"What place is safe, if not my own country?" Karel snorted.

Eudymon inclined his head. "Your law is well established here, High Lord. But I was thinking that perhaps she would find safety if taken in secret to live in the palace of her betrothed—whom you shall select, of course.''

Karel slammed his fist upon a nearby table. "That is the catch! There is that insane, worthless law my late wife sealed into the books—that the Chataine shall have the final say as to whom she marries! Regina made it law when I was in Ooster and the period of revocation passed before I was aware of it. I cannot rescind it now!" His fury at the years-old deception flamed anew. "Who knows what choice that child may make? He may end my influence upon her!"

"Surchatain—if I may remind you, you are still Ruler. You will guide her choice, gently or otherwise."

Karel stopped and let his anger dissipate in that thought. "Yes . . . and that is years away. For now, Counselor, no one must think we pay any heed to this rumor."

"Certainly, High Lord." Eudymon inclined his head again. "And I trust that your selection will prove adequate as her guardian."

"I do not trust, Counselor. I will watch him with eagle's eyes to see how he proves. You are dismissed."

That evening, Roman joined the Surchatain's table for dinner. As Deirdre's guardian, he would enjoy the privilege of eating in the presence of the Surchatain every night thereafter. He sat next to the Counselor and across from Deirdre.

As the food was served and they ate, she watched him closely. He had good table manners for a soldier, though he used the wrong hand. He ate quietly, speaking very little, and it occurred to Deirdre that he must be nervous eating at the Surchatain's table for the first time. But he picked up the right utensil for the right dish, and even used the finger bowl correctly. However, when the squid was served, he cocked an eyebrow at his plate and looked to the Counselor. Eudymon did not look up or speak, but properly sliced and ate his. Roman followed his lead.

Abruptly, Karel addressed his daughter: "Deirdre, what do you think of your new guardian?"

"I suppose he will do," she said haughtily, not looking at Roman.

"You are not pleased with him?" probed her father.

18

"Not really," she sniffed.

"Good! Then he is just what you need. You have been manipulating your servants for too long. I am glad to find someone who can control *you*." A ripple of laughter went around the table and Deirdre blushed angrily. *We will see,* she thought.

After the meal she intercepted Roman. "Take me out to Willowring Lake!" That was a great pleasure she had rarely been allowed in the past.

"Chataine, you know your father does not allow you out of the palace after nightfall."

"But with you to protect me, what could happen?"

"Any number of things."

"If you don't take me, I will start screaming." She pursed her lips determinedly. This maneuver had worked well for her at other times with Nanna.

"As you wish. But first, Chataine, consider. If you scream, the guards will come and take us to your father. He will ask what happened. You will have your say and so will I. After what he said tonight, whom do you think he will believe?" Deirdre looked away. He added, "I promise that I will take you to the lake tomorrow."

She brightened. "Very well. You are dismissed." He bowed slightly and left her. She ascended the stone stairway to her chambers in deep concentration. He was going to be a challenge. As Nanna helped her undress, she had a thought. "Where does Roman sleep?"

"In his room, Chataine."

"I know that," Deirdre said impatiently. "Where is his room?"

"That is none of your concern, dear."

"But where is it?" Once an inspiration had seized her, it would not let go.

"I think it is in the lower corridor by the kitchen. Several of the high-ranking soldiers have rooms there."

"I know the corridor. Which room is his?" She pressed the point because she knew Nanna would tell her. She always did.

The nursemaid sighed. "It is the one next to the courtyard door. The one with a door that bolts." That bolts! That was unusual. Few beyond the Surchatain's family and palace officials were given that privilege. "Now listen, Deirdre, you must not go down there at any time. Your father has made it clear that you have no business in that area of the palace. Promise me you will not go down there." Nanna's tone was so serious that Deirdre hastily promised. But as Nanna extinguished the light and closed the door, the Chataine was already plotting.

She lay awake for long minutes, waiting for the palace bustle to still. At last, when she felt things were quieted, she got up and pulled on her overrobe.

She listened at the door to Nanna's adjoining room. All was quiet, so she tiptoed to the massive outer door of her receiving room and gingerly unbolted it, opening it only partway so as not to waken Nanna with loud creaks. Then she slipped into the dark corridor, stole past the slumbering guard, and stealthily descended the stairway. She made her way down passage after passage, flattening herself against the walls or behind doors when she heard voices or footsteps. At last—there was his corridor. She had almost stepped into it when a noise froze her. It sounded like a low groan, and came from the corridor ahead. She peeked around the corner.

What she saw intrigued her. It was Hana, one of the kitchen maids, wrapped up in the arms of a soldier. They were kissing in a way Deirdre had never seen. The soldier (who was it? she could not see) whispered in Hana's ear and she said, "No, no, not here. In the small clearing. I'll meet you there straightway." With one last kiss they parted ways.

The small clearing! Deirdre knew where that was. She located the courtyard door and hurried out. If she got there before they did, she could hide in the bushes and watch. For she felt sure the man was Roman.

She slipped out the rear gate, watching for the guard, and ran fifty paces to the forest's edge. It was a chilly night, but the Chataine wore a warm overrobe and shivered, rather, from excitement. How would she handle this? She envisioned confronting Roman with her knowledge, watching his stone face drop, and hearing him beg her not to tell her father. "Well, as you say," she would at last concede, "but from now on we will do things my way!"

The imagined scenario disappeared as Deirdre halted in the forest. Now, where was it? Oh yes, over there. She hurried to a tree, but found it was not the landmark she expected. Well, now, where . . . ? A chill ran through her as she spun around. She did not recognize any of these trees. She did not know where she was.

Fighting panic, she forced herself to stop and look around. Hesitantly, she started walking again—slowly, then faster, then—what was that? There arose in her mind the faint memory of a warning that there were wolves in this forest.

She stopped to listen, but could hardly hear over the pounding of her heart. *I must get my bearings,* she thought, and looked up to search the stars. Standing very still and scanning the sky, she calmed. It was an endless April night—clear, but dark, with only a waning moon. The wind breathed gently through the trees, like a soft voice calling her name . . . Deirdre! Deirdre! Wait—it *was* a soft voice calling her name! And she recognized the voice. "Here, Roman, I'm here," she called just as softly. In utter relief she watched a dark figure emerge from the trees, and she ran to him before she remembered herself.

Silently he led her back to the palace, then to the receiving room of her chambers. Nanna, waiting there, exclaimed, "Oh! You're safe!" and hugged her tightly.

But Roman was not to be dismissed. He threw aside his cloak and asked, "What were you doing out there?" His voice was calm but his eyes were angry.

She parried the question. "How did you find me?"

"When your nurse found your bed empty, she came to me. For some reason, she believed you had come to my room." He stopped and eyed her questioningly, but she said nothing, so he went on. "I found the courtyard door open, and your footprints in the mud leading out the rear gate. It was too dark to track you in the forest. I had to call for you." Why he regretted having to do that, he did not say.

But Deirdre turned to Nanna: "You found him in his room?"

"Yes, dear. I awakened him."

What a disappointment. It had not been Roman. Then she looked up and realized they were both waiting for an explanation. "I could not sleep, so I went out to walk."

Nanna started to protest, but Roman cut her off. "Chataine, I will not warn you again to stay inside the palace at night. And I do not say that as a jest. I am telling you that your life has been threatened!'' The conviction in his voice made her start. She looked to Nanna for reassurance, but saw Nanna blanching, looking to *her*. "Stay in your room at night, Chataine.'' He walked out. Nanna gathered her in.

2

I, Penuel, continue my report concerning Deirdre, the Chataine of Lystra. The morning after the Chataine ventured into the forest there was more than the normal buzz among the servants. Her nursemaid seemed jumpy, and Deirdre had to pump her longer than usual for information. . . .

"Nanna, what are all the servants talking about?"

"Why," the nursemaid laughed nervously, "how should I know?"

"You know everything, Nanna. What are they saying?"

"Nothing important, dear, that is certain."

"But what are they talking about?"

For a moment, Nanna did not answer. Then she sat Deirdre down. "Darling, when you were in the woods last night, did you see or hear anything—strange?"

Deirdre held very still. "No. Why?"

"One of the servants was murdered last night. They found her body this morning in the small clearing." Nanna's voice was a whisper.

"Who was it?" asked Deirdre, her eyes wide.

"Hana, a kitchen maid." Nanna rushed on, "Chataine, you must not tell anyone you were out there last night. Let's forget it ever happened. Promise me!"

"I promise," said the Chataine with utter sincerity.

Deirdre did not concentrate much on her studies that morning, thinking of Hana. *Poor Hana. Why would someone kill her? Roman said someone wanted to kill me,* she thought. But then her native skepticism surfaced. *He said that just to scare me into staying out of his way at night. He has other things to do at night. The soldiers are all busiest then. . . .*

Her tutor was speaking to her, scolding her, but she paid little attention to him. She did not have to—she had him cowed. "Chataine, you must do your sums," he pleaded.

"Rory, did you ever want to be a soldier?" she asked thoughtfully.

"Mercy, no," he frowned. "It's hard, dirty, dangerous work, and a soldier's pay is miserable. They live in those horrid barracks—even the officers only have little cells, and they all have to be running off to the border all the time."

"Roman does not seem to mind it. He seems proud of being a soldier."

"I guess if that is all you can do, you have to be proud of it," he sniffed.

"Do you know him?"

"I met him once at the tavern in town, but he did not have any time for *me*—or anyone else for that matter. He just sat by himself in a corner while everyone else was having a good time."

"Why? Is he shy?"

"Not really. He belongs to that amusing little sect who call themselves 'Followers of the Way.' They believe having fun is wicked, you know."

"Oh. What is the Way?"

"That is their religion—like the worship of Mithra, though not nearly so interesting. They worship a fellow who was executed and—they say—came back to life."

24

"Did he?"

"What?"

"Come back to life!"

"Of course not!" Rory snorted. "Anyone knows that is impossible. And they never could prove it. The whole thing is really so absurd." He lowered his voice and smirked, "We call them Christians."

"Oh." Deirdre wrinkled her nose and giggled.

That afternoon when Roman took her on the promised excursion to the lake, she asked him, "Why do you believe having fun is wicked?"

"What?" he exclaimed.

"Rory says you do not believe in having fun."

"Oh," he gave a short, ironic laugh. "Something as destructive as what Rory does is not fun."

"What *do* you do for fun?"

"Well, dine and talk with my friends . . . hear their stories and tell mine . . . hunt and ride with them."

"How is that different from what Rory does?"

"Chataine, I cannot explain that to you now. But what it boils down to is that Rory and his friends have their fun using other people, even if it harms them."

"Oh," she said. "Rory says that soldiers are really bad about using the village women—"

"I try to avoid using anyone," he interrupted. "And does Rory ever teach you any history or mathematics?"

"No," she laughed, and he shook his head. She decided she might like him after all. But she had questions. "Roman, do you really worship a man who came back from the dead?"

He blinked and paused. "Yes, you could say that."

"If he is alive, then where is he?"

"In Paradise, with the Father."

"Where is Paradise?"

"Beyond the skies, Chataine."

She squinted up at the bright blue expanse dotted with clouds and exclaimed, "How did he get up there?"

He faltered. "Well—by the power of God."

25

"Who is God?"

"His Father, and your Father above. The Creator of the heavens and the world and everything in them." He paused. "The One who loves you unfailingly."

Deirdre pursed her lips, thinking she had caught him in an untruth. She had never met God, so He could not love her. Besides, no one loved her like that. Suddenly she recalled the two lovers she had seen last night. "Did you hear about Hana?"

He absorbed the abrupt change of subjects and nodded. Then he glanced at her. "Did you see her last night?"

"No," she answered carefully. He looked at her more closely for a moment, but said nothing.

The path they were riding on ended at a grove of willow trees close to the lake. Roman dismounted and helped her off her pony. They began walking toward the grove, and Roman said, "I like to come here whenever I can. It is restful and—"

But Deirdre looked down at her feet and screamed. A snake slithered in the grass toward her. "Save me, Roman!"

"Chataine," he said gently, "it is only a grass snake. It will not harm you."

"Save me!" she insisted. Roman shrugged and tossed the snake away from her. Then he carried her back to her pony. She grinned triumphantly.

"Since there are so many dangers here," he said, "we had better return to the palace." She fussed, but he was firm.

The following morning, Deirdre made a halfhearted attempt at her lessons, then wandered down to the kitchen area. She overheard the head cook discussing with her staff what they needed from the market. Deirdre popped in: "I want to go! Let me go to market with you!"

"Go ask your guardian, Chataine," the cook said. Deirdre ran off to find him. Several times a week, the cook took her kitchen help to the market in town to buy what fruits and vegetables the Surchatain's fields did not supply, as well as fish, game, herbs for the physician's use, and other household items.

"Roman!" She jumped around him when he appeared at her summons. "The cooks are going to market! I want to go!"

"No, Chataine. It would be too difficult to watch you safely in the crowds. You can buy anything you want from the merchants who come here."

"Oh, Roman. I never get out. And the crowds are just a bunch of old women." Her big eyes filled with tears. "Please, Roman?"

He weakened. "Will you stay right by my side and do as I tell you?"

"Yes, yes, I promise!"

He sighed. "Very well, Chataine. Your pony will be too slow, however—you'll ride in front of me on my horse." She jumped up and down and clapped her hands. They met the cooks at the gate and together drove to market—Roman and Deirdre leading on his bay, the cooks following in their wagon.

When they arrived, Roman let her down off the horse, and Deirdre shot like a true arrow through the crowds. "Chataine! Deirdre! Come back here!" He raced after her. Several of the women around snickered at the sight of the soldier chasing the Chataine from cart to cart. He almost had her twice, but she slipped away from him, laughing, to run elsewhere. Finally, he seized her near the flower cart and hoisted her up under his arm. She was too weak with laughter to struggle—until she saw that he was taking her back to the horse. "No! Put me down! I'll stay with you, Roman."

"That is what you said before." He plopped her in front of the saddle and swung up behind her.

"Roman, please, don't take me back. I want to see the market."

"You will when you learn to obey me, Chataine."

She pouted. "If you do not let me go, I will—" He stopped her with a menacing look. "I don't like you, Roman! You are mean and ugly!" He did not respond, and they rode in sullen silence back to the palace, where he firmly deposited her with Nanna.

"Come, dear," she said soothingly, noting their grim faces, "now is a good time for me to teach you sewing."

"No," Deirdre pouted.

At the same time, Karel was meeting in his chambers with his Counselor. The Surchatain held a letter in his hand. "I wish to avoid this invitation," he stated. "Now, of all times, I do not wish to take Deirdre traveling, especially to see her uncle!"

Eudymon paused, selecting his argument. "You are right. She shall not go. What care we if he is offended?"

Karel breathed out heavily. "I cannot risk offending him. He is too powerful."

"Then may I suggest, Surchatain, that this is the purpose for which you appointed her a guardian?"

Karel studied his Counselor for a moment, then opened his door and instructed the guard, "Summon Roman."

He appeared momentarily, bowing to Eudymon and Karel as he entered: "You summoned me, High Lord?"

"Yes, Roman . . . I am sure you are becoming familiar with Deirdre's willfulness, by now."

"She is a lively child," Roman shrugged.

"True." A look of mild exasperation crossed Karel's face. "I wished to forewarn you that we will be traveling soon—Deirdre, too—and that how well you control her could be crucial."

Roman paused, then replied, "I am not alone in protecting her, Surchatain. God is with me. He will enable me to guard her."

Karel regarded him skeptically. "For her sake—and for yours—I hope that is true. Dismissed."

The atmosphere at the evening meal was somber and restrained. Karel seemed preoccupied with troubling thoughts, and no one wished to transgress his mood with levity.

Deirdre watched Roman intently through the meal. He appeared unaffected by the Surchatain's darkness, eating calmly, without a word, as was his style. Occasionally, he glanced up at her, and she grew puzzled to see amusement in his eyes.

At length Eudymon leaned toward Roman and whispered, for her benefit, "The Chataine seems smitten with you tonight, Captain."

Roman raised his eyes to her again and Deirdre quickly lowered her burning face. Then she glanced at her father and assumed an air of authority. "I wish to go riding to the lake tomorrow, Roman."

"I will be ready at your summons, Chataine," he answered cordially.

She looked again toward her father, but he apparently had not heard.

As the dinner was finished and the dishes removed, the Surchatain roused himself and looked around the table. "You people are all stale and sleepy tonight. You need some entertainment to awaken you." He turned to a guard standing nearby. "Summon Simien the magician!" Deirdre clapped and laughed. Simien was one of her favorites—he could do so many amazing things. As the guests around the table applauded and pushed back their chairs, Simien entered with a flourish and bowed low before the Surchatain at the head of the table. Karel nodded for the magician to begin.

"Lords and ladies," exclaimed Simien, spreading his arms, "I am indeed lowly entertainment for such an esteemed assembly. Yet, as the Surchatain has so graciously given his attention, I will respond with what gifts I possess. Behold—" and he touched his forefingers together before him, then slowly drew them apart. As he did, a shimmering golden line traced the path of his fingers in the air. He snapped his wrists and dropped his hands, but the golden line still hung in space. Some guests began to applaud, but he motioned for silence. Gingerly, he reached to the middle of the line and drew down on it. It opened like a tear, and he reached inside with his free hand. The guests gasped in astonishment as his hand and forearm disappeared beyond the shining opening.

"What have we?" he murmured, as if feeling around. "Ah! Lights to enliven the table!" And he threw out a handful of lighted candles which rested in the air above the table. Quickly, he thrust his arm in again. "More?" he muttered. "Yes!" he shouted, as he flung out a flask which, like the candles, hung suspended in the air. "Wine for your enjoyment!" The flask turned and out spilled a deep red wine. It poured and poured without ending, creating a river which ran down the middle of the table. ·

"And lastly, for your pleasure—song!" He ripped the tear open wide, and out flew a throng of skylarks in full song. They flew straight to the table and lighted on the candelabras. "Are you pleased?" he queried, and his audience clapped loudly, voicing amazement. Simien bowed dramatically, then with a snap of his fingers the illusions—the candles, the wine, and the birds—disappeared. The guests gasped and clapped louder.

"Now permit me to demonstrate, High Lord, that your guests have amazing powers of entertainment as well. Behold—" he gestured to one woman, who suddenly stood and began to sing with all the strength she possessed. She was also quite off-key, and the rest of the table roared in laughter. "And look!" Simien cried, gesturing to a man. While the woman sat abruptly, red-faced, the man immediately began a remarkable imitation of a rooster. He crowed and strutted and even tried to peck the table. Deirdre laughed until the tears ran down her face, then she glanced across at Roman. He was not laughing, nor even smiling. Neither was the Counselor beside him.

Deirdre suddenly left her seat to whisper in the magician's ear. The rooster sat, bemused. Simien smiled slyly as Deirdre took her seat, and he announced, "Lords and ladies, we have a special request from the Chataine for entertainment. Witness—" and he wheeled and pointed straight at Roman. The table waited breathlessly, but Roman did not move. He simply returned Simien's glare. The magician frowned and said, "Up, soldier, and dance!"

"No," Roman replied. Simien faltered and Deirdre gazed in astonishment at Roman. The guests looked around in silence.

"I see your magic has limits, Simien," Karel said severely, though he appeared pleased. "You are dismissed." The magician bowed stiffly and fled.

As Karel dismissed the guests, Deirdre turned to Roman. "How were you able to resist his command?" she demanded.

"I obey a higher command. Good evening, Chataine." He bowed and left her.

She was dumbly pondering what he meant when Nanna approached. "Chataine."

"What is it?" It irritated her to be interrupted when wrestling with mysteries.

"Your tutor tells me you have not been attending to your studies." (Deirdre made an ugly face.) "Now you know how important this is to your father! You go directly upstairs and prepare for tomorrow's lesson, or I will have to tell the Surchatain you need a new tutor. A harder one. Like Roman!"

Deirdre glanced at her darkly, but stiffened her lip and marched ahead of Nanna to her chambers. The nursemaid stood over her while she sat at a table and began scratching out sums on a soft wax tablet. Nanna watched her a moment, then nodded and turned toward her room. "I will come back shortly to check your progress," she promised before closing the door.

8 + 8 = 16, 8 + 9 = 17, 9 + 9 =   Deirdre scratched the numbers deeply into the wax, then finished with a row of angry Xs. Everyone ordered her about like she was a peasant child! She could never do anything she wanted, only what they demanded. Do your lessons! Do not go down to the village! Stay with Roman! Do not go down to the kitchen!—Her mind halted on that one and she let the stylus fall. What was so interesting in the kitchen that she should stay away from there?

She peeked out the door of her receiving room. The guard who was supposed to be on duty there was nowhere to be seen. Immediately she was out into the corridor, working her way down to the kitchen area. She paused then—what if she encountered the soldier she had seen with Hana? What if he were her murderer, and had seen Deirdre watching them? Her heart took to pounding as she considered the dangers she might meet in the kitchen. Forcing herself to go onward made her feel very brave. At least it was not as late tonight as it was when she slipped out before. Persons passing her in the corridors nodded or bowed courteously, but showed no suspicion. Why should they? This was her palace; she had every right to be in its corridors. She lifted her chin and progressed with authority.

Nearing the kitchen, she slowed timidly as she heard clatters, voices, and laughter. Large double doors stood open from the kitchen into this corridor, and she could not approach without being seen. Her confidence evaporated at this point; everyone knew she was not supposed to be down here. But then she saw a hiding place! She scooted along the wall to one of the doors and pulled it away from the wall enough to slip behind it, then eased it back in place. Here, in the triangle formed by the open door against the wall, she was hid from both the kitchen and corridor, and could peep through the crack between door and casing to watch the activity in the kitchen.

The first thing she saw was that the actual kitchen and cooking area comprised a small part of this large room. The greater part by far was filled with tables and benches to serve as a dining hall for the soldiers and servants.

There was much eating and laughing going on. Deirdre felt somewhat envious watching through the slit. Dinner for them was a festivity—no worrying about offending so exalted a person as the Surchatain, no qualms as to whether one was proper or not.

Deirdre twisted her neck to see further through the slit, and caught a glimpse of Roman near one of the far tables. He was standing, arms folded across his chest, talking with a group of soldiers who were eating. One of them asked him something, and he began an extended answer. As he talked, the soldiers around stopped eating one by one to listen to him. The din grew quieter, and Deirdre could discern a word here and there to match his gestures—"crowed like a rooster. . . . the Chataine. . . . to me and demanded, 'Get up, soldier, and dance!' " He finished telling of the magician's failure in a low voice, and the soldiers guffawed and clapped. He broke off from the group with a wry smile, heading toward Deirdre's door, but was stopped repeatedly by someone wanting a word with him.

Meanwhile, the story he had told circulated around the room until it was told to a group directly in front of Deirdre's peeping spot. At its conclusion, a very drunken soldier who sat with his back to Deirdre burped coarsely and shouted, "Good fer you, Cap'n!" Now you can stare down ol' High Lord Tightfist to give us poor soldiers a raise?"

The hall became uncommonly still and Roman turned to the fellow with a retort on his lips. At once, though, he swallowed it and said lightly, "Come now, Forster, keg up your drivel before it gets you hanged. You are a loyal soldier when you're sober—once in a fortnight."

A laugh went around the room, but Forster lunged up drunkenly and slammed his fist on the table. "Curse it, I mean it! I'm fed up with being spit poor while that bast—"

"Forster! Silence!" Roman commanded. The imperative sat the drunken man down. Roman's glare did not let up, however, and Deirdre saw with a gasp that it was not directed at the soldier but at the crack through which she peeked.

She backed out of the door and fled back through the corridor.

She ran a straight path to her chambers and bolted the door, then sat panting and gathered up the fallen stylus and tablet.

An instant later Nanna opened her door and looked into the outer chamber where Deirdre sat. "Well!" The nursemaid looked rather surprised. "I am so glad you obeyed me for once. That is enough work for tonight, dear. Come let me dress you for bed."

"Yes, Nanna." Deirdre humbly laid the instruments aside and followed her into the sleeping room.

The following morning she studiously avoided the mere chance of encountering Roman. She summoned Rory to her chambers for her lessons rather than risk meeting Roman in the corridor on her way to the library. She worked so intently on her lessons as to amaze her tutor. When they were through, she opened the door to dismiss him and choked to see her somber guardian waiting for her in the corridor. "I am ready to take you to the lake as you ordered, Chataine," he said without expression.

Rory was watching. She cleared her throat. "Yes, Roman, I will be out directly." She closed the door and selected a jacket from the tall mahogany wardrobe, wishing she could jump in it and hide forever. But he would just wait there until she came out.

Resolutely, she opened the door. He nodded to her. She followed him to the courtyard, where her little pony stood saddled beside his great horse.

They rode at a leisurely walk in absolute silence. Periodically, Roman had to rein his horse to a stop to wait for her to catch up; his charger outpaced her pony two strides to one. "Are you well today, Chataine?"

She started. "Yes—of course. I was only worried that you would be angry—" she caught herself in confusion. It was totally unlike her to blurt out the truth so.

"Why would I be angry?" He cocked his head at her.

She cast around for an answer to satisfy him and save herself: "Umm—well—taking me to the lake after what happened last night." Had he not seen her after all?

"Oh, you mean Simien?" He smiled in his wry way. "I am not angry. I do not blame you for testing me."

"Oh, good." She was sincerely relieved. "It made a good story, though, did it not?'' she chattered, then caught her error at his abrupt look.

"Was that you, then, behind the door last night?'' he demanded.

She forced out tears. "Roman, I am sorry—'' she began to plead with him not to tell her father.

But he laughed outright, shaking his head. "Thank you, dear God!'' To her, he said, "I am so glad it was you, and not someone who would use it to bring the soldiers to grief. Chataine, I beg you—please do not tell Forster's foolish words to anyone.''

Her mouth dropped open, but she recovered enough to consider pressing her advantage—should she tell him now that it meant doing things her way? "I will not tell anyone, Roman,'' was what came out instead.

"I thank you, Chataine.'' He smiled openly at her in a way that made her feel strangely warm. "Now let us see what we can find of interest here.'' They were already at the willow grove. She slid off her pony and walked beside him toward the trees. A flock of bleating sheep scooted away from them; she noticed with mild interest a lamb which had gotten itself hopelessly entangled in underbrush. Roman noted it, too. He bent down beside it and patiently worked its little legs free. He held it just long enough to rub his face in its soft fleece, then let it down to run bleating to its mother.

Deirdre watched him, immobilized in thought. She had never seen a man evidence such regard for things little or easily broken. Lambs caught in briar and drunken soldiers sounding off their despair . . . little girls with big tempers. . . . He gestured her to follow him through the grove to a part of the lake she had not seen before. She said "Oh!'' at the sight of an array of lovely flowers with heads bowing at the water's edge. Some were red, some white, some a mottled color. "How pretty! What are they?''

"Lilies. I was told they were planted for you to enjoy.''

"Then why have I never seen them?'' she demanded, affronted.

"You have to go find them,'' he laughed. "They will not come to you.'' Then he made her bend down among the lilies near the water. "Be still and watch.''

She waited breathlessly. A solitary mosquito buzzed close to the surface and suddenly a little stream of water shot up and knocked the mosquito down. A small fish snapped it up and disappeared. Deirdre gave a little cry. "What was that?"

"They call it an archer fish, because of the way he shoots his prey down. The lake seems full of them now, though at first there were only a few. Sailors brought them from beyond the Sea for you, at your birth."

"For me?" She sat back on her heels to look at him. "I have never seen them either."

He shrugged. "They were here." He raised his eyes and looked over the lake contemplatively. "Remind me to bring bread crumbs next time we come. We will train the ducks and swans to eat from our hands." As he spoke, he nodded toward the birds dotting the far shore.

Deirdre squinted across the lake and sighed. "Are those mine, also?"

"Of course," he said, then knitted his brows. "Deirdre, do you not realize that everything your father has is yours? All will someday be in your hands, for good or ill."

She could not find words to respond, so they both were silent for a time. Then her eye caught a floating bit of brown, and she walked over to investigate. "A boat!" she exclaimed. "Roman, take me out in the boat!" He hesitated and she began her pleading. "Please, Roman, please?"

"You must sit still in it," he said sternly, dragging it up on shore. "If you tip us over and I have to return you to the palace dripping wet, I might as well go ahead and drown myself here." She snickered. He held the boat steady for her to clamber in, then he stepped in and took up the oar.

He guided them leisurely out onto the lake, and Deirdre lay back in the prow, sighing in contentment. The sun was warm, reflecting in pieces on the gentle waves. The fragrance of the lilies found her; the quacks of the distant ducks reached her ears. She turned her face up to the wide blue sky and billowy clouds. "Don't you wish you could stay out here forever like this?" she murmured, closing her eyes.

He smiled slightly. "If you did, you would miss greater pleasures to come."

She opened her eyes a little. "I do not know that any will ever come to me."

"A child of ten, already so cynical about life?" he queried, cocking an eyebrow. "Yet we have been promised, 'What no eye has seen, nor any ear heard, nor the heart of man imagined, is what God has prepared for those who love Him.' "

She squinted at him. "Do you have that?"

"Not yet. Not fully. But it is coming."

Laying her head back again and closing her eyes, she sighed, "I like to dream, too."

After a few moments of restful gliding, she opened her eyes and lazily scanned the lake. "Roman, take me to the far shore!" she suddenly demanded.

"No," he said.

"Why not?"

"There is nothing over there for you to see." He turned the boat toward their launch point.

"Not already!" she complained.

"Your nursemaid will have seizures if I do not return you to the palace by noon for your meal." She snickered again, allowing him to tie the boat and lift her out.

As they rode homeward, Roman again paused every now and then to allow her pony to catch up. "Curse it!" she muttered, kicking her pony hard.

"What?" he exclaimed.

"How can I ride with you on this little pony? He cannot stay abreast of your horse! It's not fair!"

"Do not trouble yourself about it much," he answered calmly. "Tomorrow I will teach you to ride a horse."

"Truly, Roman?" she cried, and he nodded. "A big horse, like yours?" and he nodded again. "Oh joy, oh joy!" she sang. He glanced her way, repressing a smile.

3

eirdre was awake before the dawn. Unwilling to wait for her nursemaid, she dressed herself and ran into the corridor. She pounced on the guard stationed there. . . .

"Summon Roman to me at once. He is teaching me to ride today!"

The guard bowed gravely. "Yes, Chataine." She impatiently watched him move so slowly away, then settled in her receiving chamber to await Roman. Long moments later there was a knock, and she eagerly opened the door to see another soldier standing there.

"Who are you? Where is Roman?" she asked sternly.

The soldier bowed. "Chataine, I am Captain Basner. I am very sorry that Roman is unavailable now. I have come to explain to you the schedule, set by the Commander, for all the captains. In the mornings, when you should be attending your studies," (Deirdre glanced away) "Captain Roman is required to drill his outfit and maintain his gear. He is on the grounds now, demonstrating the use of the pugil sticks."

"Is he good at it?" she asked vaguely, to draw attention away from her embarrassment and disappointment.

The Captain raised an eyebrow. "He is our champion, Chataine. You may observe him practice from that window if you desire." He pointed down the corridor.

"No, I am not interested in that," she yawned. "You are dismissed." She closed the door and listened for his retreating footsteps, then hurried out to the window he had indicated. Sure enough, below she saw Roman in the center of a ring with an opponent. They were about to begin. She looked on with interest.

The pugil sticks were five-foot poles of oak with thick round pads at each end. Each fighter gripped one horizontally with both hands, using it to strike and parry blows. Staying on one's feet required strength, agility, timing, and instant reflexes.

Roman and his opponent faced each other. They both wore only the trousers of their uniforms. On a signal they began circling. The other struck first—a lightning bolt to the head. Roman dodged it and struck him in the side with one end and the head with the other. He was obliged to wait a few seconds till his opponent had recovered enough to continue.

From then, they traded blows and blocks with such ferocity that Deirdre closed her eyes at times, fearing to see Roman killed before he could teach her to ride. But on looking closer, she saw that he was seldom actually hit. He struck a blow, then bounded back, parrying a shot and striking again. Then he would speed up the pace and deliver a whole series of blows before the other could strike back. Finally, Roman delivered a sharp uppercut that felled his opponent and the match was ended. Deirdre had almost joined in the cheers when she looked across the quadrangle and saw the Counselor in the window opposite her. He, too, was watching the match intently. When he caught her gaze, he disappeared from the window.

She looked again to Roman. Evidently her summons had reached him, for he was leaving the field. He picked up his shirt and short-coat and unfolded them as he walked. Then, curiously, he stopped in a walkway, hidden to all eyes but Deirdre's. He glanced around to be certain he was not observed, and, not seeing her in the window above, he took something out of his clothes and put it on. It was a gold medallion. She could not see it clearly from where she stood, but she easily guessed it was not a piece any soldier could afford. He then donned his clothes, safely hiding it.

At that moment she heard voices around the corner of the corridor—two guards who had been watching the match from a nearby window. "The Captain certainly can handle the sticks, eh?"

"Aye. I won't get in the ring with him. . . . Too bad he's gone as far as he'll go, now that they made him the Chataine's guardian."

The other tsked. "And I heard that he was about to be made the Commander's Second. Who will get the job now? Basner, you suppose?" Their voices faded as they walked away from her down the corridor. Deirdre reflected on what she had heard for a moment, then shook her head and ran to the courtyard entrance to meet him.

"Roman! You promised! Today I learn to ride!"

He almost smiled. "Come with me to the stables, Chataine. I have picked out a mare for you."

He left Deirdre waiting beside his horse, already saddled, while he entered the stables to bring out her horse. Her very own horse! Bobbing with excitement, she could hardly contain herself to wait for him to appear. At last he came out leading a grey mare and carrying a small saddle.

Deirdre clapped and squealed, "She's beautiful!" As Roman draped the reins around a post, she stroked the mare's shiny mane and fretted, "Now, what shall I name her?" Roman smiled. Deirdre glanced at his horse. "What is your horse's name?"

"He does not have a name," Roman answered a little disdainfully. "He is just the bay hunter."

"Well, then you call him the Bay Hunter," Deirdre reasoned. "As my mare is grey, I will call her Lady Grey. Saddle her quickly so we can ride!"

"Come here and watch," he instructed, swinging the saddle up on the mare's back. "I want you to learn how to saddle her."

Deirdre impatiently protested, "Oh, the groom can do all that! I just want to learn to ride."

"Someday you may need to know how to do it yourself. If I am going to teach you to ride, I'm going to teach you right." So she settled down and tried to pay attention to everything he said.

When he had done, he lifted Deirdre onto the saddle. How high she felt! He mounted the Bay Hunter, only a little larger, and took her reins to lead her through the rear gate. When they had gained the grassy fields, Roman let her have the reins, instructing, "Watch how I hold the reins, and imitate me."

Then at last she was riding with him out toward the hills. She was ecstatic. She could look him in the face now, when they rode, instead of up at him from the pony's low back. He kept up a constant stream of instruction to her—how to handle the reins, how to hold on with her legs, how to flow with the motion of the horse.

"The pony followed wherever he was led, but your mare has a mind of her own," he reminded. "You must keep control at all times." Then, after watching her ride for a while, he allowed her to gallop beside him, and they raced across a flat stretch of land to the foot of the hills. As they pulled up, he said, "You learn very quickly. You seem to have a natural affinity for riding."

Overflowing with the excitement of racing the wind, Deirdre recklessly stood in the saddle and threw her arms around his neck. "Thank you for teaching me!"

He laughed out, "Whoa!" and gently pushed her back into the saddle. But hugging his neck had reminded her of the medallion.

"Roman," she said, "where did you get that medallion you wear?"

For the first time ever she saw him startle. "How do you know about that?"

"I saw you put it on today, after your match." His face turned to stone, and he said nothing. "You could not have bought it. Did you steal it?" she prodded, to draw a response.

"Of course not." He glanced at her darkly. "It was a . . . gift of appreciation from . . . a friend."

"Who?" she pressed.

"It's time we headed back. Your father desires to have you seated at the noon table." With that, he wheeled his horse around and left her to catch up.

Deirdre felt very important to eat with her father at noon. True, she usually had the evening meal with him, but many others were also present then. If he requested her company now, then surely he had important things to discuss with her. She imagined her father asking her opinion about whether soldiers should be paid more.

It came as a severe disappointment, then, to see that not only Roman but also the Counselor would share the table with them. After an extended conversation with the men about some border dispute, her father finally addressed her, "Well, Deirdre, I have heard that Roman is teaching you to ride. Have you learned yet?"

Her eyes gleamed. "Oh yes, Father! He says I have a natural divinity!" Abruptly, the three men laughed. She shut her mouth, confused.

"Well said," Karel smiled. "In three days we are riding to Ooster to visit your uncle—your mother's brother. He has not seen you since you were a baby, and has pressed us for a visit."

"Does he have children?" The prospect of meeting cousins her age was attractive.

"Yes. Two sons."

Was it only her imagination that he sounded bitter? She said no more and kept her eyes on her plate. But happening once to glance up at Roman, she saw him looking at her kindly. After they were dismissed, he drew her aside. "Chataine . . . we did not laugh maliciously at you. What you said was just amusing. Please don't be offended."

She shook her head listlessly. "I'm not. I always say the wrong thing around my father. It is a curse." Roman tried to look serious. She perked up and asked, "Do you know my uncle?"

"I know of him. He is a wealthy and respected man. He has brought order to a very unstable country."

"What about his sons? How old are they?"

"Six or seven years older than yourself."

"Do you know their names?"

He reflected. "The oldest is Jason. The younger is Colin. Your uncle's name is Corneus."

Soon provisions were gathered and preparations completed for the day's ride to Ooster. Nanna made a pest of herself in her anxiety. She packed and repacked the Chataine's bags, muttering to herself about the obvious lack of judgment shown by her exclusion on this trip. The traveling party consisted of Karel, Deirdre, Roman, and ten soldiers. Deirdre happened to overhear a heated discussion as to whether more soldiers were needed, but it was finally agreed that more would seem an affront to Corneus. He would expect to assume responsibility for the safety of his guests.

The Chataine and her bags arrived at the front gate. The Counselor, who stayed in the palace during the Surchatain's absences, was receiving final instructions from Karel. Roman helped Deirdre mount her horse, and the party set off.

At first, the ride was exhilarating for Deirdre. They began travel at a fast, sustained gallop while the horses were fresh and the roads were flat. The soldiers rode in protective formation around her: four before her, Roman to her left, another to her right. Her father, behind her, was flanked by two soldiers, and the remainder formed the rear guard. Deirdre visualized what would happen if this moving stronghold were ambushed by renegades. The soldiers would spring to the attack, with Roman shouting orders and brandishing his broadsword. Hoofs would fly and villains fall in pools of blood—all on account of her. And her father, of course. It was a splendid fight to protect them.

The reality of the ride, however, was something else altogether. Twenty minutes into the trip, Deirdre was ready to stop galloping. An hour later she felt her teeth would be jarred from her head. At this point the road became bumpy and irregular, climbing hills and dropping into depressions. Even though the party slowed their pace and stopped time and again to rest their horses, Deirdre felt she was a puppet bouncing on strings, ready to collapse when released. Still they traveled on over rough, hilly terrain—ground impassable for a carriage. The cool spring morning wore on and became a hot day. And Deirdre, unaccustomed to sustained travel on horseback, grew very sore and weary.

When Karel mercifully called a halt to rest and eat, Deirdre fell from her horse and hobbled about to see if her legs still worked. She took her portion and moved off a few paces to eat standing up. Roman sent two soldiers into the forest, then came and stood beside

42

her. "How are you holding out, Chataine? I fear we should have brought you a saddle pad."

"I am fine," she bristled. "I just wanted to unbend my legs." She started to move off into the trees.

But Roman caught her arm. "Do not leave my side for an instant," he ordered.

"But . . . I have to . . . you know."

"I will go with you."

"No!" The idea appalled her. "You don't dare! It will only take a minute!"

"Chataine." He pulled her closer and whispered. "I believe we are being followed. I do not know who is among the trees with us, but I am certain I spotted someone matching our pace. Now, would you rather me observe you, or someone else who is not so concerned for your welfare?"

She winced. "You can come." They found a suitable spot, and she began to hike up the yards of skirt, then stopped. "Turn your back." His eyes scanned the forest around them uneasily. "Turn your back," she insisted. He complied. She needed only a moment.

Just as she let down her skirts, a massive pair of hairy arms from nowhere surrounded her. Roman wheeled an instant too late. Another man had sprung from the bushes and smashed him in the face with a bludgeon. As he fell, Deirdre glimpsed blood. She tried to cry out, but a heavy hand covered the bottom half of her face. She heard shouts. The arms swept her up and carried her to a waiting horse. The hairy man threw her on it, then jumped up behind her and spurred the horse to a run.

The speed at which the party had been traveling was a trot compared to the run at which this horse carried her. Deirdre gritted her teeth, shut her eyes, and clutched the saddle in terror. She opened her eyes to see trees veering by wildly on her left and right, then shut them tight.

A sudden plunge opened her eyes again. They were running down the middle of a shallow stream; the spray was soaking her skirts. Miles later, the hairy man directed the horse out onto a rocky bank that sloped steeper with every stride. When the horse began to stumble he stopped, put Deirdre off, and dismounted himself. Pushing her ahead of him, he led the horse up the bank. Deirdre's long, sodden skirts weighted her down like armor. Each time she fell, he jerked her up and pushed her the harder ahead.

At length they reached a shallow cave in the face of a rocky cliff. Deirdre sat, gasping. Out stepped a silver-haired man in fine riding clothes. He studied her an instant, then handed the kidnapper a small bag of coins. As he weighed the payment in his palm, the hairy man advised, "You best be off quick. They'll be hot after you for sure."

"Did you come the way I told you?"

"Yes, lord, I did."

"Then by the time they track you to this point, we will be quite . . . gone. Where is your companion?"

"Well—uh—don't know. I didn't see him." The hairy man looked back uneasily.

"Fool! Go make certain he does not lead them straight here!" Then, turning to Deirdre: "Come, my dear. We must be going." He led her toward his horse. She decided to faint rather than get on another horse. When she saw, however, that the gentleman was simply going to throw her on it like a saddlebag, she chose to awaken. He placed her in front of him on the saddle and pinned her with his elbows as they rode.

Deirdre could not long endure his cool reserve. "Where are you taking me?"

"We are almost there."

"Who are you?" He did not answer and she twisted in his grasp to study him. He had a smooth, hard face and ice-blue eyes. He smiled, and a fresh wave of fear swept over her.

Without warning he reined in his mount. She looked around. He dismounted and courteously lifted her down. Then he led her firmly past a few last scraggly trees. Twenty paces in front of them the ground seemed to cut into open sky. It was a cliff. He took her to the edge. Below them was a deep, jagged gully lined with debris and brush at the bottom. If she fell down there, no one would ever find her . . . if she survived the fall.

He shoved her. "No!" she cried, grabbing at him. She fell, but her hands held. Dangling over the cliff, she had caught his shortcoat and brought him to his knees. He wrenched her hands free and she caught with a last effort on an overhanging rock, straining desperately to hold on. She did not know why she did not fall. The man lifted his foot and—disappeared.

In his stead appeared a bloody brown face, and strong arms lifted her back on to the cliff. She clung to Roman and would not let him go. He touched her hair. "Are you hurt?" he asked. She could not answer. But when she raised her eyes and saw the ugly gash on his forehead, she began to sob.

It was midafternoon before the party set off again. Roman's head was cleaned and wrapped with makeshift bandages. He was a shade pale, but steady. Deirdre climbed up in front of him on his horse—she would ride nowhere else. The soldiers tied a body on Deirdre's mare, then they all pieced together what had happened.

After the initial attack, the soldiers came to Roman's aid and killed his assailant. Then Roman and two soldiers set out to follow the kidnapper. It was easy tracking him through the forest and stream, Roman said; at times they could glimpse him far ahead. But when he got on the rocky bank they had to search much harder. Finally one of the soldiers spotted him coming down—alone. They caught him and, under pressure, he directed them to the cave. Roman sent the kidnapper back with the soldiers to face the wrath of the Surchatain. From there, Roman followed the trail alone. He was almost on top of them when he heard her cry out at the cliff, and feared he was too late. But he saw her clinging yet to the rock, and sent a knife into the man's back to stay his foot. Roman thought he had killed him. But after retrieving Deirdre from the cliff, he turned to see that the man—and his horse—was gone.

The captured kidnapper was escorted back to the Surchatain's prison for later questioning. (All he could tell them, however, was that the gentleman had hired him and his partner in a tavern to abduct the Chataine. They were to be paid on delivering her to a specified place, and no names were exchanged.) Deirdre described the silver-haired man as best she could (Roman had not seen his face clearly) but no one could say he knew him. At this point, she did not care. She felt safe tucked in close to Roman.

Their progress was slowed, somewhat, from then; Roman, his wound bleeding continually, suffered some light-headedness that required more frequent rests. The air turned cool quickly as the sun dropped behind the mountains, and the travelers made yet another stop to dig out cloaks from their traveling bags. Deirdre found it more convenient, and more comfortable, to wrap herself in the roominess of Roman's cloak than don her own. Then in the growing darkness, the band tightened their formation and pushed ahead to Ooster.

4

I t was late in the evening when they arrived at Corneus's gates. The Surchatain of Seir himself met them. . . .

"Karel!" exclaimed Corneus, embracing Deirdre's father. "I was becoming concerned. I almost sent a regiment after you." Seeing Roman's blood-soaked bandages and the body on Deirdre's horse, he cried, "What on earth has happened?" Then he saw Deirdre as she unwrapped herself from Roman's cloak.

"Corneus, it is good to see you," Karel said wearily. "We encountered some ruffians on the road who delayed our trip a bit. It would be a great kindness to me if you would allow me to offer a reward to anyone who can tell me this fellow's name and village." He gestured toward the body.

"Certainly, Karel, certainly," assured Corneus. He turned to a guard. "Have him placed in the courtyard and post a notice offering—" he glanced inquiringly at Karel.

"One hundred royals," Karel answered.

"—one hundred royals from the Surchatain of Lystra to anyone who can identify this man." The guard bowed and the body was removed. "Now, you all must be weak with hunger and fatigue— you, young man, need the physician!" Corneus declared, peering at Roman. "Summon him" was directed at a servant. "Come in, come in now—" Corneus herded them into the warm, plush dining hall favored with walnut and hung with blue tapestries.

Roast duck and pottage, brown bread, red wine, cheese, nuts, pastry, and honey came out of the kitchen in rapid order. Roman paused eating long enough to let the physician cleanse his head and bandage it to his satisfaction. Meanwhile, Corneus did not press Karel for details of the incident, but talked merrily of trading profits and innovative ideas and consolidation of resources—or some such things. Finally he turned to Deirdre and said, "So this is Regina's daughter. You look so much like your mother, my dear. She had that same blond hair."

"Thank you, uncle."

"But you have not met my family!" he exclaimed. He sent a summons, and some time later a tall, slender, stately woman appeared in the dining hall with two young men beside her. "Deirdre, this is your Aunt Bedelia." Deirdre rose from the table to greet her properly and Bedelia nodded coolly. "And this is Jason and this is Colin," continued Corneus. They bowed. "This is your cousin Deirdre, boys," he winked. She nodded politely.

"Deirdre, do you want to go see the armory?" Colin asked.

Deirdre turned her eyes to Roman. He looked spent and pale. "In the morning, Colin. I—I would like to go to bed now, Father."

The room given her was as fitting as her own, with many lacy pillows and quilts. The housemaid assigned her for their stay was motherly and attentive—much like Nanna. And, as Nanna certainly would, she objected strongly when she learned Roman planned to sleep in the adjoining room. "It is not proper!" she scolded. "The Surchatain will be appalled!"

"He will understand. She is my charge," Roman replied quietly.

Deirdre lay in bed and tried to sleep, but vivid flashbacks to that afternoon kept her wide-eyed. She left her bed and pressed her ear against the door to Roman's room. Was he asleep? She opened it. Roman was on his knees in the center of the room. His head was bowed, his eyes shut, and his lips were moving. She watched him wonderingly a moment, but he did not look up, so she closed the door quietly and buried herself in the downy bed.

In the morning, when he met her in the corridor to go downstairs for breakfast, she was alarmed to see his right eye swollen and somewhat blackened under the bandages. "Roman—you look terrible!"

"Thank you, Chataine," he said wryly.

"No—I mean—you look hurt worse today."

"Not at all. My head is clear this morning. I only look worse—as luck would have it," he ended on a mutter which was lost to her. Nonetheless, he walked slowly, pausing once or twice to steady himself on the stairway.

"Roman, are you sure you feel well?"

"Yes," he said, and did not pause again.

They descended to the dining hall to find Karel and Corneus already being served. As Deirdre and Roman took their places, Jason and Colin entered to sit on either side of her. "You will be really glad you came here, Deirdre. Colin and I have a lot to show you. You are going to see how warriors train!"

"Do you have a lake?" she asked. "I would rather see a lake, with flowers around it."

Jason gave an incredulous sneer. "No, we do not have a lake. That is stupid."

"Father has a garden—" began Colin, but Jason interrupted him.

"That is nothing to see—just bushes and trees. Hurry and finish, Deirdre, so you can come watch." She looked across the table to Roman. He said nothing, but coolly assessed Jason.

As promised, the first event of the morning was a visit to the armory, which at least interested Roman. Then they sat outside in the courtyard to watch Jason and Colin spar with the pugil sticks. Growing impatient at their many feints and misses, she exclaimed, "You should get Roman to teach you at it. He is a champion!"

"Really?" Jason smirked. Roman was only a shade larger than he. "Then let's have a match." Roman declined. Jason muttered, "Coward." Roman did not respond.

So, instead, they watched the boys play a match of ground ball.

Next they watched the boys at archery. For Deirdre and Roman, sitting most of the morning as spectators at least gave them the opportunity to talk privately of the attempt on her life. She could not understand how anyone she did not know would want to kill her.

"You are your father's only heir," reminded Roman. "Someone wishing to usurp his position would need you out of the way eventually."

"But who could have known we would be on the road then?"

He shrugged. "There are spies all over, from every region. We have no way of knowing unless we can find your silver-haired gentleman."

"Why did he not kill me at the cave?" she wondered.

"To buy time, no doubt. Your father could not appoint a successor until you were proclaimed dead. That would be difficult to do if we could not find you. As long as you were missing, we would be obliged to search for you three years. Only then, if you still were not found, could he appoint another heir."

At that point they were distracted by a mild disturbance from the far end of the courtyard. It soon turned into a serious one when Corneus came stomping out of the palace. "Fool! How could you have allowed that to happen?"

"Surchatain—there was a mix-up in the guards—"

"Excuses! You are relieved of your position! Now get soldiers out to find him!" Karel then appeared in the courtyard and Corneus took on a humble tone. "Karel, a most embarrassing thing has happened." He cleared his voice. "My guards were negligent in their duties and somehow, someone has stolen the body of the man you wanted identified. I cannot imagine—"

Karel began to seethe. "It is more than embarrassing, Corneus; it is critical."

"Indeed it is. So I have offered a reward of five hundred royals to anyone who can produce the body."

"The body alone does us no good!" burst Karel. "I want to know who hired him!"

Corneus's face altered slightly. "We will do what can be done, Karel." His voice suggested no anxiety on his part.

Karel braced his jaw and inclined his head ever so little. "I leave the matter in your capable hands, Corneus."

A bell sounded, signaling the noon meal, and the party assembled in the dining hall. Roman took his seat across from Deirdre. As the food was served, she could hardly help but notice the attention a pretty serving girl paid to him. The girl smiled and leaned close to him, fretted over his bandaged head and even toyed with his hair. Deirdre felt an unreasonable jealousy. She burned slowly as she watched, but the others seemed not to notice. Toward the end of the meal, the girl put her hand on his shoulder and whispered in his ear. He smiled and shook his head. She whispered again, then sauntered off. Roman watched her go and sighed very faintly. Then he saw the Chataine's angry face and lowered his eyes.

Afterward she asked him point-blank: "What did she say to you?"

"You ask too many questions, Chataine."

"But what did she say?"

A pause. "She wanted me to come to her room tonight."

Deirdre's jealousy flared. "Are you?"

"Of course not," he answered quickly, then turned thoughtful. "Besides, I do not believe her motives were the purest, if you'll pardon the word."

"What do you mean?"

"Well, I saw her yesterday when we arrived. She served us at dinner. She did not even give me a second glance then. This sudden interest is suspicious."

"Oh?" said Deirdre thoughtfully. She was still trying to recall her from yesterday. "I did not notice her."

"I did."

During the subsequent days of their visit, Roman was especially vigilant in warding Deirdre. When Jason suggested to Deirdre a trip into Ooster to see the town, Roman immediately objected.

"If you cannot protect her in a crowd, stay here," Jason taunted. "*I* will be with her."

Roman leveled a cold stare at Jason and responded, "If the Chataine wishes to go, she may. But I am her guardian."

Deirdre raised pleading eyes. "I really want to go." Roman tightened his lips, and she whispered, "I *promise* I will stay with you!"

The four of them—Deirdre, Roman, Jason, and Colin—rode at a

leisurely walk down the broad thoroughfare from the palace into the main part of town. "What a smooth road!" exclaimed Deirdre, admiring the paving stones.

"Father says nothing helps trade like good roads," Jason said proudly. "It's better than a river."

Deirdre nodded. "But how much you must pay the stonemasons to do it!"

"Nothing," laughed Jason. "The soldiers do it. Father says it gives the lazy brands something to do." He cut his eyes toward Roman, who turned him a deaf ear.

Jason then began to point out the best businesses and shops. Deirdre listened eagerly to his boasting about all the goods available and all the money that traded hands in this town. "Father says commerce is what builds an empire," he stated.

"And soldiers protect your commerce," Roman added casually.

"That is what I always say!" interjected Colin. Jason directed a threatening look toward his brother.

"Roman, look at that!" exclaimed Deirdre. They stopped before a beautiful building of polished oak and glass. Stone steps led up to intricately carved doubled doors—which were bolted fast. "What business is that?" she inquired.

"That is the cathedral Father built for Mother. It is the most beautiful building on the Continent. The floors and pillars inside are black marble, and the walls are covered with carved panels which tell a story."

"Of what?" asked Deirdre.

"I do not know," he admitted.

"Then let us go in and see," said Roman, dismounting. "And while we are within, we can pray."

"No," said Jason. "We cannot. The doors are bolted."

"When are they opened?" Roman folded his arms on his chest.

"When Mother gives her say."

"Then what use is this building to your people?"

"Fool!" Jason ejaculated. "Can't you see how beautiful it is?"

Deirdre caught her breath at the insult and looked to Roman. But he remounted without a word. She got the definite impression he had made some kind of a point.

Jason continued them on their tour. He pointed out the bakery, blacksmith, woodwright, potter, and silversmith. At the tanner's, he paused for them to dismount and examine the goods. "He sends much fine leather to Hycliff every year," Jason boasted. As they remounted, he made no comment about a large, lovely house next door with scarlet curtains in its windows.

"What is that?" asked Deirdre.

"Ask Roman," smirked Jason. "He should know."

Deirdre turned inquiring eyes to her guardian. He paused, inhaling. "It is a brothel, Deirdre."

"A brothel?" she frowned. Roman sat still and did not elaborate. Then she remembered something Rory had once described and her face took on color.

"Want to see the inside, Deirdre?" Jason teased.

Roman abruptly leaned over and took hold of her horse's bridle, turning Lady Grey in a tight half circle as he spurred toward the palace. "This is beneath you, Chataine. I will not permit it."

"Roman!" she protested angrily, but secretly she was glad.

Corneus, Karel, and an aloof Bedelia were standing near the front gates conversing as Roman and Deirdre came into view, galloping up the thoroughfare. Corneus paused, watching them. Then he commented: "Your daughter's guardian is quite faithful, Karel—he never leaves her side. He does his job well."

"He should," answered Karel. "His life depends on it."

"Deirdre, dear," Corneus called out to her.

She and Roman gained the gates and dismounted. "Yes, uncle?"

"You will be having your coming out here, Deirdre, when you are sixteen. Did you know that? It will be grand—young men from all over the Continent will be here. Won't that be exciting?"

"Yes, uncle!"

"I can hardly wait, myself," Corneus said. Then he leaned closer and added, "And I hope you and Jason will get to be good friends, eh?" He winked.

Karel tapped him on the shoulder. "We will talk about that, Corneus."

"Aunt Bedelia, will you be chaperoning?" asked Deirdre politely.

"I regret that I will not be here at that time," the Surchataine answered. "I plan to be visiting friends."

"Who?" Corneus frowned.

"I do not know yet." She turned and reentered the palace.

The day of their departure, the party assembled in the courtyard before dawn. Corneus stood by, chatting and overseeing. "Karel, allow me to send an outfit back with you. Since we have not yet recovered the body of that ruffian, we do not know—he may yet have cohorts lying in wait for you."

"That is why we brought our own bodyguard, Corneus. No need to dispatch yours as well." Karel attempted to sound genial.

"As you wish," acceded Corneus. "Deirdre, I shall look forward to seeing you here again."

"Thank you, uncle. I shall look forward to coming. Please tell Aunt Bedelia goodbye for us."

"I shall. Goodbye, my dear. Goodbye, Karel."

Karel lifted his hand in response and the party rode out of the gates, in formation as they had come.

Deirdre was more prepared for the ride home. Roman had fitted a dainty little pillow to her saddle and now, as they rode, demonstrated to her how to ride standing in the stirrups to relieve cramping in her legs. She was anxious now to prove herself as capable as the men of enduring the long ride to Westford.

And she did well. The party achieved rapid travel until midafternoon, when a thunderstorm broke suddenly over the mountains and sent sheets of sleet and rain on the party. They stopped to don their cloaks, then resumed travel at a slower pace, for the horses were edgy and less sure-footed.

The darker it grew, the more nervous Deirdre became. A lightning bolt crashed in the forest near them and Lady Grey broke into a run past the soldiers ahead of her. Deirdre hauled back on the reins and the mare tried to stop, but slipped and fell heavily on her side. Deirdre, thrown clear, bounced once or twice in the mud before coming to rest. As soon as her breath returned, she set up a wail.

But Roman was already on his knees beside her, wiping mud from her face. "Are you hurt? Are you hurt, Chataine?"

She stopped crying to feel herself. "No—I do not think I am," she said, surprised. Lady Grey staggered up, offended but unhurt.

Roman kept wiping her face. "Hold your head back," he murmured.

"What?" The rain was pounding around them. She pushed his arm away from her face impatiently. When she saw the blood on his fingers, she began to cry again.

"It's only a nosebleed, Deirdre. Don't cry," he pleaded.

"Roman! Is she injured?" Karel called from his horse.

Roman did not answer immediately. He lifted Deirdre and carried her to his horse. "Do you want to ride with me?" he asked her softly.

"Yes!" she said, grasping the saddle. "I am not hurt, Father," she added over her shoulder. He nodded, and Roman placed her in the saddle and sat behind her. Then he wrapped her up completely in his great cloak. As they set off again, he leaned his head down to hers and murmured, "Thank you." She grinned back at him and wiped her nose.

Hours later, they arrived at the palace—a weary, bedraggled band. Roman lifted Deirdre down and carried her inside. Nanna was there waiting. "Aiiee!" she screamed when she saw the muddy, bloodied little girl. "Baby! What has happened to you?" She paused to direct a murderous look at Roman.

"My horse fell down with me!" announced Deirdre proudly.

"Come here, let me get you cleaned up—oh! poor dear!" And with one last glare at Roman, Nanna bustled her to her chambers.

Meanwhile, the Surchatain and his Counselor were conferring in Karel's chambers. Eudymon had heard from the soldiers who had brought back the kidnapper of the attempt on Deirdre's life. He posed, "Then the rumors must be true that Corneus is trying to kill her!"

"We do not know that it is Corneus," replied Karel. "We must interrogate the kidnapper and see what he can tell us." After some discussion, they also agreed to send spies to Seir and the surrounding regions to try to locate an elegant, silver-haired man with a deep knife wound in his back. That resolved, they both lapsed into troubled silence.

After a long moment of deliberation, the Counselor said, "Surchatain, I am loath to advise you on personal matters, but, as it regards the throne . . ." Karel looked up. "Will you not consider remarrying, High Lord, to provide yourself with at least one other heir—?"

"No," said Karel, in an uncommonly soft voice. "Deirdre is Regina's daughter. It is the least I can do for her, to see that Deirdre succeeds me. It is the least I can do. . . ." he trailed off, and the Counselor said, "A most commendable gesture, High Lord. Most commendable." Karel did not respond.

After another long pause, Eudymon stated, "Roman must be severely punished."

"Why? Deirdre was not harmed."

"Nevertheless, it was his carelessness that allowed this incident. He must be flogged."

"No, Roman shall in no way be punished. I have decided that. You are dismissed, Counselor."

As he stepped into the corridor, he saw a soldier leaving the armory. "Roman!"

The soldier turned and bowed respectfully. "Counselor?" For a moment they eyed each other.

"I heard you had a run of ill luck on this trip," Eudymon remarked.

Roman shrugged. "The Chataine is safely home."

"For that, I am most grateful. And how do you fare?" He eyed the broken scab on Roman's forehead.

"I will heal. I always do. I have been wounded much worse before." His face was granite.

Eudymon lowered his eyes. "We all take blows, at one time or another. There is justice in life, but not much mercy."

"Will that be all, Counselor?"

"Yes. Goodnight, Roman."

"Counselor." He bowed and walked away.

When Nanna got Deirdre into her chambers, she hugged the breath out of the little girl. Nanna, too, had heard of the attempted murder and fainted dead away. Now Deirdre began to recount to her every savory detail of the abduction. However, she changed it up just a little to save face. She did not want to tell Nanna she made Roman turn his back on her. So she said that he left her alone for only a moment.

Nanna burst out, "That bastard! Why the High Lord gave the likes of him charge over you I'll never know!"

Deirdre was mildly surprised. "Why, Nanna, I never heard you swear before."

"I am not swearing. That is what he is—a bastard." The woman was truly angry. "It's common knowledge that his mother was a prostitute, and there is no saying who his father might be!"

The Chataine was intrigued. "Where is his mother?"

"She died of disease years ago. They put the boy in the Surcha-tain's army, as there was nothing else to be done with him." As her anger cooled, she saw at once that she had said too much. "Well, dear, that all means nothing now. I am sure he does the best he can to ward you. Dear . . . please do not tell anyone what I told you. It is not important. Please promise me you will not repeat it to anyone."

"I promise," smiled the Chataine.

In the morning, Deirdre could hardly wait to spring her newfound knowledge on Roman. She dressed herself early and, ignoring her studies and his obligations, ran to summon him. She waited impatiently to see him bringing their horses from the stables. He smiled when he saw her running eagerly to meet him. They mounted and rode west, out to the hills.

"Roman," she plunged right in, "I heard that you're a bastard and your mother was a prostitute. Is that true?"

His face turned to stone. "You do not know when to stop, do you?" he said quietly.

"What?" She was suddenly uncomfortable.

"You are still trying to gain the upper hand on me—still trying to put me in my place."

He would say no more. As Deirdre studied him, the realization broke over her that her words had injured him as brutally as the kidnapper's bludgeon. But he was so strong and rocklike, she had not thought it possible to hurt him—until she saw him bleed.

They rode at a walk side by side. Deirdre tried to get him talking, but he answered politely and fell silent again. She began to feel remorse, then immediate self-justification: *I did not intend to hurt him.* But as she looked at him, another insight answered her as clearly as someone speaking: *Yes, you did. Did you really expect to say something so cruel and not hurt him?* She startled. Her conscience had never been so assertive. Did just being with him make it so?

"Roman, I—I am sorry I said that. I am sorry I hurt you."

He nodded. She felt a sudden tightness in her throat.

At the table that evening she was especially deferential to him. He spoke to her kindly enough, but did not look up much.

"Roman," she said softly, "have you ever said anything you wished you had not said?"

"Often." He looked at her now.

"I wish I had not said that."

"I know." He relaxed. "It's only that . . . is that what the palace thinks of me? Is that what they are all saying?"

"No!" she said. Some heads turned. "No," she said more softly. "I heard it from only one person." She stopped, but the question remained in his eyes. "Nanna," she sighed.

"Your nursemaid should be a communications runner," he observed. But he smiled at her.

Days later, Deirdre was watching from her usual window as Roman practiced at archery on the grounds below. *That looks like fun—I must get him to teach me,* she thought. But, for now, she was bored and he was busy. She was supposed to be doing her lessons, but she did not even know where Rory was. She sighed and turned from the window. Then an inspiration struck. Eagerly, she wound her way down to the kitchen corridors. She approached the door to his room and tried the handle. The door creaked open and she peeked in.

Rory was right. It was a small, dreary room with no rugs or tapestries. There was only one small, shuttered window. Beneath it was a narrow bed. She crossed over and sat on it. Ouch—how hard! Deirdre pulled back the blanket. What she had sat on was part of the frame, really, which had thick, rugged cloth stretched taut over it.

There was no mattress or pillow, only the thin blanket. She replaced it on the cot as it had been.

The only other piece of furniture in the room was a small stand with a wash bowl. Beneath it, a pile of clothes lay neatly folded. She fingered them, and out fell a bronze medallion. She picked it up. It was a medal of valor. She had seen her father award them to soldiers who had acted with courage in battle. She was so intently studying it, she did not hear the door open.

"What are you looking for, Chataine?"

She whirled. "Oh—Roman—I came to see if—we could go riding."

"You did not summon me? You know where I am in the mornings." He stood outside the doorway until she replaced the medal and came to the door.

"Well . . . I was really just curious to see your room," she confessed.

"This is it."

It is pitiful, she thought, but aloud she asked, "What did you get the medal for?"

"I will tell you about it sometime. Now, I must wash and change. Chataine?"

"What? Oh, yes . . ." And she stepped out into the corridor to wait.

"What are you looking for, Chataine?" a servant asked her respectfully.

"Nothing!" she snapped, and hastily moved off.

When Roman finally arrived at the gate with the horses, she almost jumped on him. "Well?"

"Chataine?"

"What did you do to get the medal?"

"Oh, that. When I was a boy, I carried water to an outfit on the border."

"Is that it?"

"Not exactly. They had been stranded behind the lines of the enemy without water for two days. With what I brought them, they were revived and able to fight their way back to the outpost."

"How old were you then?"

"I am not certain. Commander Galapos says about fourteen."

"You were in the army at fourteen?"

"I was the Commander's errand boy."

She considered. "Roman, would you do that for me? Would you risk your life to save me?"

He looked at her almost in disbelief. "Haven't I already, Chataine?"

She remembered with sudden clarity the details of the recent attack and blushed at her large forgetfulness. "Yes."

5

I, Penuel, continue this account. . . .

Deirdre sat listlessly leafing through her books. This new tutor Father got for her certainly cut into her free time. History, geography, mathematics, law—she slammed the books shut and gazed out of her window. It had snowed again last night. The barren ground was hidden beneath a shimmering skin of white. She set her mind to planning how to persuade Roman to take her to the lake in the sleigh. Roman had promised—

Roman. It had been almost two years since he had become her guardian. Was that right? Yes, because in a few months she would turn twelve. It only seemed as if he had always been at her side.

She remembered the trip to her uncle's and shivered. None of the spies Father sent out could locate the silver-haired man. But from the description they believed they found who he was. His name was Stase. He was an assassin for hire. There had been not a trace of him since the attack, and some believed he must have died from his wound. But Roman would not chance it, so she had not been away from the palace environs since. And she was getting restless.

Deirdre said "Pooh!" to the books and ran downstairs to summon Roman. The errand boy could not locate him, but one of the guards told her he was at the palace gate. She found him heading up a group of soldiers who seemed to be waiting. "Roman! Let's go sleigh riding! Let's go to the lake!"

He glanced at her. "Chataine, please, let's go later. Not now." Excitement seemed about to crack his usual cool reserve.

"Why not? What is happening?"

"There is an outfit coming in for leave from the border. Galapos is with them."

"Galapos?" She did not know him.

"Commander Galapos, the Field Commander. He is second in charge of the army, under your father."

So? she thought, but she let him wait. Presently a shout sprang up from the soldiers as the outfit was spotted up the road. The wide gates swung full open, and a tired group of men entered to whistles and cheers.

She spotted Galapos immediately. He was right out in front—the biggest man Deirdre had ever seen. Roman ran forward to meet him. The Commander was shaking hands and receiving friendly slaps as he dismounted, but when he saw Roman his face changed. "Roman, my boy, how are you?" The two men embraced.

"Well, Galapos, quite well," he answered, then extended his arm toward Deirdre. "Galapos, this is my charge, Chataine Deirdre."

"Eh? Yes, I heard you had been made her guardian. Come, sweetheart, let me look at you." He bent to study her. He was so big! He had flowing hair streaked with grey, a large moustache, and deep lines around his mouth and bright blue eyes.

"How do you do," she said, lifting her hand.

"Oh! And how do you do?" he returned, with a wink up at Roman. He took her hand in his big bear paw and kissed it solemnly. "I hope I shall have your company at dinner tonight, Chataine. We have much to discuss."

"Oh?"

"Yes. I am most anxious to know what trouble that lazy, ignorant, irresponsible jackass is making."

"Who?" she cried.

62

"Roman!" he burst, and all the soldiers standing around roared. *Roman won't like that,* she thought. But he was grinning broadly. "Roman, may we go out in the sleigh now?" she asked politely, in spite of her impatience to get him away.

He tossed an aside to Galapos: "We will talk later." The Commander nodded, eyes twinkling. "Wait here, Chataine, while I harness your mare to the sleigh," Roman instructed over his shoulder.

Deirdre smiled in satisfaction. Glancing self-consciously at the soldiers, she moved away from them to wait for him, but they paid no attention to her. Except Galapos. She pretended not to see when he turned her way and studied her reflectively for a moment.

When Roman at last appeared driving the sleigh, she scurried up beside him and began asking questions before she had sat down: "Who is that man? Why did he call you those names? Where—?"

He raised his hand in mock surrender. "Give me some air and I will tell you everything. As I said, Galapos is Commander of the army. He is the one who took me off the streets and brought me here, years ago. He had no reason to do it, but for the kindness in his heart. He made me his errand boy, and personally taught me riding and archery and combat with all types of weapons. He treated me as his very own son. But when I was still a child, the Border Wars broke out and he had to assume command from Outpost One. I had hoped to join him, but . . . well, he has been away from the palace for most of these years. There is peace along the border now, so he has returned on leave."

"Why did you let him say such terrible things about you?"

"Because I know and everyone else knows that he does not believe those things about me at all. You saw he is fond of me. But he prefers to cover his tender heart with droll talk."

She considered all this. "Did he give you the gold medallion?"

"No." They were both silent while Roman skillfully guided the sleigh to a point near the shore of the frozen lake. "Here we are, as you requested."

She dug a pair of skates out of hiding in the sleigh. "I have a surprise for you!" she laughed, strapping them to her feet. "Wait till you see what I can do!"

"Where did you get those? What do you think you are doing?" His tone became threatening.

"Watch," she said, stepping from the sleigh in her skates.

But he grasped her arm firmly. "You are not going out on the ice."

"But, Roman," she faltered. "I learned to skate. I wanted to show you what I learned."

He dropped her arm in surprise. "Who taught you to skate?"

"The merchant who was here the other day. I bought the skates from him to surprise you," she said anxiously. The look on his face was not pleasant surprise.

"Where did he teach you?" he demanded.

"Here—at the lake. We sneaked out for just a little while so he could teach me. I wanted to surprise you," she whimpered.

He abruptly lifted her up and sat her back down in the sleigh with a plop. "Deirdre, that was very foolish. You know you must never leave the palace without me. Have you forgotten the assassin? Anyone could be in his hire. If you do not value your own life, at least consider mine."

Her lip began to quiver. "I only wanted to show you what I could do."

He looked at her for a moment, then sighed, "So show me."

Elated, she stepped onto the ice and began gliding in shaky circles. He stood on the very edge of the shore to watch her. "See, Roman, see?" She waved as she skated in a straight line. He smiled and nodded. Then she boldly built up speed and skimmed the ice in a whoosh toward him. Unable to stop properly, she crashed into him, laughing. "Did I do well, Roman?"

"You did well," he laughed, picking her up. "I am proud of you."

"So am I!" And she set her skates on the ice again.

That evening, when Deirdre came down for dinner, she found to her surprise that Galapos had been given a seat between her father at the head of the table and herself to his right. There had always been a gap there and she had wondered about it; now she knew. She paused timidly at the doorway, but Roman saw her and stood.

Galapos, turning, declared, "Chataine! You have come at last!" He rose and escorted her respectfully to her chair. "How gracious of you to insist I have this seat, sweetheart. But let us not tell the Surchatain." His voice dropped to a sly whisper. "We do not wish to arouse his suspicions." Deirdre giggled.

The Surchatain entered and they all stood until he was seated. Galapos picked up his goblet and said, "To the Surchatain!" The table did likewise. "We drink to your good health and long life, High Lord, as we profit from your good graces." Karel smiled tightly as they drank their goblets down, and Deirdre, remembering the drunken complaints she had overheard in the kitchen, wondered how much Galapos was paid. The Commander added, "And I thank you, Surchatain, for allowing the captains to share your table during my furlough. I must needs check up on these men by the minute!"

As the servants brought out white bread and roast lamb, an officer down the table demanded, "Tell us news from the outposts, Commander."

Galapos raised his bushy eyebrows and said, "Harumph. Nothing much. We have caught Loren and his band of merry men."

"Loren the outlaw?" queried Roman.

"Who terrorized half of Lystra?" added the officer.

"The same, Captain Dyek."

"How did you do it?" asked Roman.

"Blind luck, actually," Galapos laughed. "He thought to rob two of my scouts I'd sent out dressed as merchants. He did not know they were armed and fronting for a unit following on horseback. It was a short fight." He stopped to bite into a shank. Deirdre watched him, spellbound.

Dyek exclaimed, "That demands a song!"

Galapos froze for an instant with upraised finger, eyes to the ceiling, composing. Then he sang,

> Sound a cheer for Loren!
> (May he rest in peace.)
> Got his fill of robbin',
> Got himself deceased!

Those at the table—excepting the Surchatain and the Counselor—laughed riotously. Deirdre giggled and choked on a mouthful.

Galapos slapped her gently on the back to clear her throat and said, "Tell me now, sweetheart, about this villain"—nodding toward Roman—"and what he has done with you." Suddenly everyone was quiet, watching her, smiling.

"Well . . . " she began timidly, and her mind blanked out. What had he done that she resented most? "He makes me mind him!" she blurted, and the roar that followed made her hide her face. The Surchatain looked from Deirdre to Roman with raised eyebrows and even the Counselor smiled.

"Such heartlessness," growled Galapos, when he could catch his breath. He added mildly, "Then he's done no more than a nurse-maid would."

"Actually, Commander, the Captain saved her life," Captain Basner said calmly, and the table stilled.

"Aye?" inquired Galapos casually, but his face took on a different cast.

"Spring before last, when we were traveling to Ooster. On the road, he had suspected we were being followed and sent Kam and Marc into the forest at the noon rest to have a look. Before they had gotten around, though, a pair of renegades bludgeoned him and stole the Chataine." He paused, but Galapos was quiet. "We caught one at the site, but the other got away with her and we had to give chase. Captain Roman insisted on the lead, though he was bleeding like a—" he caught himself and glanced toward Deirdre—"rather badly. We chased him a ways, lost him on the cliffs, then caught him coming back without the Chataine but loaded down with silver. While we took the prisoner, the Captain chased a third kidnapper to the edge of a cliff where he was about to throw down the Chataine. The Captain knifed him and recovered her hanging from the edge of a rock.

"Taking up the ride to Ooster, though, we thought for sure we'd lose him. His head bled the whole blasted time. Those snatchers almost killed him after the fact." At that, Galapos made no comment and the table sat in silence. Deirdre gazed in dismay at Roman. She had never been aware he had come so close to dying.

Finally Roman himself blurted, "But they improved my face!" And he pulled back his hair to show the scar the bludgeon had left. Galapos laughed appreciatively along with the others. But Deirdre felt his laughter was subdued.

In all the merriment, Deirdre could hardly help but notice the Counselor. He alone did not laugh, and seemed only mildly interested in the Commander's tales. She thought he looked rather like a lone grown-up at a children's gathering. It appeared that he did not much care for the Commander.

At one point, a guard came to Karel's side and whispered in his ear. The Surchatain paused, then declared, "Well, why not? Send him in." The guard bowed as Karel told his guests, "I am informed we have a traveling minstrel passing through offering entertainment. Let us hear his songs, then decide if he is worthy of a few royals." This plan was enthusiastically approved by all the guests.

Immediately a thin, pale man in ragged motley stepped up to the table and bowed low to the Surchatain. From the corner of her eye, Deirdre saw Roman give a little start. The minstrel said, "Surchatain, I have been given a song for you. I pray you to heed it." Then he strummed his guitar and began to sing in a minor key:

> Hear a sad tale that I tell to be free
> Of warring and honor and flights to the sea,
> Of ills unforeseen,
> Of fathomless dreams,
> Of battles that ever were cast upon me.
>
> I never had courage and never was bold
> Till I saw my dream in a woman unfold.
> She became mine,
> But perished in time,
> And the grieving grew stronger that should have grown old.
>
> The rage and the power I did not deny,
> But gave them such sway that my spirit did die.
> By slow degrees
> It trickled from me,
> And all that remains is this shell of my pride.

Fleeing forever the face of the sun,
I chose to run till my lifespan was done.
Who can I face?
Who will send grace?
Where is the mercy for what I have done?

Hear my lamenting and know it is true:
My warning will ever depend upon you.
Think you are wise?
With no one besides?
Note now that I myself thought once as you.

The last line had barely left his lips when Karel stood glowering and commanded: "Guard! Take him and—and—" the guests were gaping at the extremity of his reaction. "Take him to the whipping post—give him twenty lashes and send him away," he finished. "You are dismissed," Karel waved at his guests. Deirdre promptly went up to her chambers. She did not like to be underfoot when he went sour this way.

Roman and Galapos went to the Commander's chambers, provided for him while he was on leave. "So . . ." began Galapos slowly. "How goes it—warding the Chataine?"

"Well enough," answered Roman with downcast eyes. "I have not suffered yet as the minstrel did for his song."

"Aye." Galapos raised his thick brows and coughed. "And how long shall this appointment run?"

"Until she marries . . . four, maybe five more years. If God sees it fit to preserve my life that long."

"God!" Galapos uttered the Name in exasperation, turning on Roman. "Where was He when you were almost clubbed to death? When the Chataine was hanging over the cliff?"

Roman swallowed. "He preserved us then; He will do it again."

"Roman, how long will you cling to this—this myth? This wish? There is no God! Your own skill and strength delivered you, with a sweet helping of luck!"

"You are wrong, Galapos. I did what I could, yes, but God intervened. I felt it." At Galapos's look, he rushed on: "I cannot explain it, but there have been times in my life that I have felt God's power, that I knew with certainty His hand was upon me."

"Next you will be telling me that God directed me to take you in as my errand boy."

"Of course. You saved my life."

"I did, Roman! Not God!" His exasperation turned to anger. "I need a Second whose eyes are open, Roman. I am sorry. You are dismissed." The Commander turned his back, and Roman, stony-faced, withdrew.

Deirdre's new tutor, Olin, liked to start unreasonably early every morning, so the morning after Galapos's arrival she yawned through her lessons till Olin scolded her. "Do you not understand how valuable your lessons are? One day you will be Surchataine! You will need to know all this, and much more. So few people ever have the chance to learn. Few can even read! Is that worth so little to you?" It was, but it gave her an idea. Here was something at last she could do for Roman.

Immediately after her lessons, she sent the errand boy to summon him. The boy was gone so long, she finally went downstairs to look for him herself. She met the boy, then, returning to tell her he had found Roman, alone, at the fenced pasture near the stables. He was inspecting a new bunch of wild horses captured that morning. Deirdre hurried out to catch him, but was irked to see that Galapos had just joined him. "Roman, my boy, forgive me," Galapos was saying.

Roman turned to face him as Deirdre interrupted. "Roman, I want to talk to you!" she insisted as she drew him away.

"Chataine?" He looked annoyed for an instant, and she became suddenly tongue-tied.

"Roman—had you like—don't you think it would be a good idea if you knew how to read and write? I could teach you!"

"Thank you, Chataine . . . but I do read and write already."

She released his arm, surprised. None of the soldiers had any such learning. "What? Who taught you? Galapos?"

"No, the Counselor."

"The Counselor! Why?"

"As you said, Chataine, he thought it was a good idea."

He turned back to the Commander, who nodded toward the horses and remarked, "A promising lot." Roman silently agreed. Deirdre, meanwhile, had slipped into a most sour mood. She slapped at the arms of her heavy jacket. Then she noticed a horse penned by himself, away from the others. She started over to have a look at him when Roman stopped her: "No! Chataine, do not go near that horse. He is untameable and dangerous. Come back here."

"I just want to look at him," she said crossly.

"No. He is very wild and easily provoked. Come stay right by my side."

She reluctantly obeyed, bristling at the sharpness in his voice. "What are they going to do with him?"

"He is to be destroyed." He made no effort to soften the statement.

Deirdre stared at the beautiful horse in dismay. He was so still and regal—surely they would not kill him! Then she had a thought. She was an excellent rider for her age; everyone commented on how well she rode. She felt certain she could tame this horse. A vision came to her mind of the astonishment on everyone's face—especially Roman's—as she triumphantly pranced the horse around his pen. *Untameable? We will see.*

Galapos had begun speaking to Roman again in a low voice, holding his attention. Her eyes narrowed in determination as she waited for just the right moment to slip away from his side. In an instant she was by the pen of the beautiful stallion, talking to him gently.

He watched her with impossibly bright eyes. His sleek body was taut and trembling; his ears pricked high. The steam from his nostrils gave him the appearance of some mythical dragon. Deirdre slipped inside the fence and reached out to touch him. . . .

Someone shouted and the horse erupted. Rearing and screaming, he knocked her to the ground and reared again to trample her. Suddenly Roman was standing over her, bearing the crushing blows of hoofs on his chest and shoulder. He grasped the legs and heaved with all his strength, throwing the horse enough off balance that it fell backward on the frozen ground. Gasping, he scooped her up and tossed her to Galapos outside the pen. He had barely time to throw himself over before the horse had rammed itself into the railing, teeth bared and ears flattened.

Deirdre screamed, holding her bleeding hand. It had been gashed when she threw up her arms in defense of the flailing hoofs. Galapos shouted for the physician. Roman lay face down in the snow, wheezing. With an effort he sat up, clutching his chest in pain.

The physician appeared, and at his side was the Surchatain. At the sight of Deirdre, he called for the guards. "Take him to the whipping post!" he ordered, pointing to Roman. Two guards helped Roman to his feet and he stumbled a few steps to face Karel. Livid, the Surchatain shoved a finger in his face and growled, "I warned you, soldier. Twenty lashes!"

Deirdre leaped to a stand. "No! Father, it was my fault! He told me not to—but I waited until he was not looking—and I—don't beat him, Father! Please!" She was screaming now, but he ignored her. Roman was dragged off and everyone around followed.

The physician ordered Deirdre to be held still until he could wrap her hand, then she ran for the courtyard. He followed close behind. There was already a large crowd around the whipping post. Deirdre pushed her way through till she could see him. Stripped of his shirt and coat, he stood gripping the cold chains on the post. The deep marks of hoofs showed bright red on this chest and left shoulder. He seemed to be struggling to breathe. There was no sign of his medallion—then she saw that Galapos, next to her, held it clenched in his fist.

At that moment the Counselor pushed his way through the crowd. "What is happening here? Who—?" He stopped as if shot when he saw Roman on the post.

The physician pleaded, "Counselor, stop them until I can look at him. If he is badly injured, they may kill him!"

Eudymon shook his head helplessly. "Can I rescind an order of the Surchatain?"

"Twenty lashes," the Surchatain commanded. "Now."

A burly soldier stepped up with a metal-tipped whip and began the count. One . . . the whip cracked and Roman jerked. Deirdre screamed. Two . . . three . . . his face contorted at every blow, but he made no sound. Seven . . . eight . . . nine . . . Deirdre pounded her head with her good hand. "Stop, stop!" she cried. "Roman, I swear from now on I will obey you!" Fourteen . . . fifteen . . . Usually anyone on the whipping post got heckled by the crowd, but now there were no jeers or taunts. Eighteen . . . nineteen . . . twenty. Roman sagged to his knees. Two soldiers released him and carried him toward the infirmary, shadowed by the physician. Deirdre followed too.

They laid him face down on a narrow bed. The physician gingerly lifted him and felt his chest, then dressed his wounds front and back. "What can you do for him?" Deirdre whispered.

"Nothing now, but watch him. Amazing that he seems to have broken no bones. But how deeply he is injured, I do not know . . ."

Deirdre felt her own arm throb as she sat by his bed. He lay face down, breathing as if it were the greatest effort of his life. His face was gray, and the sweat trickled down his head and neck. She cried softly in remorse as she watched him, then took his hand gently. He opened his eyes a little. "Roman," she whispered brokenly, "I am so sorry. I swear I will never question you or disobey you again. Please get better. Please, Roman." His lips moved and his eyes shut again.

The next few days they watched him anxiously. He slept most of the time, and did not seem to worsen. Yet he lay very still and drew in shallow, uneven breaths. The Chataine hounded the infirmary to do what she could for him until the physician chased her away. The best thing for him, he said, was to be left alone. She sneaked back in whenever she was able; the burden on her conscience was too great for her to stay away. If he should die—why, she would have killed him. She envisioned herself being hanged for murder.

Days later when she peeked in the infirmary, she saw him awake and sitting up. "Roman!" She ran to his bed and would have thrown her arms around him if he had not caught her.

"Chataine—you were hurt," he whispered hoarsely, examining her hand.

"No." She pulled it back. "Not like you were. Roman, I am so, so sorry. Are you going to be well?"

"Certainly. But I am weak. I cannot go riding with you for a while . . . Oh, what about the horse?"

"What?"

"What happened to the horse? The stallion you were concerned about?"

"I do not know," she answered darkly. "I hope they killed it."

Deirdre spent most of the next several weeks in the infirmary, doing what she was allowed to succor him. She had been assigned a replacement guardian, but refused to go out at all. Galapos, also, kept appearing at his bedside. The Counselor came, and even the Surchatain. He seemed somewhat subdued on seeing Roman's condition, but said nothing remotely akin to an apology. He did not prohibit Deirdre from spending so much time ministering to him, however, even when her lessons lapsed.

After this incident, she began to think differently of her father. Before, she had always considered him unreachably wise, beyond her in judgment. But her child's sense of justice was offended that he had punished Roman so severely for her disobedience—after Roman had saved her by sacrificing himself! She could have forgiven her father readily if he had only admitted the possibility of error. But such a confession never came.

The Counselor came often to see Roman, although he never stayed more than a moment. He had pressing business, of course. But Deirdre stayed. She relayed all the palace gossip to him; she brought him a book he had requested from the Surchatain's library; and she played board games with him. She brought soap and water for him to bathe and shave, and helped change his bandages. She even brought his meals and took away the dishes.

After a fortnight, he grew stronger quickly. He got up more and more and began stretching and loosening up his stiff muscles. When Deirdre peeked into the infirmary one day and saw his bed empty, she went running in alarm to the physician. "It is well, all is well," he reassured her as she tried to tell him Roman was gone. "He only went to the service in the chapel. He will be back soon."

Deirdre said nothing of it when Roman returned to the infirmary, but she thought it a little silly that a grown man—a soldier yet—made such a point to attend services. Her father allowed them disdainfully because they had been requested, but he had said that only old women bothered with such things. So why did Roman go? She wondered about it, but was not yet interested enough to investigate.

6

*pring came early that year, and the first scent of it made
Roman restless to get out. And Deirdre was sick of the infirmary.
Then the news came that this was the week of the Fair.*

*Twice a year, in the spring and the autumn, merchants from all
over the Continent and beyond the Sea gathered in the port city of
Hycliff to show off their finest merchandise. Since it was only a
few hours' ride from Westford, the Surchatain gave Deirdre permission to go for one day and an allowance to spend. Roman
eagerly agreed to go now, and the physician gave him leave to
ride. . . .*

Deirdre was up at dawn, ready to go. Roman was still rather weak
and winced as he mounted the Bay Hunter, but would not hear of
forfeiting the visit. (She was glad for that.) By the time they arrived
at Hycliff, the Fair had consumed the city. The merchants—hundreds of them—had raised their booths in the grassy fields just north
of the city proper. The booths were open-sided structures with

thatched roofs in which the sellers displayed their goods. Some of the booths were no larger than stalls—others the size of Deirdre's sleeping room. It was truly said that anything which could be had for money could be found at the Fair.

Deirdre and Roman left their horses grazing in a field under the eye of an errand boy, and turned in hesitant wonder to the fields crowded with booths. Pausing at the edge of commotion, they watched as buyers haggled over prices, sellers called to passersby to stop and look, merchants argued loudly over the placement of booths next to their own. It was a motley scene. Deirdre glanced excitedly up at Roman and he grinned and pointed ahead. A minstrel was strumming his lute and singing straight at Deirdre: "Come join the Fair! Come join the fun! And buy! Buy! Buy!"

They stepped into the field. Deirdre quickly located booths of jewelry and expensive cloth goods. She fingered a pile of rich brown leather. "This would make a nice dress coat for you," she said, casting a sidelong look at the simple deerskin shortcoat he wore.

He glanced at it, saying, "It is kind of you to think of me, Chataine, but I do not need a dress coat. My uniform suffices."

"Oh, but you do!" she insisted, unfolding some of the leather. "You must have it for festive occasions." He began a protest, but her mind was fixed. "Nanna keeps insisting I must learn to sew. I will let her teach me so I can sew it for you." Roman shut his mouth and inclined his head to her. She turned to the merchant at her elbow. "How much of it do I need for a soldier's dress coat?" Roman looked away as if embarrassed.

"We sell it by the hide, Chataine," answered the merchant. "At six royals a hide—" Roman looked back.

"That is a high price for leather," he observed coldly.

"But this is the finest, from islands across the Sea," the trader protested.

Roman ran his hand over a hide, noting the tanner's imprint. "This is from Ooster."

"And Ooster sends us fine leather also!" he agreed. "But since your pretty mistress wishes it so, I will give it to her for four royals a hide."

"Taken!" exclaimed Deirdre, paying him out of her father's purse. Stepping out of the booth, she asked, "Don't you like it?"

"Yes, Chataine, of course—and I appreciate your generosity, only . . ." he fumbled, "it is so much to spend . . . I am not accustomed to luxuries such as this."

"Nonsense," she said firmly, choosing to ignore that his discomfort was real. She began to look around for something he might really want, however.

They paused to watch a puppet show, then ate their fill in booths of cheeses, sausages, and pies. Roman stopped to gaze in a booth of shining weapons, and Deirdre urged him to select something. "I noticed you broke your bowstring last time you practiced," she led him on.

"That is true." He smiled a little shyly, then she watched with admiration as he expertly tested the strength and flexibility of several longbows before choosing one. It made her feel good to buy this for him.

Following that, they were off to examine booths of ornate saddlery, tapestries, metal wares, and tools. One booth they passed caught at her heart like an old friend. There, lining shelves and shelves, were beautiful little dolls that winked and smiled. She longed to look, but—she glanced at Roman self-consciously— surely she was too old for dolls. But Roman pretended to be looking elsewhere. So she shyly stepped in and scanned the rows, then bought herself a new friend. Roman joined her outside the booth, and never once questioned her or mentioned it.

Even more intriguing to Deirdre than the booths were the crowds. She had never seen so many different kinds of people at once. Lords and ladies brushed with peasants, soldiers, merchants, seamen— Deirdre stared so much, some people stared back. She stuck close to Roman's side.

As they stepped from a booth of perfumes and spices, their attention was drawn by a loud, angry voice and derisive laughter attending it. The voice belonged to a sharp-eyed man dressed in a robe like a holy man. Catching sight of Roman, he pointed a bony finger at his face and demanded, "Repent, sinner, or burn forever in hell!"

Roman quietly replied, "I have repented. I am a follower of the Way."

The man widened his eyes and declared, "Liar! You are a soldier—a murdering, blood-loving soldier!"

Roman's face began to harden. "Yes, I am a soldier. But I am also a believer. I do not kill for lust—I do not murder. I do not extort money. I do not rob. I perform my duty as it is required of me, and I follow our Lord in all that He commanded."

"No soldier can be a follower. It is a profession for the damned!"

Roman's face was flint and his eyes were sparking. "Do you know the Scriptures?"

"Certainly!"

"When soldiers came to be baptized of John, they asked him what was required of them in their new life. He told them not to rob or extort, but to be content with their wages. And our Lord, when the centurion in a foreign army asked Him to speak a word and heal his servant, proclaimed the soldier's faith the greatest He had ever seen. Were these damned?" A listening crowd had gathered by this time.

Roman's accuser sputtered, "You cite Scripture to cover your own blackness!"

Roman shot back, "Are you God, to judge the heart?"

The man turned and fled into the crowds. Someone nearby murmured, "Well said." Deirdre gazed at her guardian in new respect. He paused a moment to regain his usual air, then looked down at her. "Would you like to see the livestock now?" She grinned and nodded.

It was late afternoon when Roman began to show his fatigue. Deirdre was tired also; she could hardly hold on to everything she had bought (even though Roman was carrying most of it). They trudged back to the remote field where their horses had been left grazing. As they passed the last booth, she turned to speak to him, but stopped in mid-sentence as she saw a silver-haired man at Roman's back raising a knife. The expression on her face caused him to wheel, scattering merchandise, and he caught the man's hand as it plummeted. Roman threw Stase to the ground but was pulled down with him. "Run!" he rasped. "To the horses! *Now!*"

She could not. She was frozen in horror as she watched them wrestle. The assassin gained the advantage and raised his dagger again for the kill. Roman stayed his hand for a moment but, weak and hurting, he could not hold him long. Deirdre screamed. The dagger came down. Then it stopped in midair. Stase froze in a crouch, staring at Roman. Then he slumped forward. The shaft of an arrow protruded from his back.

Roman pushed the dead man away, and Deirdre rushed to his side. At that instant a robed figure came running from a booth toward them. It was the Counselor: "I heard you scream, Chataine—" he halted abruptly as he saw the assassin. "What—is that Stase?"

"Yes—he tried to kill Roman. Counselor, he—Roman—may be hurt. We must get him back to the palace straightway," she gasped.

"Certainly. My carriage is here. We will return in it . . . your boy can ride your horses back." He paused. "You should not have killed him, Roman. Now we will never know who hired him."

"I didn't," Roman panted.

"No? Who did?"

Roman shook his head. Deirdre answered, "I did not see who it was."

Eudymon left to summon his carriage. A merchant rushed past him to look over Roman and Deirdre and the dead assassin. The man gave a low whistle. "Good shot! Who'd have thought a fellow like that could handle a bow? You all right, Sonny?"

"Who was it? Who shot him? Did you see him?" grilled Deirdre.

"Sure, didn't he tell you?" The merchant looked surprised. "The High Lord's Counselor shot him. Saw them fighting, grabbed a bow, and let one fly. Perfect shot."

When the merchant returned to his booth, Roman cautioned her, "Deirdre, do not say anything to the Counselor about this. And do not tell anyone that he shot Stase."

"But shouldn't Father know?" she asked.

"I will speak to him," Roman replied. So, difficult as it was, she held her peace. The long, silent ride to the palace was somewhat awkward. At every bump and jolt of the carriage, Deirdre looked anxiously to Roman. "I am not hurt, Chataine. Only winded. Warding you is quite a challenge," he smiled. She returned a little smile to him, rubbing her hands nervously. The Counselor made her so uneasy.

When they arrived at the palace, Deirdre took his arm firmly. "I want the physician to look at you."

"I will go see him now, Chataine. You must take all these things you bought and show them to your nursemaid." Deirdre thought that was a fine idea, so he called a boy to carry the goods for her. "Nanna, look!" she commanded, bouncing into her chambers. The nursemaid came scurrying, and Deirdre laid out her treasures.

"Oh!" exclaimed Nanna. "How lovely!" She smiled and nodded as she examined the doll, jewelry, trinkets, and cloth. But she picked up the leather with a questioning frown.

"That is for Roman," Deirdre said proudly. "I want to make him a shortcoat. You must teach me to sew now."

Nanna put down the leather slowly. "Chataine . . . that is so dear of you . . . But it is unseemly for you to make clothes for a soldier—"

"Roman does not want it, and you do not want me to, but I want to!" Deirdre insisted, her face screwing up.

"Certainly, dear, certainly! I will be happy to teach you!"

Meanwhile, as he promised, Roman went to the infirmary and looked in the door. The physician turned to him. "We have returned, and I am well," Roman told him. He nodded.

Then Roman walked slowly to the Surchatain's chambers. He addressed the guard at the door. "Kindly tell the Surchatain I have a report for him."

The guard nodded and went within. Roman heard Karel say, "Send him in," so he entered. "Yes, Roman, how did it go at the Fair?"

"Well enough, to a point, High Lord," he answered, then coughed. "We were attacked by the assassin as we returned to the horses."

Karel startled. "Deirdre?"

"She is unharmed. He attacked me. But, as we were fighting, someone shot and killed him."

"Yes?" Karel frowned. "Who?"

Roman bit his lip and said, "I did not see who shot him. Nor did Deirdre. It could have been someone aiming at me."

"Indeed. Well, we must assume that Stase's employer will have to hire someone else now. Blazes! We must find out who that is! Well, you are dismissed." Roman bowed and turned. "Er— Roman."

He looked back inquiringly. "Surchatain?"

"Well done." Roman bowed.

At dinner, Deirdre was pleased to find herself the center of attention as she recounted the incident to the guests at table. She described how she had turned to see the assassin at Roman's back, and how they had fought. "Then he raised his knife, and poor Roman was so weakened—I thought he was good as dead," she sighed to a hushed audience. "Then from nowhere comes this arrow, and kills the assassin!" A murmur went around the table, and Roman sat watching her fixedly.

"A lucky arrow, to be sure," remarked Galapos. "But it could not have come from nowhere. Who shot it, sweetheart?"

"Well, that is the strangest thing!" she exclaimed, forgetting Roman's caution. "It was—" She caught Roman's intense gaze and paused. *He asked me not to tell,* she remembered. *But shouldn't I always tell the truth, Roman?* "It was—" *Why shouldn't I say the truth?*

Her conscience answered: *What do you wish to gain by saying all you know?*

"It was no one that we could see," she ended weakly. Galapos cocked an eyebrow at her. Roman breathed out and looked at his plate. The Counselor looked at Roman.

Oblivious to all this, Karel commented, "Yes, that is what Roman said," and proceeded to spear a chunk of venison. The guests sat quietly looking from face to face.

Shortly after the Fair, Galapos gathered his men to return to his outpost on the border. New disturbances were continually arising, and the army required his coordination on the field. Deirdre chanced upon Roman and Galapos conferring one last time before his departure. She could not prevent herself from eavesdropping. "Galapos,"—Roman's voice was even lower than usual—"I wish more than anything to go with you and fight by your side, even as just your errand boy again."

Galapos shook his head slowly. "I have an errand boy. I do not need another." He paused. "I need a Second in command. I need a good fighter and a quick thinker. I need a man loyal to his Commander and his troops." Their eyes locked. "Christian or not, you're the best soldier under my command. When you have done with your babysitting, ride on out. The position will wait for you."

"Galapos—" Roman choked. He was actually beaming.

The Commander shook his head in mock disgust. "Don't go soft on me now, boy." His voice dropped to a whisper. "May your God ward you well until we ride together again." He departed.

Roman stood watching him go, his eyes frozen on the middle distance. Deirdre stood in shock. She had always assumed that he would rather be her guardian than anything else—that it was the greatest honor he could have. But now it was clear he would rather be with Galapos, off fighting some bloody war. Why? Did he not have everything here? Was he not happy?

Then the inaudible voice of her conscience spoke again: *Why should he be happy? What has he received but injury and abuse? And what have you yourself done for him but try to control and use him?*

That is not fair, she argued. I cared for him in the infirmary. *To console yourself for putting him there . . .*

Roman turned from the door and saw her, "Chataine—did you—"

"Roman," she rushed, struggling to control herself, "do you— are you happy taking care of me?"

"Happy, Chataine?"

She struggled harder. "You would rather be with Galapos, would you not?"

"I am a soldier under orders, Chataine. I have been given my assignment—my purpose—in guarding you. If I desert my assignment, how useful could I be to Galapos?"

It required seconds for her to understand his meaning. "But—I thought you had volunteered to be my guardian. Did you not want to be?"

He whispered, "No."

She let out a great sob and ran from the room. He called after her, but she ran harder, straight up to her chambers. She refused even to talk to Nanna, but bolted her door and cried on her downy bed.

An hour later, she had stopped crying and started thinking. It was true. It was all true. Why should he care for her? What reason had she given him? She rose from her bed and studied her reflection in the looking glass. Determination formed inside her. From this time on he would have a reason—she would give him one. She would treat him with appreciation and respect, the way she saw him treat Galapos. Then perhaps he would feel the same about her as the Commander felt about him.

There was a knock on the outer door. Roman's voice said, "Chataine, please come out. I have been too harsh—"

She flung open the door and threw her arms around his middle. "I love you, Roman."

Riding together that afternoon, she was so exuberant, he was smiling in response. When they dismounted to hike up a small hill, she took his hand in hers and swung it as they walked. Toying with his fingers, she marveled at how big and brown they were next to hers. When they sat to rest at the top of the hill, she put her arms around his neck and kissed his cheek. She felt that here, in him, was her one true friend—someone to take care of her and stay with her regardless of how badly she acted at times. For the first time, she felt genuine gratitude to him.

But he cautioned her gently, "I value your affection greatly, Chataine, but someone else seeing it might not understand. It would be best if you did not hold me or kiss me." Deirdre's face burned as she released him. He did not care for her—he was only doing his job, as he said. She would never be anything more to him than a chore. Tears filled her eyes and she jumped up to stumble to her horse.

As he helped her mount, she saw his dismay: "Chataine, I am sorry to make you cry . . . But you must understand that I could be put to death for such a small thing. We will show our affection in other ways. Deirdre?'' She nodded, sniffling. And he made her see his affection in the way he was gentle and open with her. Even though she did not want to admit he might be right, by the time they arrived at the palace she was smiling at him again.

By dinner her high spirits had returned. She understood him better now—of course he cared. She could see that. They would always be friends. Roman, for his part, was marveling at the flexibility of her moods.

Her father spoke little until they had finished the beef pie. Then abruptly he said, ''Roman, I have heard a disturbing report today. It seems that you were seen embracing my daughter. Is this true?''

''Not entirely, High Lord,'' replied Roman calmly. ''The Chataine put her arms around my neck and kissed me.''

Before Karel could reply, Eudymon threw down his cloth and exclaimed, ''High Lord, this is outrageous! This soldier must be punished!''

''I will decide that,'' the Surchatain said peevishly. ''Deirdre, why did you do that?''

''I did it because I wanted to!'' she flared. ''He has taken care of me and saved my life and I felt I owed him—something! Will you ever trust him? Or do you have spies watching us, too?''

''Enough!'' Karel bellowed. After pausing to gain control, he said, ''I merely wanted to give him the chance to deny it. You shall not be punished, Roman,'' with a glance at the Counselor. ''And you, daughter—keep your hands to yourself!'' Deirdre burned as a titter went around the table. Roman was not smiling.

She sat very still and sullen until she was dismissed, then she went straight upstairs to her chambers, wishing she never had to come down again.

The next day she did not leave her rooms at all until Roman knocked on her door. ''Chataine, come riding with me. It will be all right.''

''No,'' she shouted through the door. ''I do not want anyone watching us.''

''I have something to tell you about that. Open the door.'' When she did, he said, ''It seems your father reprimanded the servant who gave him that report yesterday. I believe we will not be watched as closely from now on—or at least not be reported to your father. We can still ride together."

She hesitated. "They were all laughing at me last night," she said glumly.

"And I am sure by today they have all forgotten why. Chataine," he said, "humiliation can be a good thing if you accept it straightforwardly. It tends to keep your perspective true." He added, lower, "That is a lesson I learned not long ago myself." She remembered his embarrassment over Nanna's gossip.

Relenting, she took his hand and began to walk with him down the corridor, then remembered something. "Wait! Wait right here!" She rushed back into her rooms. When she came out again, she was carrying a bundle rolled up in her arms. Shyly, she held it out to him.

"What . . . ?" He unrolled it and then smiled broadly to see a nicely sewn leather shortcoat. He shed his old one to try it on. "It fits well," he noted, straightening his shoulders.

"Nanna helped me with it," she admitted, "Do you like it?"

"Very much," he smiled. "I thank you, Chataine." She grinned proudly and took his hand to swing it as they walked.

A few days following, when she had finished her morning lessons, Deirdre wandered downstairs to look for something to do. Her first inclination was to find Roman, but little whispers and smiles were going around the palace about how much time she demanded of him. So she took her embroidery to the garden and began to work, but the sweet spring air, the scent of apple blossoms and the sight of robins would not let her do that for long. She put it aside and wandered back toward the kitchen. From within, she heard his voice and froze. He was saying, "We will need some fruit . . . some bread, too. We may be gone all day." A girl's voice answered him with some words in laughter, and he said, "It will do us both good to get away from the palace for a few hours."

Deirdre wanted to feel jealous, but could only droop her head. *He has the right to be with other people and do other things.* Before she could move away, he came out of the kitchen with his pack, a comely, black-haired serving girl behind him. They saw her and paused in surprise. Seeing them standing together, Deirdre felt suddenly awkward and conspicuously out of place.

"Chataine, are you well this morning?" Roman asked in genuine concern. She nodded. "Good, because we are doing something different today. I think we have both seen enough of the fields and hills around Westford. I am taking you out farther today, to see more of the countryside."

"Me?" she exclaimed. "You are taking me?"

His brow furrowed in mild perplexity. "Yes, you, if you wish to go. Do you want to go with me?"

"Yes, yes!"

"Well, come!" he gestured, then lifted his hand to wave goodbye to the girl.

He took her on a northeasterly route towards plains and gentle hills. They found a rough road which straightened to the east. Roman pointed out scurrying foxes and silken-antlered deer, and they laughed at magpies fighting over a berry bush. They passed the fuller's field and Deirdre wrinkled her nose at the odor.

"Must they work so close to Westford?"

"You had better be glad they do," Roman laughed. "They clean your clothes, and mine. We wouldn't be able to endure the smell of each other if they didn't do their smelly work." She laughed a little ashamedly in response.

Farther out, they began to pass little cultivated fields. Peasant farmers paused in their planting to call greetings to Roman, and he always lifted his hand genially in response. "Does everyone love you?" she wondered aloud.

"No," he said. "Delmar, though, remembers when I spoke in defense of him against Lord Farquehart, who was trying to take his land. And Taine recalls when I helped him pull his prize cow out of a mud pit. Your actions come back to you. You reap what you sow." He said it with the confidence of having lived it.

They rode on, and talked, and ate from his pack, and Deirdre considered how the light cast from just one person could color her world so intensely.

1

The spring of Deirdre's fourteenth year heralded major turning points in her life. She was disappointed not to be able to see the Fair that spring, as there were still concerns for her safety. But many of her favorite merchants brought their goods to the palace for a private showing. And as always, after her lessons, she and Roman rode out to the hills or to the lake to explore. Often, they brought crumbs for the birds, and Roman took her boating on the crystal water.

They returned many times to their favorite resting place on the edge of the lake, under the willows. The lilies were in bloom now, their heads drooping down to the water as if to drink. This place of theirs was quiet and sheltered from the hot sun of summer as well as from curious eyes and ears. She and he could talk without fear of being overheard. Often, Roman would lie in the grass as she sat reading or sewing. Other times, when his head throbbed from the bludgeoning years before, he would prop his head on her knees and she would massage the pain down to a murmur.

They talked of many things. Once, when Roman had mentioned his mother in passing, she felt the itch of curiosity. . . .

"Will you tell me more about your mother, Roman?" Deirdre asked delicately.

He shrugged, tossing a crumb to the ducks. "It is true that she was a prostitute at one time, but when she met my father, she stopped seeing other men. She said he loved her too, but he never married her. Yet she was as faithful to him as if he had."

"Roman, I have always wondered . . . was he a believer?"

"No," he said emphatically.

"And Galapos is not, is he?"

"No."

"Then, how did you come to be one?"

His eyes went back over years. "You did not ask me if my mother was." She began to stumble over words in her surprise, but he waved it off. "Of course not. Not a prostitute. But this is what happened: One afternoon, some months before she died, I came home to find her crying on her knees. It frightened me—I thought she was hurt. But she looked up at me from where she knelt, and I saw her eyes shining with unspeakable joy. She hugged me and said, 'Roman, all is well now. All is forgiven. God is with us and we will be cared for.' I was really confused. I thought she was talking about the money my father was sending us to live on. But then I learned that a holy man had come and talked to her about God. She had believed his message.

"That holy man came back to our hut a number of times to instruct my mother in the Way and pray with her. I shunned him, though—I did not trust him. But listening to my mother's prayers was comforting. They mostly concerned me. By the way, do you remember the minstrel who came to the palace, the man your father had flogged for his song?" She paused, then nodded. "That was the holy man who had taught my mother. I am sure of it."

"How strange! Did he teach you also, then?"

"No—I would have none of him. It was not until a year or so later, after I had come into the army. . . . I was cleaning Galapos's buckler and sword one day, listening to a group of soldiers nearby. One was telling the others about another soldier who had died the day before—he had taken a blow meant for that fellow, and it had killed him. So this one was telling all the others about his valor and sacrifice. He kept saying over and over, 'He died for me. He died for me.' Those words—they pierced me to the bone. I remembered then something the holy man had told my mother. So I went and found the holy man, Tychus, who holds services here—he was here then, too—and asked him who had died for me. He told me the story of the Christ. I believed then, and was baptized."

He sat still, recollecting. She said, "What is that story?"

He looked at her in some surprise, and said, "Many years ago, God sent His only Son to earth as a man, born of a virgin, to live among us and teach us about God. He performed many miracles, healing the sick and giving sight to the blind and even raising people from the dead. He taught us how to love God and love others, and called us to repentance—"

"What is that—'repentance'?"

"It means to admit that we have gone wrong, and to come back to God and obey Him. You repented to me, after I was whipped because of the horse—remember?" She winced and nodded. "Well, same thing, only it is God who forgives us. As I was saying, He went about teaching of God. But the established leaders hated Him, for they were evil and He called them so. Therefore, they condemned Him by trickery and executed him by torture." She held her breath. "Yet they did not triumph over Him, for it was in God's plan that His only Son should die to pay the penalty for our crimes, that we might live. So on the third day God raised Him to new life. He went up to the Father in heaven, but promised to send His Spirit to live in us until He should come again Himself to take us to live with Him forever."

He fell silent, gazing over the lake, and she studied him. It was the strangest story she had ever heard. She did not wish to question his gullibility for believing it, so she changed the subject: "Will you tell me . . . how your mother died?"

He looked back to her in surprise, but began slowly, "The winter following her conversion was very hard. Some of our neighbors fell ill, and mother took them food, as poor as we were. But then she became sick. It was so sudden . . . in the morning I found her dead." He shook his head at the memory. "I went to our neighbors—they came and buried her, then left me alone.

"The next few weeks were terrible for me. The money my·father had been sending suddenly stopped. Yet I did not know where he was or how to reach him. I lived on what I could scavenge, then went to the neighbors again—the ones my mother had taken food to. They turned me away.

"I went to the town, then, and passed by the bakery. . . . I saw all that bread through the window, and I determined to steal me some."

"They hang you for that!" exclaimed Deirdre.

"I did not know that then," he said wryly. "And I was starving. But a strange thing happened. Galapos came out of the bakery with a basket of fresh, hot buns. He was swinging the basket very carelessly, and a bun fell out. He did not see it (so I thought), so I grabbed it up and ate it. I began following him. Another bun fell, and I ate that one. Then another and another. I followed him clear to the blacksmith's doing this. At the corner by the smith's he dropped the last one, and I bent to pick it up. He grabbed me and shook me. 'You little thief!' he said, 'If you are going to eat my bread you are going to work for it!' It was then he took me into the army as his errand boy."

"What luck!" she marveled. "What was the Commander doing at the baker's?"

"He had some swords on order at the smith's and had gone into town to get them himself. While he was waiting, he decided he was hungry, so he walked down to the bakery. Inside, he saw me looking through the window and guessed what I was about to do. So on his way out he dropped the buns deliberately to lure me away from a hanging."

Deirdre sat pondering the union of fate and kindness that had favored Roman. "No wonder you love him so," she murmured. He nodded, his eyes keen with light.

When they returned to the palace, Deirdre sighted the archers practicing on the grounds. "Roman!" she pulled on his arm, "teach me to use the bow!"

He followed her gaze to the grounds and began to protest: "Chataine . . . that is not fitting pastime for a young lady—and it is not so easy as it looks—"

90

She pouted, "You are ashamed to be seen teaching me."

"Certainly not!" he insisted, but he looked a little guilty. "Come, then," he said, and led her to a weapons stall on the grounds. He selected the lightest bow he could find and, taking his bow and quiver, escorted her to the target area. "Watch me first, Chataine; this is how it is done." He fitted an arrow to the bow, drew back, and released it. The arrow buried itself in the center of the target. She picked up her bow eagerly. "Here—let me show you," he murmured. He placed her fingers and helped her fit the arrow. Several soldiers turned to watch. "Now pull back, as hard as you can—hold tight!" She drew back with all her strength and the arrow fell limply to the ground. The soldiers snickered.

"You are not holding the bow correctly." He placed her fingers again. "Hold it up high—like this." She drew back again, and the arrow covered half the distance to the target before falling. A few soldiers clapped encouragingly.

"That is hard!" she complained.

"I told you it was," he said. "Have you had enough?"

"No!" He raised a brow, smiling, and moved the target up to where the arrow had fallen. He placed her hands on the bow again. She drew it back intently and shot. The arrow hit the target. The soldiers cheered and clapped. "My arms are tired already!" she said.

"It takes practice, day after day, to build up the strength in your arms. It is not something you can master at once."

"If I practice enough, will I get to be as good as you?"

He smiled. "Perhaps. If you practice." Determinedly, she put the arrow to the string again.

It was late in the spring when an unsettling request came to Karel. Tremaine, Surchatain of the neighboring state of Seleca, had a son he wanted Deirdre to meet. Would she come for a visit? Karel said she would.

Roman earnestly protested to Karel himself: "High Lord, it is much too dangerous. That is a two-day ride! If he wishes his son to meet her, have him come here. Your daughter's life is still in jeopardy."

But Karel was adamant. Tremaine was one of the most powerful rulers on the Continent. A marriage between the two families would end Karel's worries over the safety of his little country. He would certainly accommodate Tremaine at this time. "You are responsible for the Chataine's safety while traveling," he reminded Roman. "You were appointed to guard her on just these occasions, remember?"

"Certainly, High Lord," replied Roman grimly. "Then, as I am responsible for her, I ask full freedom to arrange our travel as I think safest."

"Granted."

The Surchatain might have reconsidered had he known the guardian's plans. Roman had decided that he and Deirdre would leave quietly on horseback from the rear gate of the palace. No soldiers would accompany them. They were to travel in disguise.

The morning of their departure, Roman brought some clothes up to Nanna. "Have her put these on."

Nanna stared in horror at the old peasant dress and shawl, stockings, and worn slippers he gave her. "Never!" she asserted.

"You put them on her, or I will do it," he said firmly. "And use this." He handed her a small pillow.

When dressed, Deirdre ran to the looking glass and laughed at her reflection. In the old clothes, she could have been a real village girl. Nanna packed her good clothes in some old traveling bags and she skipped downstairs to show herself off to Roman.

He, too, was in disguise. He wore the frayed breeches and open shirt of a peasant farmer, and an old wide-brimmed hat. They looked each other over. "Where is the pillow?" he asked.

"I do not know what it is for," she said, handing it to him.

He handed it back to her. "Tie it around your waist." Frowning, she began to obey. He bit his lip and stopped her. "Chataine . . . *underneath* your dress."

"Oh." She blushed at her own denseness and tied the pillow on as he said. Suddenly she was a pregnant peasant girl.

"We are traveling as husband and wife," he said. "We are going to Corona to find you a midwife." She giggled. He smiled too, then his face clouded and he took her hands. "Chataine, I have great misgivings about this trip. I do not know if I can protect you adequately. You must promise that if we are attacked you will flee in the time I give you. You must not hang back for my sake, but ride home as hard as you can. Will you do that?''

"Roman . . . I could not leave you.''

"Chataine, what good would it do for you to die? You will have made me a failure. Swear to me you'll ride.''

She choked out, "I swear it.''

"Then let's go.''

Roman loaded up Lady Grey and the Bay Hunter, then they mounted and quietly rode out of the gate. They wound their way around to a well-traveled market road. Along the way, they met several fellow travelers who nodded or waved, and some smiled at Deirdre's big stomach. She kept glancing at Roman. His disguise was certainly clever, but somehow unconvincing. He looked like no peasant she ever saw. What gave him away? Suddenly she knew. His attitude betrayed that his clothes were a lie. He rode too straight, too easily, and his eyes flashed keenness and purpose.

"Roman,'' she murmured, "you ride too straight for a peasant.'' He cocked his head questioningly, then caught her meaning and slumped in the saddle a bit, pulling his hat down. But the alertness in his eyes still divulged itself from under the brim. She sighed. Some things just could not be hidden.

When they had passed the slow carts clogging the road, they spurred to an easy canter. Deirdre was most grateful that this route was flatter and smoother traveling than the road to Ooster. Also, she was a more experienced rider now. Proudly, she flicked the reins in just the manner Roman did.

After several hours of unremarkable travel, they were slowed again by a cart blocking the road. It was driven by a fat, richly dressed merchant carrying cheap wares. "Well, hello there, fellow! And such a pretty little wife! Where be the two of you headed, eh?''

"Corona,'' answered Roman.

"Fine city, beautiful city, been there often myself. Why, they have the prettiest wh—'' he coughed and glanced at Deirdre—"the finest wares of any city around. You going there for business?'' He looked at their horses. "You don't have anything to sell.''

93

"We are going for a midwife," Roman answered, looking to maneuver around his cart.

"Oh, well certainly! Say, you don't have to go all the way to Corona for one! I know a great little midwife who lives only a few miles from here. Just follow me and I'll take you to her."

"Thank you, but we are going to Corona," Roman answered him flatly.

"Well, sure you are, if you say so," agreed the man. Roman was directing his horse off the road to pass him when the merchant said, "Those are certainly fine-looking horses you got there. I'd give you a good sum for those horses."

"No," Roman answered. Deirdre thought he looked apprehensive.

"Well, as you say, certainly," the merchant responded brightly. Then, "Well, look, here's my turnoff! Good traveling to you both!"

As soon as he was off the road Roman barked, "Ride!" and they spurred their horses to a run. At a fork in the road on the edge of the forest, he led her up one trail twenty strides. Then they circled back and hid in the trees.

"What—?" she began, but he gestured for her silence and pointed to the road. Seconds later she heard hoofs, then caught a glimpse of two armed riders thundering up the trail he and she had just been on. Then Roman and Deirdre quickly mounted again and galloped up the other fork. They ran the horses to a lather until Roman felt it was safe to stop and rest.

"They will not chase us this far," he panted. "It is not worth that much to them."

"Who are they? What did they want?" She could hardly get the questions out fast enough.

"Renegade soldiers, of course. The merchant is in league with them. You don't think he bought all those fine clothes by selling that junk in his cart, do you?" She was starting another question when he stopped her. "He is a lookout for them. He spots chickens—unarmed folk—determines their valuables, then alerts his friends. They split the profits."

"They wanted our horses?"

"Only thing of value we have."

They continued their travel until dusk, when they made camp in a tiny clearing in the forest. Roman would have preferred to spend the night in the outpost on the way, but that would have rendered their disguises useless. For safety's sake he did not build a fire, so Deirdre huddled close to him as they ate. Night in the forest was very black and cool. She began shivering uncontrollably. He unwrapped the blankets and made her a little bed beside him. When she continued to shiver, he put his arms around her. She snuggled up and dropped off to sleep.

He woke her in the grayness of early dawn for breakfast. Now he did build a small fire, and they ate standing over it to shake off the chill of the morning fog. With the reassurance of daylight, Deirdre began to feel a great sense of adventure and cunning—regardless of what *he* said, she could not imagine any danger surpassing his abilities. She tied her pillow back in place as Roman saddled the horses, and they began the second day of their trip.

The cool of the morning carried into the day, and the road was flat and fast. The ride would have been most pleasant if it were not for Roman's constant wariness. He seemed particularly uneasy while they crossed the plain and rode through Falcon Pass, but relaxed somewhat once they were past the Fastnesses. They talked then, and he even sang her a silly drinking song:

> A man and his love had a terrible spat:
> She scratched his face and he knocked her flat;
> She spit at him and he threw her around;
> She jumped from behind and he fell to the ground.
> How sad to see such trouble as that
> Between a man and his household cat.

Deirdre laughed. "I'll wager you learned that from Galapos."

"No," he admitted, "from my father."

"Shame on him for teaching a young child drinking songs!" she scolded.

"Oh, no," he laughed, "it was not until years later that—" He cut short, but Deirdre had caught his slip.

"Then you saw him again after your mother died?"

"Yes."

He gave her a warning look, so she only asked: "Did he give you the medallion?"

"Yes," he sighed. "Deirdre, please do not ask me any more about him." Momentarily satisfied by this new bit of information, she allowed them to ride on in silence.

They entered Corona late that afternoon and blended into the city. Deirdre strained her neck staring—narrow, dirty streets crowded with merchants, milling crowds, sinister figures darting out of sight. The scene reminded her of the Fair, only so much more tawdry. They stopped at an inn to change into their good clothes, then slipped unobserved out a back way.

Shortly, they stood in front of the imposing gates of Tremaine's residence. A guard in a glittering tabard escorted them to the audience hall. Accustomed as she was to luxury, even Deirdre gaped at the splendor of this room. At the far end stood an awesome golden throne, resting on the backs of four golden lions, all facing outward. The throne was detailed in spiraling patterns of precious gems. The wide expanse of floor between her and the throne was completely covered in a brilliant mosaic of sapphire, jasper, obsidian, amber, amethyst, and more. Like a mural, it seemed to depict a story—she noted many bloody battle scenes, and long rows of people in chains. There were beheadings and pictures of torture. Entranced, she followed the scenes until they ended in the center at a colossal representation of a man in a golden robe, holding a sword in one hand and a globe in the other.

"Supposedly, that is Tremaine," Roman said through her thoughts, nodding toward the mosaic. "The tenor of his rule is apparent." Deirdre looked toward him, but her attention was distracted by the paneled mahogany walls which extended up at shifting angles to golden chandeliers. Light from thousands of candles reflected off every surface until Deirdre became dizzy in the brilliance. Roman steadied her.

Moments later Tremaine himself appeared, wearing the golden mantle depicted in the mosaic. Tall and bearded, he walked in power, and Deirdre stood in trepidation as he approached them. He stopped before her and looked down with eyes of seizing intensity. "Chataine Deirdre, my dear, I am so pleased to greet you at last. You are welcome in the palace of Corona."

Roman squeezed her arm gently and she came to life. "Thank you, Surchatain." She bowed unsteadily.

Tremaine turned to Roman. "And this?"

"This is my guardian, Roman, Surchatain." She began to breathe with some regularity now.

Tremaine eyed Roman as he bowed. "Karel is a cautious man," he mused.

"He deemed it necessary, High Lord," Roman answered.

"Come, then. Dinner awaits you." Tremaine turned in a swirl of gold and led them to a dining hall that mirrored the luxury of the audience hall—literally. For this hall was paneled with seamless sheets of glass on silver that reflected the entire room and its people more truly than any looking glass Deirdre had ever seen. Gazing at the endless reflection of mirror in mirror caused her vertigo to return; Roman directed her to the chair Tremaine indicated near his own. As they sat, the Surchatain introduced his son Rollet—a tall, proud eighteen-year-old. He looked Deirdre over, then nodded curtly to his father.

"Deirdre, my dear," began Tremaine. "This is a long-awaited pleasure for me. Your father and I have been discussing your future since almost the day you were born."

"I know Father respects you very much," Deirdre said carefully—Rollet was irritating her with his cool, haughty stare—"but it is law in Lystra that I choose my own husband."

"Truly?" Tremaine looked genuinely surprised. "How interesting. I shall endeavor to make a good showing, then. You know, dear, an alliance between us would greatly profit Lystra."

"There are other provinces which claim that. My uncle Corneus wants me to marry his son Jason." Deirdre felt he should know Rollet was not her only choice.

"Indeed?" Tremaine raised a finger toward a servant behind him to order more herbed bread from the kitchen. Deirdre felt pressure from Roman's knee, and she turned to see a discreet, cautioning look in his eyes. She understood at once that she was talking too much.

When Tremaine turned back around, Deirdre asked, "Surchatain, will you explain the beautiful mosaic in the audience hall?"

He smiled. "That is the history of my conquest of this region and the expansion of its borders. When I assumed the throne, my dear, Seleca was smaller than Lystra, our northern border being the Fastnesses. But through a series of brilliant campaigns, I extended our region to three times its former size. Yet, we are still landlocked, and the Passage does not flow strongly enough for large vessels until well into Lystra. . . . So you see, we are serious about an alliance." He raised his eyes, and Deirdre was again shaken by their intensity.

"What do the sword and the globe in the mural mean?" she sputtered in confusion.

He leaned back, smiling again, though he did not relieve her of his gaze. "The sword represents my power. The globe represents my domain. Both are invincible."

Servants brought in savory dishes of delicate roast dove, but Deirdre was too distracted to pay much mind to the food. Tremaine then turned to Roman. "So you are her guardian. That must be a shamefully pleasant task."

"At times, Surchatain," Roman answered.

"Or does it bore you—to wait at the door of fests while your charge dances?"

"She is only fourteen, High Lord. Her first fest is not for two years yet."

"Ah, yes, I had forgotten," though he obviously had not. "You look mature for your age, dear—like a Surchataine already. Do you not agree, Rollet?"

"She has promise," he conceded. Then, as bowls of creamy custard were set before them, Rollet suggested, "When you finish your dessert, I will take you to see the Sorcerer's Rooms, Deirdre."

She glanced in panic toward Roman, who said, "Chataine, it would be rude of us to leave the High Lord."

"Not you. Her," Rollet articulated.

"Forgive me, Chatain," Roman answered without a tinge of

remorse, "but I have been charged with her safekeeping at all times."

Rollet opened his mouth but Tremaine interposed, "Of course. We certainly do not wish you to forsake your charge. Rollet, I am sure Roman would find the Rooms most interesting also." He gave Rollet a look which Deirdre could not interpret, but Rollet suddenly understood something that made him smile. Tremaine stood, signaling the end of the meal.

The others stood and Rollet said, "Come with me, then." He held out his arm to Deirdre. Roman moved to her side. Then Rollet took a torch and led them to a back room of the palace. He walked right up to the far wall of the room and pressed a panel. The wall came open, and Deirdre saw a narrow flight of crude stone steps. Roman took her arm.

Rollet turned in the eerie glare of torchlight and whispered, "Climb them carefully." He began to ascend them first; behind him, Deirdre gathered her skirts nervously and proceeded. Roman followed her closely. They were treacherous steps, steep and slippery, but he kept a steadying hand on her back. At the top was a rough-hewn wooden door. Rollet produced a silver key from his coat and unlocked it. "This is the blue room," he whispered. He pushed open the door, and Deirdre felt a waft of cold air. They stepped into a small room completely of blue—a blue so intense it seemed to vibrate the air.

Deirdre stood rooted in a confusion of senses. The light in this room did not come from Rollet's torch—it was a blue light, and colored everything vivid blue. The room had two doors—the one through which they had entered and another opposite it—but no windows. It was empty except for a small table and chair. The table held a thick, old book and a statuette of a naked man with the head and feet of a goat.

Deirdre looked up at Roman. His skin was deep blue and his hair was blue-black. His brown soldier's uniform had also taken on varying shades of blue. He was staring at the statuette.

"Blue is the color of power from knowledge—of hidden things locked deep in the heart of man," whispered Rollet, his face as blue as Roman's. "Blue is the key." He held up the key, and it shone a bright silver in the blue light. It alone kept its natural color in the room.

Rollet took her arm and guided her to the opposite door. "This is the green room," he whispered, taking the handle, but she felt something amiss and turned to look back at Roman.

He was standing in the same spot, motionless as the statuette which held his eyes. "Roman," she said. He did not move. "Roman!"

He looked to her as if snapping out of a trance. "What? Chataine—" He blinked and shook his head, hastening to her side.

Rollet seemed irritated at the disturbance. "The green room!" he insisted, opening the door. The air that wafted from it was heavy and perfumed. Inside, it vibrated with green—lush, rich green. The room had in it a couch, on which was placed a nude figurine of a woman.

Deirdre felt Roman suddenly step away from her side. He was drawing deep breaths, keeping his eyes away from the figurine. She gaped at him, wondering what was troubling him. He looked disturbed and anxious, yet his eyes were drawn irresistibly to the couch.

"Green is the color of desire," Rollet whispered, "and of all sweet things of the earth." Deirdre looked again with real concern at Roman. The agony of resisting forbidden desires was painted vividly in his face. He tore his eyes from the couch and breathed out one word. Then she suddenly felt him relax. He squeezed her hand and nodded reassuringly. She sighed in relief.

But Rollet had his hand on the next door. "This is the red room," he chuckled. He swung open the door and Deirdre felt herself immersed in hot, sticky air. This room had in it a table which held a sword and shield. "Red is the color of blood, of war, and of death," said Rollet.

"Oh, no!" Deirdre wheeled to Roman. He looked as if he were bathed in blood—trembling and sweating, clenching and unclenching his fists. She could almost see the violence raging inside him. "Roman!" She grasped his arms and felt his tense muscles hard as iron. He wrenched free of her grasp and staggered backward, covering his eyes with his hands as if to gouge them out. His lips formed one word over and over again. Then, when she thought he was lost, he opened his eyes and nodded at her, drained and shaky.

"Rollet!" she spun on him angrily. "I do not know what is happening but I do not like it. You get us out of here!"

He restrained his satisfaction. "There is only one room left. We can go through it, or return the way we came. Do you wish him to repeat what he has just been through?"

She turned her eyes to Roman's blood-red face. He looked numbly at her. "No," she said.

Rollet put his hand to the last door. "This," he said slowly, savoring the moment, "is the black room." He pushed the door open into a black, yawning abyss. His torch died suddenly. The room was utterly black and still—yet, she sensed something building from its corners. Rollet's voice came in an echo: "Black is the color of hell."

With a mighty rush something gathered and threw itself full force on Roman. The odor of it made her gag. She felt Roman thrown back and heard him choking. She opened her mouth to scream, but heard him cry, "Jesus!"

At once Rollet's torch blazed fiercely to light. He dropped it. The outer door flung itself open and pure white light poured into the darkness. Deirdre stood blinking in the middle of a small, plain, unremarkable room.

She bent beside Roman who was raising himself from a sprawl on the floor. "Roman, are you hurt?" He shook his head. Rollet looked dazed.

As they exited the room into a normal sitting room, Tremaine turned to greet them. He startled to see Roman step into the room behind Deirdre. Forgetting her fear of him, she opened furiously to Tremaine: "Your Sorcerer's Rooms are not interesting! They are horrible! Who are you to abuse your guests in such a manner?"

He seemed taken aback. "I am so sorry to cause you unpleasantness, Chataine—you should not have been affected by the little spells they contain. They are harmful only to persons with a certain weakness."

"What weakness?" She could not imagine a flaw in Roman that she did not share.

"Those who claim a belief in God," he said evenly.

Deirdre stared at him in silent astonishment, hardly able to comprehend the import of what he said. Roman spoke: "You would have no power over us but what God allows, to serve His own purposes."

Tremaine narrowed his eyes. "You tread dangerously, young man."

Deirdre said stonily, "I have had enough entertainment for the evening, High Lord. I wish to retire."

He bowed. "I shall summon a servant to show you to your chambers, my dear. My profound apologies that your guardian suffered ill in our little rooms," he uttered.

They were taken to a stately suite, and Deirdre was most relieved to see that Roman would occupy a small room adjoining hers. Before retiring, he searched carefully around her room, examining in particular the carved paneling on the walls. He pushed and poked and knocked all around them, then stood back, shaking his head. "This is not to my liking at all," he muttered. "Bolt your outer door, but not the one between us."

She lay down to sleep, but could not relax for fear of the darkness of the room—how much it was like the black room! Eventually, however, fatigue closed her eyes.

Later in the night, Deirdre roused half awake. In the darkness, the wall of her room seemed to be moving. Then she heard muffled footsteps and sensed someone coming toward her. In an instant, she was fully awake: "Roman!" The intruder lunged for her, but was too late to stifle her scream. The door crashed open and Roman appeared. Two forms pounced on him and covered his face with foul-smelling rags. They needed only a moment. He sagged and collapsed on the floor. Then a flickering light appeared, revealing an opening in the wall. Tremaine stepped into the room, carrying a torch and swearing at his guards. He glanced down at Roman and muttered, "That man is a thorn in my eye!"

"What did you do to him?" Deirdre cried.

"Oh, it is just a little something my sorcerer discovered quite by accident. He will come to himself wholly in the morning. Except for a slight headache." He brightened. "No harm done, my dear. I only needed to talk to you privately. Since we were never given an opportunity, I had to create one myself.''

"What do you want from me?" she gasped.

"It is very simple. I must tell you that I decided it would be wasteful—and unnecessary after all—to kill you. Your father's province will join our alliance in the end, regardless. But you have the power to decide if it shall be done forcibly, with much bloodshed, or peaceably."

"Me?" she choked.

"You. And you shall have a choice about it. If Rollet does not please you, you may marry Merce's son Caspar or Savin's son Artemeus. Our purpose for your country will be accomplished if you take one of these three. Your province will be left intact, though of course it will no longer be—independent. And no lives shall be wasted."

"What if I want none of them?"

"Then you will leave us no choice but to attack. It is true that your father has a well-trained army, and Galapos is a fox, but we have five times his numbers. We would crush his small forces. And everyone you know will die. Beginning with him''—he gestured at Roman's form on the floor.

"I merely desired to give you something to think about, Chataine, before your betrothal fest. The lives of many are in your hands." He turned to leave. "Oh yes," he said, noting Roman, and gave orders. Roman was laid in his bed and the door bolted. "He will awaken in the morning, and should recall nothing of this incident. If he does, you will tell him he merely suffered nightmares. That is all. After the dreams that potion will give him, he will believe you. For if you tell him—or anyone—what has passed between us tonight, you will start the slaughter early. If your father moves against us, we will spare no one. Not even you. And if you are wondering, Chataine, there are others in this alliance I have not mentioned. If your father plans to strike, we will know. Good night, my dear." He exited through the passage and the panel slid smoothly closed. Blackness engulfed the room again. Deirdre huddled awake the rest of the night.

8

efore daybreak Deirdre heard a rustle and groan from Roman's room. Instantly he was pounding on her door. . . .

"Chataine, are you in there? Chataine!"

She hastily opened it before he broke it down. "Are you all right?" he demanded. "What happened? Why did you bolt the door?"

"Nothing happened, Roman," she said uneasily, lighting an oil lamp on the table. In her nervousness, she had to strike the flint several times before it would spark right. "I bolted the door because I became frightened." She cursed herself for not noticing they had bolted it.

He sat on the bed, holding his head, trying to gather his thoughts. "I heard you scream. I opened the door, and—and—"

"No," she said. "You must have been having a nightmare."

He studied her face. "If you were frightened, why did you not come to me? Why did you shut me out?"

She stammered, "I—was not thinking clearly. I—"

"You are lying, Deirdre," he said softly, then anxiously, "What happened? I remember now—I was attacked—they put something on my face, and I could not breathe. . . . Deirdre, what did Tremaine do to you?"

"I don't know what you mean!" she cried.

He grabbed her shoulders. "Deirdre, don't play games with me now! We are in danger here. You must tell me what happened!" She sat on the bed and began to cry. He held her tightly and said, "Listen to me. If you do not trust me, I cannot protect you—I may unwittingly play right into his hands. You are not strong enough to carry this burden by yourself. Let me call on my resources to help you. Let me be your defense!"

She broke. In a hushed voice, she told him everything the Surchatain had said. When she finished, he sat in silence for a minute. Then he said, "We will let Tremaine think his threats have kept you quiet. He is right about one thing—if your father knew, he would be likely to charge unthinkingly, and that would be fatal. You have told me; that is enough. Do not tell anyone else."

"Yes, Roman."

"Go back to sleep now. We are not supposed to rise for hours yet." He rose heavily with a wobble, and returned to his room. She soon dropped off and slept as one of the dead.

Late in the morning, she awoke with a start from a dream in which she had been suffocating in thick blackness. After a moment of coming to, she realized the room was rank and stuffy, so, with a wary glance at the paneling, she lifted herself from bed to the window.

The draperies were heavy and would not open at first, so she gave them a mighty yank. They parted unwillingly. She stifled a little scream to see an ornate iron grill which closed the window fast up. It was wrought in the shapes of tortured faces.

Deirdre yanked the draperies closed again and dressed with remarkable speed for shaking so. She opened Roman's door, but he was gone. Whimpering, she flung open the outer door to see one of Tremaine's glittering guards standing outside. He looked at her with eyes of cold stone.

She straightened and met his gaze. "You may take me downstairs now."

On the way down, she observed artwork hung on the paneled walls which she had not noticed the night before. Tremaine had not only needleworks, but paintings, many of them, rare and costly. He had greater wealth than she had ever seen, or even imagined. The thought crossed her mind, *I wonder why Roman's God cannot do all that for him.* She also considered that if she accepted Rollet she would share in this wealth. But this prospect could not make itself pleasing to her after what she had seen of Tremaine.

When she appeared in the mirrored hall for breakfast, Tremaine turned from Roman to greet her. He was courteous and casual—the perfect host. "Did you sleep well, my dear?" he inquired.

"Not really, High Lord. I had nightmares," she answered coolly.

"Ah, that is a pity! Your guardian here was just saying the same thing." He gestured to Roman, who rose from the table, stroking his head.

She sat down beside him. "Does your head hurt?" she whispered. He murmured, "Ummph" and looked at her with one eye. "Well," she said, "we will not go riding today." She turned to Tremaine. "May we have a cold cloth for his head?"

"Of course, Chataine." He summoned a servant and soon a compress was brought. "I should have known better than to put you in that suite," Tremaine sighed regretfully. "It is haunted by the ghost of a soldier who tried to betray me. He hid in the lesser room, waiting to escape. But of course, we found him and severed his head on the spot. So his spirit lingers, seeking revenge on anyone who sleeps in that room."

"He is satisfied now, High Lord," muttered Roman.

Tremaine beamed. "Is he now? Well. Come to the lower pasture, now, Chataine; we have captured some wild horses I wish you to see. Perhaps your guardian will show us how well he can ride."

Deirdre opened her mouth to protest, but Roman was already standing: "Certainly, High Lord."

Before they reached the door, Rollet hurried up. "High Lord—" he drew his father aside without a word or glance at Deirdre. They talked in whispers a moment, then Rollet disappeared and Tremaine turned to Deirdre. "My dear, something very inconvenient has happened . . . some northern villages have gathered soldiers and revolted. They require my personal correction—Rollet will be accompanying me, of course. I cannot say how long we shall be gone, though you are welcome to remain here in our absence.''

"No—thank you, High Lord," Deirdre said quickly. "We must return to Westford. I think that our purpose in coming has been met.''

"It has," Tremaine said with a tight smile.

"Then we will take our leave." She could almost feel Roman's relief in with her own.

"As you wish. Farewell, Chataine," he nodded.

"High Lord," she nodded in response. He directed his eyes to Roman a moment, but turned on his heel without a word.

Roman and Deirdre were out of the palace within a quarter hour. "Whew!" she sighed, as they galloped up the thoroughfare. "I feel like I am coming out of a bad dream!"

"I, also," Roman said with a trace more intensity in his voice than usual.

"But what shall we do about his threat? I will not marry into that alliance!"

He shook his head slowly. "I do not know what to tell you. I will discuss it with the Counselor, first. He will know best how to advise us and your father.''

"Are you sure you should tell him?" she asked doubtfully.

"Yes.''

They stopped at the same inn as before to don their disguises. Deirdre thought it unnecessary, since Tremaine was no longer trying to kill her, but Roman overruled.

After they had changed, he led her out through the dining room of the inn. It was crowded even at this hour, and a number of patrons were already drunk. One man they passed made an obscene comment to Deirdre. Roman shot him a black look but did not intend to stop. The fellow's drinking companion, however, took umbrage at the remark and swung his fist at his partner's face. He was wide, and came instead within inches of Deirdre's nose. Roman intercepted his arm and flung him against the wall. His fellow jumped Roman from behind, and suddenly everyone was fighting.

Deirdre looked around her in astonishment. She had never been in the middle of a drunken brawl before. Men were punching and kicking and gouging each other, overturning benches and crashing onto tables. A fellow close to her was smashed over the head with a bottle, and a little wine spilled on her old peasant dress. She absently wiped it with a cloth as she watched the melee.

Roman kept trying to get close enough to shove her through the door, but he was too deeply embroiled in the fracas. Everyone seemed to want to take a shot at him. As soon as he knocked one man away, another would jump on his back or grab his legs to trip him.

Then of a sudden Deirdre realized Roman was in trouble. They were ganging up on him; she had to help! Looking around, she spotted an iron skillet hanging on the wall. She gripped it with both hands and started swinging at everyone around Roman. Wham! Blap! "Ow, ow!" "Hey, girl—what?"

They began falling away, and Roman caught Deirdre's hand and rushed her outside. They leaped to their horses and spurred them hard away. When they had reached a small hill safely out of Corona, they paused to breathe.

"I had no idea you were so dangerous," panted Roman. He gingerly touched his bleeding lip and stroked his throbbing brow. "Thank you, Chataine." She beamed at him. Then he said, "Fix your stomach."

"My stomach?" She looked down—her pillow was sitting crazily off to one side. "Oh," she laughed, and straightened it. They smiled at each other.

Then Roman's face darkened again and he said, "We must get back to Westford without delay." She nodded, and they kicked their horses to a gallop. They spoke little on the return trip, intent on making good time, and reached the palace by afternoon of the second day.

Deirdre was immediately summoned to the Surchatain's chambers. "Daughter." He kissed her as she entered. "I am relieved to see you home safe. But why are you back so soon?"

"Tremaine and Rollet were called away by a revolt along their northern border," she answered casually.

"I see. Well, tell me all. How do you like Rollet?"

She hesitated a moment. "I do not, Father, not at all. Nor Tremaine—he scares me."

"Well, he is a powerful man, and you are just a little girl. I am sure he would awe you at first."

"It is not that," she insisted. "He is cruel, and proud, and—devious."

"Well." Karel raised his eyebrows as if she had insulted him instead of Tremaine. "That is not really a matter of yours to judge. Deirdre, I must explain something to you. We are a small country surrounded by others who would eat us alive if they could. Now, that means it is crucial to our survival whom you marry and thus form an alliance with. Tremaine has given me his personal assurance that an alliance between our two families would honor the integrity of our province—"

"And you believe him?" Deirdre asked, amazed. "Father, he told me straightforwardly that one way or another he was going to annex our province to his own!" she blurted, then gasped to realize that once again she had said too much.

He stared at her with fire building in his eyes. "Deirdre, I have endured enough of your lies and disobedience. You will not risk the future of our province to have your own way. You will do as I tell you!"

"I will not marry Rollet!" She defied him squarely, relying on that blessed law to back her up.

He paused, then retreated. "Perhaps not. Your coming out is two years away and your betrothal fest a year after that, so we have time enough to discuss it."

She felt giddy at his sudden concession, and soaked up the feeling of power before a little pain hit. "What will happen to Roman when I marry?"

"He will be retired from the army—with honors, of course."

"Could he not come with me?" She missed him already.

"Of course not. He will no longer be necessary. Your husband will ward you then."

She suddenly recalled the conversation she had overheard be-

tween Roman and Galapos. "He does not want to retire. He wants
to go fight with Galapos."

"What you think he wants is not important."

"But will you not even consider letting him go?"

"The Counselor believes he should be educated in the law, to
train for a counselorship."

"Is the Counselor now responsible for planning Roman's ca-
reer?" she asked sarcastically. She could not conceive of Roman
draped in those pompous, crimson robes, studying those dry old
books. He was too real, too alive to play that tired role.

"You are dismissed, daughter!" he ordered. She swallowed her
resentment, bowed, and left.

Late that night, Roman slipped quietly into the Counselor's
chambers. A messenger was dispatched. The Surchatain was not
awakened.

The following day as they rode out to the hills, Deirdre told
Roman of her conversation with her father. When she mentioned his
defensiveness about Tremaine, he frowned. "I am surprised your
father puts so much faith in him. Obviously, he does not think
Tremaine could ever be a threat. That is most disturbing."

They sat silently for a few moments, while Deirdre explored the
possibilities and found them all undesirable. "What does the Counselor say?" she asked.

"He says to bide our time and build up our defenses. He has sent
word of the situation to Galapos."

"What is he going to tell Father?"

"I do not know."

That prompted a new question from Deirdre: "Roman, I do not
understand the Counselor. Why does he do the things he does?"

Roman shrugged. "I do not understand him either. At times he
has helped me . . . other times he has not."

"Do you think he can be trusted?"

"With matters of state, certainly. He is loyal to your father. But I
would not put my life in his care," he replied. Deirdre detected a
trace of bitterness. Remembering how the Counselor had killed the
assassin at the Fair, she began to ask another question. But for once,
seeing his face, she swallowed and kept quiet.

At that very moment, the Counselor was in private conference with the Surchatain. "High Lord," he was saying, "a most disturbing report has reached me. It seems that Tremaine himself was the one who hired Stase to kill your daughter."

Karel looked incredulously at his Counselor. "That is absurd. Who told you that?"

"Deirdre said he admitted it to her freely—"

"Deirdre!" her father laughed and relaxed. "She has an untameable imagination."

"Apparently, High Lord, there is some truth to it. Roman says Tremaine took extraordinary measures to disattach him from her side so that—"

"Did Roman hear it?"

"No, not directly; but he feels she was telling the truth—"

"Young men are prone to believe anything a pretty child tells them. I will hear no more slander of Tremaine, Counselor. Dismissed."

Eudymon paused, reluctant to leave. But under the Surchatain's fierce glare, he bowed and withdrew.

Weeks slipped quietly by, and the menace of Tremaine seemed to fade into the remote. One summer afternoon Karel summoned Roman to his chambers. "High Lord?" Roman bowed.

"Roman, I heard just this morning that a daughter of one of the nobles drowned recently in the lake—you take Deirdre to the lake often, do you not?"

"Yes, Surchatain," Roman said uneasily.

"Perhaps from now on you should not."

Roman hesitated. "High Lord, have I not warded her well up until now?"

"Yes, you have."

"Well, Surchatain, you can be assured that I am most watchful of her near the lake—"

"I have heard her talk about how you take her boating. That too must stop."

"As you wish, Surchatain. But . . . there are so few enjoyments we allow her, and the lake is one of her greatest pleasures. . . . As her father, will you be the one to tell her she is now forbidden that, also?"

Karel eyed the guardian, thinking. "You will teach her to swim," he said suddenly. "Today."

Roman's eyes widened but he bowed quickly. "Yes, Surchatain."

Deirdre was summoned, and squealed her agreement when told of the plan. Nanna found her some modest bathing clothes, and Roman stopped by his room to don some old sparring breeches. Then he took her to the lake for her first lesson.

First, they waded out into shallow water, and he made her practice holding her breath and going under. Then he took her to deeper water. "No, Roman—do not let go of me," she said anxiously, clinging to him.

"Don't be afraid, Chataine; I am right beside you. I want you to learn to keep yourself afloat."

"Roman, I've decided I do not want to learn to swim after all. Please take me out."

"You can get out when you can swim to shore," he said, lowering her in the water.

"Roman!" She began to thrash in panic.

"Be still!" he insisted. "Just lie still and you will float!"

She went limp, holding her breath, and her face broke the surface. Roman stood beside her in chest-deep water as she floated like a lily pad.

"Now stroke—like this—" he demonstrated, "and kick your legs." She found to her delight she could swim while looking at the sky.

Then he turned her over and showed her how to swim face down. Soon she was splashing all around the lake, as far as he would let her get from shore.

Too soon he called, "Lesson over. Come out now."

"Oh, Roman, I was just getting good at it! I need to practice more."

"You've done well. Come out for now," he insisted. She splashed to him in a circuitous manner and they climbed up on the shore. She turned to him dripping and triumphant, but stopped abruptly. Frowning, he followed her eyes. His wet breeches were clinging tightly to his body, and she was staring at him. Hastily, he covered himself with his dry clothes.

Deirdre looked away, embarrassed. Sometimes she seemed to forget that he was a man. It was a shock to rediscover it. Her attention was drawn to him again as he attempted to untie the horses. He had to fumble considerably with the reins before he could get them untangled from the bushes. She stared at him in amazement—his face had blushed crimson. He glanced sidewise at her and said, "Get on your horse."

She quickly obeyed and they turned silently toward the palace. The novelty of seeing him react so humanly to embarrassment caused a mischievous little smile to appear on her face. Dare she press it? "Roman, I am so ignorant about many things . . . there is so much you could teach me—"

"And there is much I cannot teach you," he interrupted. "Do not even ask." And he abruptly spurred to a gallop. When they reached the palace, he ordered, "Get yourself upstairs and dry off. I am through with you today." She searched his face anxiously, fearing she had angered him, but saw a slight smile. She bowed low to him and ran upstairs.

At dinner the Surchatain asked how her swimming lesson went. "Very well, Father," answered Deirdre innocently. "I learned much more than swimming." Roman's fork clattered to the floor.

"Oh?" said Karel.

"Yes," resumed Deirdre. "I learned that I must get out of the water before I get tired, and that I must not ask Roman to show me things he cannot." Roman stared at her. She alone could see his panic.

But the Surchatain only muttered, "Amazing someone could quash your curiosity." No one else at the table noticed anything awry, and her father addressed another.

But afterwards Roman caught her before she could escape. "What did you think you were doing?"

"Oh, no harm done," she said casually. "No one pays any mind to what I say."

"Nonetheless, if you ever try an experiment like that again, I will—I will—" (she was smiling at him) "I will not take you swimming again." He finished the threat in some confusion, but she put on a sober face.

"I will not, Roman. I promise." He left shaking his head, and she went smiling up to her chambers.

Gradually, over the next few days, Deirdre began to notice a slight change in him. He talked little when they rode and seemed to lose interest in exploring the hills. She abandoned her lessons one morning and went to the window overlooking the practice grounds to watch him. She did not see him at first, then finally spotted him off to the side by himself. He was fidgeting with his longbow, apparently tightening it. Suddenly he threw it down in exasperation and walked away.

When he came at her summons later, she asked, "Ready to go riding?"

He sighed. "Must we today, Chataine? We go every day."

Her stomach tightened. "I thought you enjoyed it."

"Well, I do . . . but every day . . ."

"What is wrong with you, Roman? Why are you behaving so strangely? Are you sick?"

"No. I am sound. We will go riding if you wish."

She became angry. "I want to know what is wrong with you!" He crossed his arms on his chest and just looked at her. At that instant she knew. She had felt that way too often herself. "You are bored," she said slowly. "You are sick with boredom."

He inhaled and looked away, resting his hand on the balustrade. "It's not that only. I have been your guardian for over four years now, and I still have years to fulfill my vow. It's not that I do not enjoy your company—I do—but I wish I were . . . *doing* something. I feel as though I am just waiting around for the next time you get into trouble. There is so much I could be doing now to help Galapos . . . so much I could be accomplishing . . ." he trailed off, and Deirdre was silent. His words stung, although she knew he was right. After some moments he said, "Forgive me. I have no right to burden you this way. It is something I must work out for myself. Come—let's go riding.'' She looked up at him dubiously, but he smiled and cocked his head, extending his hand to her. She took it.

The coming of autumn brought the Fair, and Deirdre was allowed to go for the first time in two years. Roman had little trouble assuring her father that she would be safe enough with him.

It was like going home again. A number of the merchants remembered her and welcomed her back. Her father had given her an extra amount to spend, and she was resolved to spend it all. Recalling the penury of Roman's room, she asked him repeatedly what he would like to have, but he kept saying he had no needs. He weakened when they came to a booth of fine woolens, however, and they were making selections when Deirdre heard a shy voice at her side: "Hello." She turned to see a pleasant-faced, well-dressed girl about her own age. She had dark, thick curly hair under her cap, and green eyes fringed with black lashes.

"Hello," said Deirdre eagerly. "Who are you?"

"I am Laska, daughter of the Surchatain of Calle Valley. And you?"

"I am Chataine Deirdre of Lystra. This is my guardian Roman." He nodded. There was a momentary silence.

Then Laska asked, "Have you been to Anson's jewelry booth yet?"

"No!" And they proceeded with haste to Anson's booth. By the time they arrived, the girls were talking and giggling like old friends. They compared notes on almost every item on display.

Eventually, Laska selected several pieces and said, "I am going to wear these at my coming out year after next. When is yours?"

"The same time!" exclaimed Deirdre.

"Oh, we will be there together! Won't that be splendid? I have heard all about it from Caspar, my older brother. He went to his first fest this past spring, and he told me everything!"

"Well?" cried Deirdre.

"Oh, it is so exciting—so many men! You spend the days playing and meeting young men, and Corneus has a beautiful garden where—" she broke off and glanced at Roman, then whispered in Deirdre's ear.

"Truly?" she squealed.

"Yes," breathed Laska. "If you are really beautiful, a man might fall in love with you the first night. And then he will not be able to look at anyone but you, and he will always want to be near you. Best, he will do anything for you. Anything!"

Deirdre sighed. "It must be wonderful to have someone love you like that."

"Oh, it is!" Laska said it so confidently that Deirdre looked at her in surprise. "My older cousin got married this past spring. She told me all about it," she hastened to explain.

Deirdre's eyes began to glaze. "What does a man do when he falls in love with you?"

"First, he asks you to dance." Deirdre made a mental note to get Olin to teach her to dance. "He holds you close and gazes into your eyes and never once has to look at his feet. Then he tells you how beautiful you are and that he must have you forever. And that is it."

Deirdre blinked. "That is all?"

"Well, sometimes they go about it a little differently, but usually that is what happens," Laska explained. Deirdre watched the crowds with unseeing eyes, dreaming. A handsome young seaman passed by and winked at her, but—catching Roman's cool stare— did not slow his stride. She immediately put the seaman's face on a royal body and imagined him fighting his way through a crowd to beg her to dance. She sighed, taking Laska's arm. "Tell me more."

The girls spent the next few hours in secret conversations, giving cursory attention to the booths they passed. Roman followed unobtrusively. At one point, when Laska mentioned that Caspar would be at the fest with them, Deirdre said, "But, I thought you said he had already been."

"He has," Laska replied. "But Father will not let him marry until he goes to our betrothal fest. And the men can go as many times as they wish until they find their choice."

"Why is your father making him wait?"

"I do not know," Laska frowned. "Caspar said he understood,

but he would not tell me." No insights struck Deirdre, either; Tremaine's threats seemed for the moment to have been forgotten. The remainder of the day slipped away while the girls shared all their treasured secrets.

"I dream sometimes," confided Laska, "of what it would be like to be Surchataine. To have everyone do exactly as I tell them. To make laws and appointments and execute people who displease me. To be the most important person in the country! Why, you could have any man you wanted, just by saying so. As many as you wanted!"

Deirdre nodded, absorbed in her own thoughts. "I dream of being Surchataine, too. . . . I dream of being favored of someone very powerful—the wife of someone who would love me more than all his power and wealth, and prove it. And I dream of being free to travel. . . . to see other places, learn new things . . ." Suddenly she caught a vision of freedom. How would it be to go anywhere she wanted, any time she desired, with no one forbidding her? The possible avenues dazzled her. And at once she wanted that freedom intensely.

Roman was speaking to her: "Chataine, it is time we left. Your father expects us for dinner."

And Laska was saying, "Oh, Deirdre, this has been so nice. I wish you could come visit me. It is a long time until the fest."

"Perhaps I will come see you soon," Deirdre said. Then she whispered, "Are you leaving Hycliff tonight?"

"No," Laska answered in a whisper. "We are staying at the inn here and leaving in the morning. Why?"

"I may go with you tomorrow—if I can get away," Deirdre whispered. Laska nodded excitedly.

"Goodbye, Deirdre!" she called as they mounted their horses.

"Goodbye, Laska," Deirdre winked.

As they rode easily side by side up the broad market road to Westford, Deirdre was quiet, making plans. Roman said, "It was good to see you finally able to spend time with a girl your own age." When she did not reply, he said no more.

She was preoccupied at dinner, also, and asked her father if she could speak with him in his chambers. He walked with her there after the meal. As he closed the door, he said, "What is on your mind, Deirdre?"

"Father, I met Laska today, Surchatain Merce's daughter. She asked me to visit her in Calle Valley—she is staying at the inn in Hycliff tonight, and leaving tomorrow morning. . . . I would like to go with her."

The Surchatain considered. "I see no reason to deny you this. You and Roman may meet her party in Hycliff early tomorrow."

"Father . . . I want to go alone. We will be safe—she has guards traveling with her."

"You cannot go without Roman. He is your guardian."

"Father, I do not need him anymore! I am not in danger. And he never leaves me alone! Let me go without him."

"What possesses you to demand this?" he queried sharply. "You are not going anywhere without Roman! Dismissed!"

She stomped to her rooms and dismissed Nanna curtly, then undressed and lay in bed. It was not fair! She only wanted to be free a little while.

Abruptly, she threw off the covers and found her clothes. She packed a small bag, fastened on her cloak, and opened the door to peek out. She paused. Roman might be punished if she just disappeared. She would leave a note. Deirdre stepped back inside, then thought, no, a note would let them find her too quickly. Her father would reason out where she had gone.

She opened the door again and quietly slipped down the stairs. She passed through the kitchen corridors and unlatched the courtyard door—it squeaked so loudly! She shut it hastily and slipped into the darkness. There was the guard, occupied with a bottle. It was not difficult getting past him unseen to the rear gate. She drew it open.

"Chataine, where are you going?"

She whirled. Her heart sank to see her guardian. "I am leaving. Alone." Deirdre made a stand, knowing it was futile.

He shut the gate and took her hand. "No, I am sorry, you are not. Come back inside."

Furious, she yanked her hand away. "I want you to stop ordering

118

me around! I do not need you anymore, and I am indeed leaving!''
She shoved him away and spun around to the gate. Roman caught
her and lifted her over his shoulder. As he carried her thus through
the courtyard, she struggled desperately, but he easily restrained
her. In a rage, she beat his back and screamed, ''Let me down! Let
me go! I hate you, Roman! I hate you!''

''If you must,'' he said calmly, ''but you still cannot leave.'' He
carried her all the way upstairs and pounded on Nanna's door. Some
of the servants gathered, laughing. Nanna came to the door and
shrieked at the sight before her. Roman put Deirdre down, saying,
''The Chataine attempted an excursion alone. You had best watch
her tonight.''

As he turned away, Deirdre shouted, ''I will never forgive you
for this, Roman!'' Then she flung herself into her room.

The next day she refused to go riding or even speak to him, and
carefully avoided looking his way at dinner. After three days of her
unyielding silence, he respectfully requested an audience with her.
She granted it. When he came to her receiving room, she asked,
''What is on your mind, Roman?''

''Chataine, I talked with your father yesterday. He told me that
you had requested to go to Calle Valley without me.''

''So?''

He hesitated, searching for words. ''I know how you must feel—
almost like a prisoner, bound in chains to me. I feel that way myself
at times. But there are some things we have no control over. Our
circumstances are often beyond our choosing. We just must live the
lives given to us as best we can—otherwise we will make ourselves
miserable . . . as I was doing, wanting to go with Galapos when I
could not.'' She did not respond, so he continued: ''I want you to be
happy, Deirdre, but I cannot forsake my vow to protect you just
because you want me to.'' He stood watching her as she studied the
floor for several long minutes. ''Will you go riding with me today,
Chataine?''

''Let me get my jacket.'' When she reemerged, she added, ''You
know I do not hate you.''

''I know, Chataine.''

Outside, as they led Lady Grey and the Bay Hunter out of the stables and mounted, she noted unusual activity in the courtyard. The palace overseer was vainly attempting to organize servants and villagers into groups. A large cart filled with empty bushels stood nearby. "What is all this?" she asked Roman.

"It is time to harvest the orchard—the apples are falling off. But your father is shorthanded for workers."

"Oh." She stopped to watch, then looked beyond the courtyard to rows and rows of heavily laden trees. "We can help, can we not?"

She thought he was going to fall off his horse. "Yes—of course!" He lifted her down and took her—proudly, she thought—to the overseer. Taking a basket from the cart, Roman said, "The Chataine has offered her assistance in the harvest." The overseer gaped at them. Without waiting for him to recover, Roman led her to the first row and selected a tree. "I will climb up, and—"

"No, no! Let me climb, Roman!"

He shook his head in helpless bewilderment. "As you wish, Chataine, but take care. I will stand beneath you." Eagerly, she thrust her skirts aside and let him lift her to the lower branches. "Pick only the ripe ones and throw them down to me one at a time—"

"I know, I know," she said impatiently. She began to pick and toss. He caught them and placed them in the basket. Then she decided that was too easy. She began throwing them down more rapidly, sometimes two at a time.

"Deirdre—wait—" he sputtered. One caught him perfectly on top of the head. She shrieked in laughter and he made a sudden rush at the tree. "Do that again, and I will come throw *you* down!" he threatened. She suppressed a barrage of giggles.

They filled the entire bushel and carried it back to the courtyard together. Deirdre lifted out another empty basket. "We need to help until they finish," she said sternly.

Roman stared at her open-mouthed, yet in his face was something else besides astonishment, something unreadable to her—a look almost of pain. He blinked and said, "That will take several days. It will be enough for us to pick one more bushel." They took it out to the trees and worked in earnest silence.

She caught him again looking at her with that same sad expression, and asked, "What is wrong?"

He cleared his throat and said, "You are changing—growing so. You surprise me every day with something new . . ."

"What do you mean?"

"I mean, soon you will be grown, and I will no longer ward you . . ." He turned his back on her, and she sat pondering why that would disturb him so.

9

ixteen-year-old Deirdre stood before the looking glass and carefully combed her long hair. She studied the reflection and smiled. Some of the guards were looking at her appreciatively now. And she drew attention whenever she went into town. It was a little overwhelming to be noticed so suddenly. She took an overall survey in the looking glass and, after smoothing a stray curl, decided she presented an acceptable sight. She stepped out of her chambers. . . .

The guard in the hall stood at attention as Deirdre passed him. He looked younger than most. She smiled and he nodded. "What is your name?" she asked sweetly.

"Arin, Chataine," he responded.

"Are you required to stand here all day?" she wondered wide-eyed.

"Unless I am ordered elsewhere, Chataine," he smiled.

She began to reply but Roman's voice to her left said, "Guard, you will stand at attention at all times in the presence of the Chataine" (he snapped to) "and if I ever see your eyes leave the wall in her presence, I will put you in charge of cleaning the stables for the next six weeks. Understood?"

"Yes, Captain!" The guard became a statue.

Deirdre turned to Roman in exasperation. "Are you everywhere?"

"Only where I am needed, Chataine. Would you care to go riding now?"

"No, Roman. I am much too busy today." She returned to her room and checked herself in the glass again as Nanna came bustling in.

"Here it is, darling! Isn't it beautiful?" And she held up a long, full gown of creamy silk and lace.

"Oh, yes!" exclaimed Deirdre, and held the dress under her chin in front of the glass. Her first fest—her coming out—would be next week in the palace of her Uncle Corneus.

Nanna clapped. "You are beautiful! No girl there will be lovelier than you! And who knows"—she rolled her eyes and gave a naughty smile—"but that some young chatain will decide he cannot wait until your betrothal fest to ask you to wed!"

Deirdre started, suddenly remembering Tremaine. His threat had been sleeping peacefully in her mind, but now the reality of it loomed near. "Oh, Nanna, I do not want to get married yet!" she said, while thinking, *I have another year before I must face that*. "Nanna, I want to be free now, to live for myself. I do not want to think about being someone's wife, and—and—" an unplanned rush of tears came.

Nanna, confused, gathered her in. "Dear—of course you are free to do as you please. No need to run ahead of ourselves here. You are the one to say when and whom you will marry. No one can say that for you—not even the Surchatain."

Deirdre groaned and fell on her bed. "Tell Father I do not feel up to dinner tonight."

She was there, nonetheless, at the dinner table that evening. Roman glanced at her from time to time as she picked at her food, but no one else seemed to notice her malaise. She smiled at him. Good old Roman. He was always there. He always cared. A thought struck her: *I wonder how much I can make him care?* She finished dinner smiling and laughing as she planned the assault.

Late that night, when the palace was quiet, Deirdre rose from bed and pulled on her overrobe. On second thought, she loosened it somewhat around the neck. She stuffed pillows under the quilts to resemble her sleeping form; it would not do for Nanna to come searching for her. Then she took up a candle, slipped out of her chambers, and descended the cold stone stairs. Cautiously, she found her way to the corridor by the kitchen. Remembering when she had done this before almost made her giggle, but she hushed herself and went on. She came to Roman's door and listened. Not a sound within. Trying the door, she found it bolted. She hesitated, then knocked softly. No answer. She knocked again, louder. Roman opened the door sleepily. When he saw her, he woke up fast. "Chataine! What is wrong? What is it?" She came in and he shut the door. As she placed the candle on the small table, he peered at her. "Why are you here, Chataine?"

"I wanted to see you, Roman." She opened her overrobe.

He watched her. "My life is worthless if you are found here."

"You're jesting. I only wanted to talk." She looked him over appreciatively; he wore only loose, lightweight breeches. Then she came up close to him and put her arms around his neck as she had seen the maids do with the soldiers. Roman seemed utterly immobilized by her touch.

"Why are you doing this?" he whispered.

"Because I care for you, Roman." She reached up to kiss him.

He backed away. "No. If you cared for me, you would not put my life in danger just for your fun."

She looked at him crossly. He was spoiling everything. "Father is not going to do anything to you."

"No? Remember the horse?" The scars showed plainly on his chest.

She released him. "If you do not want me, just say it," she huffed, throwing her head back.

"That is not the point. I can never have you, Deirdre; we both know that. Why are you tormenting me?"

"Tormenting you! Is that what you call it?" Yet even as she said it she could see he was really in pain. "Very well, I certainly will not torment you!" She stalked out and slammed the door. Hearing it echo all over the palace made her scramble for her chambers.

Safe in bed, she buried her head in a pillow. That had been foolish and stinging with shame, she knew it. She should not try to use him like that. He had taken enough abuse from her—and for her. She would apologize to him in the morning.

After breakfast in her chambers, she sent the errand boy for him and waited. As the minutes passed and he did not come, she grew slightly uneasy. At that point she received a summons to her father's chambers. When she entered, she saw to her alarm Roman standing stiff and stony-faced before the Surchatain.

"Deirdre," her father began, "Roman has requested to be removed from service as your guardian. He says he is no longer effective in his duties. Do you know of any reason that this should be so?"

She gulped. "No, Father, none at all."

"Do you see that he is losing his effectiveness?"

"No, of course not, Father. He has always been capable and faithful."

"Has he behaved improperly toward you?"

Her eyes stung. "Never, Father."

The Surchatain raised his shoulders. "Well, Roman, since I cannot determine exactly what fault there is, I must deny your request. You have proved yourself too useful. Whatever the trouble is, I trust you will work it out yourself. You are both dismissed."

As they walked through the corridor, Roman neither spoke nor looked at her. She caught his arm, and he glanced at her sharply. She let go. "Roman, please, I want to apologize for last night. I do not know why I did it. I did not realize it would affect you so. Please forgive me."

"Done," he said, then added, "But you must never touch me again."

Deirdre's chagrin over the incident was forgotten in the next few days of preparing for the fest. Her finest clothes were packed to wear for the three days of festivities that would precede the gala event on the final night. Even Roman, going as her chaperon, was offered splendid new clothes, which he refused. "I shall wear the shortcoat made for me by the Chataine," he said. Nanna was particularly hurt that she would not chaperon, but the Surchatain's decision was final.

They departed for Ooster in the morning, escorted by an armed guard. As they traveled, Deirdre's anticipation mounted higher and higher. No need to waste time trying to flirt with Roman—Uncle Corneus's fests were notorious for the romancing that went on. And instead of the Cohort to admire her, there would be a palace full of royalty. She envisioned herself in her new gown surrounded by a crowd of young men. She could hardly endure the slow pace of their travel to Ooster—a pace that had once left her giddy.

When at last they came within sight of the palace, Deirdre spurred her horse to a gallop, surprising the soldiers who rode with her and forcing Roman to spur after her in pursuit. She arrived at the gates with him on her heels. There, servants took their horses and directed them to the wide audience hall. Deirdre laughed in recognition of her uncle's flamboyance in decorating for the festivities.

At the heart of the hall was a five-tiered fountain that flowed with wine. Long, thin tables circled it like a maze—set with aromatic dishes of pheasant, beef, and ham; fruits and pies; pastries; and more she could not see. Enormous bouquets of spring flowers marked the entrances to the maze. The crowd of guests already there were eating and laughing as they watched several venturous young men attempting to find their way through the maze to the fountain of wine.

Deirdre scanned the room excitedly for familiar faces. She recognized Jason and Colin, and Rollet on the far side of the fountain.

"Deirdre! Over here!" called a voice, and she spotted Laska waving to her. Deirdre hurried over to greet her.

"Laska! Hello!" They embraced. "I received your last message but had no time to send a reply—"

"Do not give it a thought," interrupted Laska. "Have you ever seen anything like this in your life? Oh, hello, Roman." He nodded.

Deirdre laughed a shade too loudly. "No, I have not. Uncle

has—" she broke off as she caught sight of one young man surrounded by girls. His perfectly sculpted face surrounded by chestnut curls riveted her attention. Deirdre touched Laska's arm and nodded. "Who is that?"

"You do not know? That is Chatain Artemeus. Do you like him?"

"I certainly do." Deirdre could not take her gaze from him. Suddenly he looked directly at her. He smiled, and broke himself from the group to walk over to her. She felt suddenly panicky.

He took her hand. "Laska, will you introduce me to this lady?"

Laska smiled. "You are greeting Chataine Deirdre, daughter of Karel of Lystra. Deirdre, this is Surchatain Savin's son, Artemeus."

He kissed her hand. She said, "I am honored to meet you."

"I am spellbound by your presence," he answered. "I beg you to sit with me at dinner tonight. Please."

"Of course. Thank you." She desperately hoped she appeared cool and poised.

As they dressed for dinner, Laska, who shared Deirdre's quarters, advised her confidently on how to handle Artemeus. "I have heard that he is quite a lover. But do not give in directly—make him work for it. You will hold his interest longer."

"Laska!" Deirdre was shocked.

"This is how it is done, Deirdre," Laska insisted.

Deirdre came down for dinner in a daze. As was customary, the girls' chaperons stood behind their chairs during the meal. Artemeus seated himself next to her and leaned close to whisper, "Deirdre, you look lovelier than all the flowers in this palace." She blushed at the look in his smoky grey eyes, and he added, "I am sure that any other chataine would be ashamed next to your beauty."

"Artemeus, there are many lovely girls here," she protested happily.

"Not as you are," he countered firmly. "Your skin is so fair and perfect—your hair is like silk—your eyes are so wide and deep a man could drown in them."

She giggled. "Please—you will turn my head."

127

"I hope to turn it my way," he said earnestly, taking her hand. She drew it away to eat.

"So you are Savin's son." As she said it, she suddenly recalled he was one of the choices Tremaine had given her.

"Yes," he said proudly. "He is the greatest ruler on the Continent, next to Tremaine."

"And my father."

He smiled. "We rule Goerge from a palace built high on cliffs of solid rock—Diamond's Head. Have you ever been there, Deirdre?"

"No."

"You must come soon. It is one of the wonders of the world. It is an impregnable fortress, worthy to house the most desirable Surchataine." He was gazing into her eyes again. He had not even touched the aromatic dish sitting before him. She raised the goblet to her lips, and he drank in her every movement with longing eyes. She was thinking hard. What would it be like to marry him? If she did, she would save her country from invasion by Tremaine. But . . .

"I could not leave Westford—that is my seat to rule Lystra."

He laughed. "Deirdre, my love, why should you worry about little things like that? Lystra will be well in hand."

"In whose hand?" she grew serious.

He laughed again. "Oh, I love a clever girl! You are so entrancing. . . . I must have you, Deirdre," he ended in a murmur.

She felt Roman, behind her, shift. *I have time yet,* she thought; *I need not think about marriage yet, only the pleasure before me now.* "Perhaps you shall," she smiled enticingly, and his eyes lit up with anticipation.

As dinner ended he stood and took her hand, kissing her fingers. Wordlessly, he led her out to the palace gardens. Roman followed. Artemeus swung open the wrought-iron gates and Deirdre stepped into a paradise of color and fragrance. She sorted out scents of jasmine and honeysuckle, but before finding them stumbled upon a trellis of climbing roses in blazing yellow-orange. The pebble-lined paths into the garden curved in a circular fashion, some of them ending abruptly. It took her a moment to recognize that the garden mimicked the maze of the audience hall—or vice versa.

Artemeus led her to the end of one path and they sat on a velvet-covered couch. "Deirdre," he whispered, "you are the one I must have—will you give me your love?" He bent forward to kiss her lips.

She was considering an answer when she saw Roman step from the shadows toward them. Obeying his steady gaze, she avoided Artemeus's embrace and he almost toppled off the couch. "Deirdre!" he complained, regaining his balance, then caught her eyes and followed them to Roman. He swore under his breath. "You are dismissed. You can go," he called to Roman. Her guardian did not move.

"Let me speak with him," said Deirdre. She rose and walked over to face him. "Roman, you really do not have to stand over me this way," she said softly. "I am not a child any longer and my life is not in danger now."

"No," he answered, "but your honor is. Your father made clear to me what my duties are." She nodded and returned to Artemeus's side.

"I am sorry," she said. "He is not leaving."

Artemeus looked toward him darkly. "No?" He sallied up to Roman and said, "Well, there is no doubt that you are a good chaperon. The finest. I know you earn your pay. As a matter of fact, I am sure you are not paid near your worth. So listen"—he drew out a bag of coins—"I have twenty royals in here, and they are yours if you will leave us for an hour. One hour. Here . . ." and he held them out. Roman did not move, nor even answer. "Go on, take them," urged Artemeus. No response. "Damn you!" he burst, and strode back to Deirdre.

"Is it so important that he is here?" she asked. "We can talk and he will not eavesdrop—"

"Be quiet and let me think!" he snapped. Deirdre was stunned. His face smoothed. "I'm sorry," he said tenderly. "You wait here. I will return immediately." He left her standing by the couch. Undecided as to whether or not to wait, she looked toward Roman. He was still as the stone walls around them, and she could not read his face in the darkness. In minutes Artemeus was by her side again, smiling and relaxed. "Everything is taken care of," he whispered.

Deirdre felt vaguely alarmed. "What did you do?"

"Just arranged a little entertainment for your friend." Suddenly two young men armed with clubs sprang over the garden wall onto Roman. But he merely shook one off into the rosebushes and threw the other up against the wall. He seized Deirdre's hand, but Artemeus held on to the other. Roman hesitated just an instant, then punched him in the ribs hard enough to leave him gasping on the couch. Then he led Deirdre firmly to the well-lighted banquet hall.

"I see why Father would not send Nanna," she said, subdued. "I am sorry that happened, Roman."

He smiled. "Do not apologize. It was quite satisfying."

Later in the evening she spotted Artemeus with some of his friends. She took a deep breath and approached him, intending to make amends, but he eyed her coldly and turned his back. "Do you know what I really hate?" he asked his friends. "A wench who won't deliver what she promises!" They laughed, and Deirdre turned away in tears.

She began the next morning with the resolution to forget Artemeus and start all over. After breakfast, she found most of the other guests gathered on the grounds. She brightened to see the men showing their skills at archery. Boldly, she approached the weapons stall and selected a bow and quiver. One of the young men saw her and laughed, "Hey, fellows, move up a target!"

"That is not necessary," she smiled. She fitted the arrow to the bowstring, drew back smoothly and shot. The arrow planted itself firmly in the bull's-eye. The men around her gaped.

"I'll wager you cannot do that again," one of them said.

"You lose," she answered, and shot again. An impromptu competition was set up, and she bested all challengers. The crowd of men shooting quickly dissipated, as did the girls who had been watching them. Deirdre looked around. "Where did all the men go? You would think I was shooting at *them!*"

"You might as well have been. Nothing is wounded so quickly as one's pride," Roman said, then beamed at her, "I am proud of you. Your practice paid off."

"How?" she muttered, canvassing the deserted grounds.

Before dinner that night Deirdre made another resolution to begin again. So she listened bright-eyed as her dinner companions told of their exploits. Otto, seated across from her, was saying, "It was a dangerous plan, but we had to recover the money those villains had stolen. So we—just my brother and I—lay in wait in the forest until we heard them riding up. We gave chase to the edge of a cliff, where they had to stop and fight us. There were three of them, and we had only our hunting knives to their swords. It was very bloody —my brother lost a finger. But we overpowered them and threw them off the cliff, then took their horses and money."

"How exciting!" exclaimed Deirdre. "When I was ten, we were traveling here to see uncle, and I was abducted by two kidnappers who took me to an assassin. He tried to throw me over a cliff, but my guardian Roman caught me . . . and . . ." she faltered as Otto turned to speak to a girl seated next to him. ". . . saved me," she mumbled into her goblet.

A fellow next to her spoke up. "Deirdre, have you ever been to Corona?"

"Yes! Tremaine invited me—"

"Well, I stopped there on my way here. I was traveling alone, you know. I told Father, I said, 'Father, I do not need guards traveling with me! Just give me expense money and I'll be off!' So I stopped in Corona to see Tremaine's palace. You should see his audience hall!"

"I have! He invited me to visit his son Rollet there two years ago. Roman thought someone might still be after my life, so we traveled disguised as peasants! He put me in a tattered old dress, with a pillow underneath to make me look pregnant!"

She stopped to laugh, and he resumed, "Yes, well, as I was saying, Tremaine's audience hall is something to behold! The floor is set with a mosaic of diamonds and rubies . . ." he continued to talk, but Deirdre shut his voice out and concentrated on the delicious quail.

Later, one young man named Morin asked her to walk through the gardens with him. "No—thank you—" she said quickly, glancing toward Roman. "I would rather stay in here and talk."

"Very well," he said, and a tentative silence ensued while they searched for something to talk about. He then said, "Do you ride?"

"Yes, fairly well."

"I train wild horses to the saddle and bridle," he remarked. "I suppose I have trained fifty horses in my life."

"How interesting! I know that is difficult. I thought I would try it once, but the horse reared and knocked me to the ground before I ever got on him. He would have trampled me if my guardian had not saved me. He threw himself over me and let the horse strike him instead. It was so courageous of him . . ."

"Really?" queried Morin, peeved. "Isn't it his sworn duty to protect you?"

"Well, yes," stammered Deirdre. "But that does not make it easy."

"Or interesting," he said, taking his leave.

At that point Laska drew her aside and said, "Deirdre, you must stop talking about Roman. They are not interested in him."

"I cannot help it," she said. "He has been with me in everything I have ever done."

"Then do not talk about yourself. Just listen to them."

So she listened. All night long she listened, and went to bed very tired.

In the morning she awoke with a headache. Tonight was the night of the fest—the grand finale. This was her last chance to make good. She invested her time that day admiring the men in their activities, and managed to gather several beaux for the fest that night. But when the guests gathered in the banquet hall, and she talked and danced in her beautiful silk dress, she found she could not really concentrate. Her eyes kept drifting past her partners' faces and her ears just barely caught what they said. For some reason, she kept glancing toward Roman, who was watching from his position against the wall.

The fest wore on interminably. Deirdre stopped dancing to stand apart and watch. This was the night she had been dreaming of ever since she had first talked with Laska at the Fair. *Why did I believe it would be so wonderful?* she mused. Laska paused between dances to encourage her: "You are doing splendidly! I think Gastin is interested in you."

"I wonder if he can dance," Deirdre murmured.

"You tell me," Laska frowned. "You just danced with him!"

"Not him. Roman."

Laska grabbed her shoulders and almost shook her. "Deirdre, you stop that now! Remember who you are and concentrate on what you are doing! You are going to marry one of these men soon!" Deirdre left the fest and went up to bed.

The following morning they departed for home under heavy grey skies, riding in utter silence. Roman kept glancing at her.

I tried, I really tried, she thought. *What went wrong?*

You expected them all to be like him.

Her eyes went quickly to Roman. He returned her look quizzically. *It is true; there is no one like him,* she thought. And she considered how she felt about him.

In the afternoon the clouds grew darker and the rain came heavily down. The travelers stopped and donned their thick cloaks, but still got wet and chilled as they rode. The rain slowed their pace considerably.

Deirdre shivered, then laughed, "Remember when you used to carry me in front on the Bay Hunter?" Roman reined the horse to a sudden halt. The soldiers halted. Deirdre stopped. He reached over and lifted her onto his horse as easily as if she were still a child of ten, then wrapped her up in his cloak. As they continued homeward, she laid her head on his neck. "Roman," she began thoughtfully, "the night after I was attacked, on our first trip to uncle's—you remember?" He nodded. "That night, I opened your door and saw you on your knees. . . . Were you praying to God?"

"Yes, Chataine."

"Do you pray often?"

"Every night, Chataine."

"What do you say?"

"Whatever is on my heart."

"Does God answer you back?"

"At times. Not in words, but impressions, usually. I find insights."

She sat up. "Like someone speaking without a voice to you?"

"Sometimes. Most often when God chooses to speak to me and I am listening, I am given peace, or new understanding, or just the certainty that He is in control. And often I think God has given me a guardian, like I am guardian to you."

"Why do you think that?"

"Because we are both still alive."

She laughed, "Do you suppose I have a guardian too, besides you?" The thought of a heavenly guardian scrambling around trying to keep her out of trouble amused her.

" 'The angel of the Lord encamps around those who fear Him, and delivers them,' " he quoted. That turned her thoughts serious again.

"Roman . . . could God speak to me?"

"He speaks to whomever He wishes."

"Even if I had not asked Him anything?"

"Sometimes He has to get your attention first, Chataine."

She considered this. "Roman, do you pray for me?"

"Every night, Chataine. You are always on my heart."

She looked up at his face. It was the most handsome face she had ever seen.

10

Only days after they arrived home, Deirdre's father informed her at dinner that she had received a marriage proposal. . . .

Karel opened a letter and said, "It proposes your marriage to the Chatain Gastin. What province does he rule, Deirdre?"

"Gastin?" she frowned. "I do not know. I do not even remember who he is. Send him a refusal." He nodded, apparently relieved.

The entertainment after dinner that evening was a group of singers whose repertoire favored sighing love songs. Deirdre listened enthralled:

> You have bound me with your eyes;
> I am captive of your smiles;
> Your tears rend my heart
> You are such a part
> Of me, my dove, my love.

If I loved you when we met,
I will love you ever yet,
For that love of mine
Was naught as it is
Now, my dove, my love.

What then shall I do
To win such a maid as you?
Is there hope for me
To ever touch your
Heart, my dove, my love?

Her rapture with the beautiful melody was marred only by Roman's fidgeting. "Shh!" she hissed. He glanced at her and stilled, but a moment later leaned back to whisper to the Counselor. Deirdre glared at him and he sat quietly through the remainder of the performance.

When they were dismissed, she meant to take him aside and upbraid him for his uncharacteristic rudeness, but he left the table immediately with the Counselor.

An hour later Roman emerged from Eudymon's chambers and stopped in the corridor to think. Hesitantly, he headed toward the servants' dining hall and looked in. They all had finished eating, and only scattered groups remained. He scanned the groups from the doorway. A healthy-looking serving girl approached smiling: "Good evening, Captain! Who are you looking for?"

"Ah, in fact, you, Angelina."

"Yes?" her smile brightened.

"If you are finished, I thought—you would perhaps walk with me out to the orchard."

"I am finished now," she said, tossing her apron to a group of maids who giggled and waved her out. She left the hall on his arm.

Over the next several weeks Deirdre grew irritated at Roman's increasing aloofness toward her. He took her riding only when she specifically requested it, and he deliberately avoided the willow grove. He reverted to his taciturn manner of their early months together. Moreover, he began to leave the table every night immediately when dismissed by the Surchatain, not even pausing to say goodnight to her.

She took a careful inventory to see what she might have done recently to offend him, but found nothing. She then determined to find the root of the trouble with him. Accordingly, she summoned him one afternoon to her chambers. When he entered, he bowed formally—something he had rarely done with her. "You summoned me, Chataine?"

"Yes, Roman," she said as formally, "I require your assistance in the garden. Will you be so kind as to help me?"

"Of course, Chataine." They walked with three feet of space between them to the small courtyard garden. He unlatched the gate and she entered, then directed him to the corner of the garden where new rose bushes had been planted this past spring.

"I am in a quandary as to whether the pink or the red roses complement this dress best. What do you say?" she asked. He just blinked at her. Then she dropped all pretense and asked earnestly, "Roman, what is wrong between us? Why are you suddenly so distant?"

He gazed at her and replied, "I believe the pink favors your complexion more."

"Thank you," she said, breaking off a pink bud and placing it in her hair. "And I believe the red favors yours." She broke off a red bud and tucked it in the top eyelet of his shortcoat. "Now—"

"Cap'n Roman! Captain!" They heard the voice of the errand boy outside the garden gates.

"Here!" Roman called. As he turned, he withdrew the bud.

"Captain, the Surchatain has granted your audience now."

"Thank you, Kevin." He bowed to her: "Excuse me, Chataine," and she nodded.

Deirdre stayed in the garden a few moments after he had departed, smelling the roses and lilac. On her way out, she saw the little red bud lying crushed on the path.

The following morning Nanna wakened her cheerful and singing: "Up, up now, Chataine! It is going to be a lovely summer's day!" Deirdre groaned and rolled over. "I heard an interesting piece of gossip from the servants today," Nanna continued. "Do you want to hear it?'' Deirdre mumbled something. ''One of the housemaids is getting married—Angelina. Do you know her?'' Nanna teased.

''Umm. She is very sweet.''

''Do you know who she is marrying?''

''No,'' yawned Deirdre.

''Roman!'' said Nanna triumphantly.

Deirdre came wide awake. ''He cannot get married!''

''Yes, he can. They said he went to the Surchatain and asked permission to marry, since you will soon be married and need him little now anyway. Your father gave him permission.''

Deirdre felt sick. ''When are they marrying?''

''As soon as possible, is what I hear,'' Nanna chuckled.

Deirdre put her head in her hands. So there was the cause for his coolness! He had fallen in love with someone else, and wanted no more part of her. The thought of losing him—her battle-scarred babysitter and confidant, teacher and protector—made her heartsick. He could not marry! She must stop him. How? She could get Angelina sent away from the palace. She could send her to Laska as a gift.

No, that would not do. Roman deserved more gracious treatment than that. The only thing to do was confront him. She dressed in urgent haste and ran down the stone stairs to summon him. He was gone—away from the palace. One of the soldiers said he thought Roman had gone to the village, or the town.

Was she too late? Had he already taken Angelina to the town notary? She waited at the gate for him, chewing her lips. Before long, he came galloping up and dismounted with a leap. He ran up the steps. When he saw her, he took on a guilty mien. ''Chataine— did you summon me while I was away? Forgive me—I returned as soon as I was able.''

''Where have you been?'' she asked softly.

''To the village. Taking food and medicines to the villagers.'' He rushed on to explain: ''They are having another plague—each is worse than the last. I am afraid they will have to leave the branch of the river altogether. It is becoming too foul—but they just will not listen.''

She felt a flood of relief. ''May we go riding now?''

"As you wish, Chataine."

On Lady Grey, Deirdre headed for the lake, and Roman followed on the Bay Hunter somewhat reluctantly. They dismounted by the willow trees. As they tied the horses she watched him, waiting for an opening, but he never looked up. He turned idly to the water and began skimming stones. She walked to his side and watched the little rings widen on the glassy surface. Then she opened her mouth and forced out, "I heard you are getting married." He nodded, flinging a rock. "Roman! Why?"

"I am a man. I need a wife, Chataine."

"I need you, Roman!"

He stopped throwing and gripped the stones in his palm. "I will be here when you need me. That will not change. But in the short time left before you marry, there is little more I can do for you."

"You swore to guard me until I marry," she accused.

"I will." He looked her in the eye.

"But if you are married, you will have other interests to protect." He weighed the stones in his hand without speaking. "Roman, I ask one thing of you. If you do this, I will not burden you with any more demands." She paused to meet his eyes. "Wait until I marry before you do." The heaviness of her request sagged his shoulders. "Please, Roman! I beg you."

"As you wish, Chataine. I will wait," he capitulated. Deirdre closed her eyes in sweet relief.

But Roman was moving toward the horses. "Where are you going?"

"We," he said. "Back to the palace."

"Already?"

"I must tell Angelina immediately," he said tightly. "She deserves that much consideration." For the first time, Deirdre came face to face with her own selfishness, and she lowered her head in humiliation. But she would not relent. He was too important to her.

They arrived at the palace and parted wordlessly in the foyer. This was one scene she had not the slightest desire to overhear.

Roman trudged to the kitchen and looked in. "Angelina?" She turned from a large kettle to smile warmly at him. "Can you come away from your duties for a moment?"

"For you, yes." She took his arm and he paused, then led her to the empty chapel. He shut the doors and turned toward her, but before he could speak she entwined her arms around his neck and pressed her lips to his. He held her lightly. She opened her eyes, drawing away. "What is it?"

"Angelina . . . I, uh . . ." he stammered as she tightened her lips, sensing bad news. "The Chataine has asked me to postpone our marriage."

"She has?!" Angelina exclaimed. "Why?"

"Well, she fears I will become lax in my duties toward her."

Anger crossed her face. "That is hardly likely, knowing you. Anyone can see how faithful you have been. Almost anyone."

"I tried to reassure her of that, but she still had fears . . . of being abandoned, I believe. I am her only friend in the palace, other than her nursemaid."

"Small wonder," muttered Angelina. "Roman, you are not her slave. She has no right to order your personal affairs. The Surchatain gave you permission to marry—isn't that enough?"

"Ordinarily, yes, of course," he said anxiously. "But as she felt so strongly about it, I felt . . . I should . . . accede . . ." He could not meet her gaze.

"Roman." She turned his face to make him look in her eyes. "Is it really me you want?"

"Certainly!" he insisted. "I would not ask you if I did not mean it." But his eyes wandered from her face again. "Besides, she will certainly marry next spring, then I will be free."

"I will wait, then," she said softly. "For a while." She left the chapel to return to the kitchen.

He remained a moment in thought, then sighed and shook his head. "I need never fear dying by the sword," he muttered. "These women will tear me apart long before then."

The following day, Nanna brought the noon meal to Deirdre in her chambers, setting the tray down with a thump. "I heard more gossip today, dear," she said darkly. "Do you want to know what they are saying?"

"I do not care what they are saying," Deirdre replied.

"They are saying you forced Roman to postpone his wedding. Is that true? Deirdre, look at me!"

"What is it to you? Why are you so angry?"

Nanna sat her down. "Deirdre, they say you are in love with him. Tell me that is not so, dear!"

"What difference does it make? Why are you so upset?"

"If this gets around to your father's ears, it will make a great difference! You know what will happen to Roman! And you—why do you risk your future for the sake of a—a bastard soldier?"

"Stop it!" Deirdre cried, leaping up. "I do not ever want to hear you say that about him again!" She ran from the room, spilling the tray.

That day, as they rode, Roman was quiet and Deirdre downcast. She longed to talk to him, to make him understand. *I do not want to run your life, Roman. I just want you near me,* she thought. But she could not put her feelings into words. Nor did she feel the slightest curiosity to know Angelina's reaction to his news. She did not want to hear of Angelina nor talk of her.

He found a nice grassy hill and they dismounted, releasing their horses to graze. Then he wordlessly threw himself down on his back in the sweet green grass. As he lay gazing up at the sky, she leaned over and began rubbing his temples. Then, on impulse, she kissed him on the forehead. He did not push her away. "Roman . . . do you care for me?"

"I care for you greatly, Chataine. I have a strong interest in your welfare."

"No, I mean, besides being my guardian. How do you feel about me just . . . as me?"

It was a minute before he answered. "I am interested in only the best for you, Chataine. And that is all I am allowed." He stood and helped her to her feet. "Time to go."

She studied his face. There was a tenderness, a vulnerability in his eyes that she had never noticed before. Had it always been there, and she just had not seen it?

Suddenly, she realized she finally had it. She had power over him—not to make him do what she wanted, necessarily, but to affect him. To change his life. To possibly destroy it. Moreover, she had not gained it by manipulation or cunning. He had given her that power himself.

It was a different, older Deirdre who returned with him to the palace. Roman was different, also. He dropped his formality and no longer attempted to avoid her, but things were not the same. He was still quiet and withdrawn, carrying a habitual countenance of sadness or resignation. It baffled her, but the more she tried to solace him, the more he withdrew. She began to yearn to understand him better.

Some days later, she coaxed him out to the lake again. As they gained the shore and looked out over the sparkling water, she asked brightly: "What shall we do today? Go swimming?"

"No," he said quickly.

"Then take me out in the boat," she demanded. "Roman, why will you never take me to the far shore? What is over there?"

"Nothing that is not over here," he stated, then squinted across the water. "On second thought, let's do go have a look."

"Well said!" she agreed. He held the small boat steady while she clambered in, then he took up the oars and began stroking. Deirdre leaned over the prow and trailed her fingers in the water. "How fast you are rowing! This is fun!" she laughed. He grunted.

The boat scraped ground and he leaped out, dragging it up on shore. But he sprinted to the nearby trees, leaving her sitting in the prow. By the time she managed to climb out and find him, he was studying the remains of a little camp. A fire still smoked on the ground. "What is this?" she exclaimed.

"An uninvited guest," he said grimly. Deirdre then saw strange markings in the dirt and pebbles arranged in patterns. Figurines with grotesque faces were lying as if abandoned in haste. Roman began obliterating the designs with his foot, scattering stones and ashes. He broke the figurines in pieces and threw them into deep water.

"What are you doing? What are they?"

"A sorcerer has been at work here. He must have seen us, also." He spat out a curse.

"Roman!" She was profoundly shocked.

"I am sorry, Deirdre, but this is an evil omen. Sorcerers at work in the land are like leeches sucking the lifeblood. They are extremely dangerous—they can bring a whole country to ruin in short order if they influence the right people. God has forewarned us.'' She listened soberly, but wondered at the intensity of his foreboding.

The winter of that year was the worst Deirdre could ever recall. The cold and snow were unrelenting as wolves. Although every fireplace in the palace was kept loaded with wood, an icy chill pervaded every room. Everyone wore heavy outer garments even while inside.

Deirdre was not permitted to even leave the palace proper in such weather. And she soon found that Roman would not be there for a time. Early one morning Nanna brought her a note given her by an errand boy. In bed, Deirdre opened it and read: "To the Chataine. From Roman. I wished you to know that I have been accepted to carry communications between the palace and the outposts for a short time. I had to leave before you awakened. Please pray for my safety. I am ever your respectful guardian." She closed her eyes to hold back the tears. What idiot would volunteer for such dangerous riding?

There were four outposts positioned around the border, not including the soldiers stationed in Hycliff and Westford. Each outpost was a fortress in itself, well stocked and buttressed to withstand attack or siege. All scouting and patroling parties were dispatched from these, and all units were coordinated from Outpost One, Galapos's field headquarters. In fair weather, covering the distance from one outpost to the next closest might require half a day. But in the killing cold and obscuring snow, a rider who made it within a day was considered superb. Those who did not were dead.

But communications were the lifeblood of the army. Galapos could not command if he did not know what was happening elsewhere. And Roman thought so little of expending his life for Galapos. "Please pray for my safety," he had written. He knew the risks. Then why, oh why did he go?

Resigned to waiting, Deirdre set tasks for herself to consume the time that he was gone. There was a quilt to sew and many books to be read. Immediately following breakfast, she set herself to busyness.

Dressed in layers of woolens under his thick cloak, Roman pushed the Bay Hunter to the limit of his endurance galloping through deep snow. He felt the cold sear through him as he plunged over the East Passage toward Outpost Three. At length, it seemed unbearable—the wind never stilled. And what would it be like to perish in this cold waste? *Oh Lord, that may be best—to die out here and not have to face her again.*

His horse suddenly hit a hidden hole and fell sideways to the ground, pinning Roman's leg. Sharp pain shot through his knee, and the Bay Hunter could not seem to regain his footing. In the distance, Roman heard the howling of hungry wolves. *Lord, I was wrong—I do want to see her again,* he prayed desperately. The horse staggered up, snorting. Roman limped to remount and pushed him forward again. He considered himself reminded to pray as sincerely as he wished to be heard.

Deirdre sat at dinner, staring at Roman's empty place. Why had she taken for granted his being there night after night? Why had she assumed he would be around forever? She picked up her fork, sighing. This was only the first day. "Counselor," she opened quietly, "how long do we expect Roman to be gone?"

He furrowed his brow and inhaled thoughtfully. "Well, to make two full circuits between the outposts . . . I would say a week, at the outside two." She nodded. He whispered, "I miss him also."

Day after day, Deirdre worked to exhaustion on the quilt, but that gave her too much opportunity to think about Roman. She searched out the required books from her father's library, but could not concentrate enough to read for long. Gradually, she began to pass the hours wandering through the palace and peeking out the shutters.

Roman pounded with weary relief through the gates of Outpost One. Galapos greeted him joyfully: "Well done, well done, my boy! Come in, get warm and fed, and give me your messages."

They hustled him blue and shivering into the dining room of the fortress, and he stood almost on top of the fire to thaw. A soldier broke out a keg of ale and Roman drank great gulps where he stood. Then he sat to devour a plate of stew under Galapos's shining eyes. "What do the outposts say, Roman?"

He swallowed his mouthful. "Outpost Three has been able to recruit eight hundred men from Hycliff, Westford, and the country villages, but they are short on arms—particularly bows and broadswords. They have leather jerkins, but few chestplates. Outpost Two is meeting resistance from the villagers in recruiting men— they are largely sympathetic to Savin, as opposed to Karel or Tremaine. Also, the outpost lost forty horses to lameness from the rocks. They have not arms to send elsewhere, either. What does Four say?"

"They are gaining strength under Basner. But still, they are the most vulnerable, in the valley." Galapos paused to calculate, watching Roman eat. "It is strange," he resumed thoughtfully, "that I have received no directive from the Surchatain regarding our defense against Tremaine—only from the Counselor. What are the High Lord's thoughts on this?"

Roman stopped chewing. "I do not know. After our trip to Corona, Deirdre told me he did not believe Tremaine had any intention of attacking us. I thought that the Counselor would have enlightened him by now. . . . I wonder, what shadow has darkened his ability to see Tremaine for what he is?"

Galapos shook his head and they were silent a moment. Then he asked, "And how is the Chataine?"

"She is beautiful, Galapos. A beautiful young woman."

"Is she now?" he smiled broadly, then his face clouded. "But not for you, my boy

"I know," Roman replied.

"Tell me though—do you have a clue as to whom she plans to marry in the spring?"

"No. Rollet she refused at the outset. Artemeus has fallen from her favor, I believe. Caspar has not yet approached her, though when he does she may favor him. She is good friends with his sister."

Galapos nodded. "So little time, and so much yet to do, to be ready to fight. If we only had allies, also." His eyes widened. "Surely a man who values commerce values the freedom in which to conduct it!" Roman met his eyes in a flash of recognition. "My boy—can you ride to Ooster today?"

Roman stood. "Give me your message and I will be gone."

Deirdre sat in her room, staring at the nearly completed quilt. Three weeks. Twenty days he had been gone now. Or was today twenty-one? She picked up the thread with tired fingers. Nanna entered, lugging more wood for her grate. "Is it warm enough in here, darling?"

"Warm enough," Deirdre sighed.

"Here—you bought this lovely shawl at the Fair and haven't even worn it yet." She draped it around Deirdre's shoulders.

"Thank you, Nanna," she mumbled.

Nanna stood back and sighed at her dejection. "Angelina tells me Roman has returned, and—"

"He has?" Deirdre bounded out the door before Nanna could utter another word. She raced to the kitchen and flung open the door, but saw only the maid. "Angelina! Where is Roman?"

"Chataine," she acknowledged, bowing. "He has gone to the villagers with provisions."

"What? After just returning from the border?"

"Well, Chataine, he passed through the village on his way here and saw the need was urgent."

"Oh—" Deirdre muttered in exasperation, "well—" she backed out of the door and went to the foyer to wait for him.

It proved to be a long wait. She sat and fidgeted, then walked to the foyer fire and threw a stick on it. That accomplished, she sat again to fidget some more.

After what must have been years, the heavy wooden doors swung open with an icy whoosh and a muffled figure entered. She stood up eagerly, but it was only a bearded stranger. Disappointed, she sat again. The man paused shivering before the foyer fire and spoke: "Are you waiting to greet me, Chataine?"

"Roman?" she gasped. He let down the hood of his cloak and

grinned at her. Between the black beard and dark circles under his eyes, he was hardly recognizable. She stepped toward him, wanting to throw her arms around his neck—but dared not. So she took his icy fingers in hers to warm them, and kissed them.

"Deirdre—don't," he murmured. From the corner of her eye she saw Angelina enter the foyer, then abruptly turn and leave.

"I missed you so," she whispered.

"And I you. . . . You will never know—" he jerked his hands away as the Surchatain came into view.

"Ah, Roman, you have returned. Are things well at the outposts?"

"Yes, Surchatain." Roman bowed as he passed by.

"Good—I will want a complete report soon—Guard, summon Lord Farquehart to my chambers."

Karel remained within earshot as Deirdre asked, "How do the villagers fare?"

Roman shook his head. "Poorly. The plague worsens with the cold, and many are dying. There is so little we can do for them. The children—" he closed his eyes and leaned back against the wall. Deirdre understood. He wanted to do for them what Galapos had once done for him.

"Stay here before the fire and I will bring you hot soup." He nodded gratefully. She hurried to the kitchen and began ladling out soup from a large kettle in the fire. Then she heard a strange scratching noise at the rear door of the kitchen. Angelina was not around, so she opened the door herself and looked out. A shabby child stood knee-deep in the snow outside. He stared at her. She stared back.

"I didn't get none," he finally said.

"What?"

"Roman came and gave stuff to the others and I didn't get none!"

"Oh!" Deirdre scolded herself silently and pulled him inside. "Wait here," she instructed. While the child gazed, she filled a leather bag with victuals and gave it to him. She wrapped her own lambswool shawl around him and hung a sack of coal over his shoulder. Heavily laden, he had begun to stumble out when he stopped and turned to look at her. Wide-eyed, he pulled on her hand till she bent down, then gave her a sloppy, resounding kiss. She returned it on his little grimy face and sent him home.

She carried the soup to Roman, who thanked her and gulped it down. She began to tell him about the child, but then decided, no, this was something she did without looking to him for approval. He handed the empty bowl back to her. "It is good to be home," he said.

At dinner Deirdre was delighted to see him rested and clean-shaven again. He even wore the leather shortcoat she had made for him. He hardly spoke a word, as usual, but she could read content-ment—even happiness?—on his face. "Roman," she smiled won-deringly, recalling a question of long ago, "are you happy here?"

"Exceedingly," he said easily.

She felt a thrill run up her spine and the Counselor said, "Of course! He has just survived three weeks of the most perilous duty in the army! Surchatain, may we toast in honor of this soldier's courage?" Deirdre stared at the Counselor. She had never heard such praise for Roman fall from his lips. Eudymon caught himself in confusion, as if recalling something crucial that had slipped from his mind.

The guests at table waited, then looked at the Counselor and Roman in embarrassment as the Surchatain made himself deaf to the proposal. Roman did not seem offended, however. He was studying his plate—and the Counselor—with the intensity of sudden appreciation.

Now that Roman was home, Deirdre intended to hoard his time, but found that he again had other plans. Every afternoon he departed the palace with supplies and spent hours at the village. Once, she appeared downstairs in heavy clothes and cloak as he was about to leave. "I am coming with you."

"No, Chataine, you are not," he said emphatically. "As I told you, there are many ill. I will not have you down there."

"But—*you* are going—Roman!" she shouted after him as he raced out the door. "Curse it," she muttered, removing her hood.

In two weeks' time the weather was unchanged, and Deirdre felt really tired of being kept inside like a prisoner. Listlessly she roamed from room to room of the palace, searching for something to occupy her. Roman was out for the afternoon, of course.

At dinner she did not want to eat anything. It all looked liked so much mush. She drank, though, for her throat was parched and her head was pounding.

"Deirdre? Answer your father. Are you ill?" It was Roman's voice. He was looking at her intently.

"What? Oh, Roman. Did you address me, Father?" Strange that she could not focus on him. Roman was standing now, coming over to her chair. He was saying something about her face. She felt hands on her forehead and heard an odd buzzing . . . that was the last she knew as she fell unconscious into Roman's arms.

Her skin burned with heat and for days she drifted in and out of fitful sleep. The physician was helpless to succor her. "It is the same disease the village folk are fighting," he reported in distress.

"What?" cried Karel. "How could she have been stricken—she and no one else in the palace? Roman!" He turned on the Captain. "Where have you been taking her?"

"High Lord, she has not set foot out of the palace walls!" declared Roman.

Nanna added shyly, "Surchatain, that is the truth. She has not been out." As Deirdre's fever burned her life away, there was much pacing and crying, but no one could restore her. Nanna cared for her continually, hardly eating or sleeping herself. She gave the Chataine water when she could take it, and bathed her forehead with wet cloths. Still Deirdre grew weaker.

For her part, Deirdre was being terrorized by feverish nightmares. She dreamed she lay in an open coffin placed in the center of the courtyard. Her father looked at her and screamed, "She is dead! Guards! Take him to the whipping post!" She saw Roman dragged before the coffin and forced to look down at her. "Chataine," he pleaded, "I know you are not dead. If you do not rise, my life is worthless. Why are you tormenting me?" As he was dragged away, she tried to call after him, but her tongue was leaden.

Then she saw Tremaine standing at the foot of her casket holding a torch. He said, "No harm done, my dear. You'll wake in the morning with a headache. Now, which do you prefer—red, green, or blue?'' He pointed to the side and she saw a red Rollet, a blue Jason, and a green Artemeus holding hands and dancing around a maypole. Suddenly, a silver-haired man leaped on top of her casket, wielding a shining dagger. He plunged it into her chest, and she saw her blood pouring in torrents from the wound. Then she was falling fast into a terrifying blackness. It engulfed her, choking her, pressing down on her so that she fell faster and faster into some unnamed horror. Rollet's voice came in a whisper: ''This is hell.''

''Roman! Roman!'' Deirdre bolted upright in bed, screaming. Roman, who was in the receiving room of her chambers, heard and pounded on the door. ''Nurse! Let me in now! Now!'' Although he had tried to see her for days, Nanna had insisted that a man could not be allowed in the Chataine's sleeping room. Now Roman insisted, ''Nurse! I will break this door in if you do not unbolt it!'' She opened it quickly, scolding him as he rushed to kneel at Deirdre's bedside. He seized her hands. ''Chataine, it's Roman. I'm here. I'm here!'' But Deirdre did not even see him. She flopped back down in her bed to more restless sleep. Roman, still holding her hands, studied her pale face. ''She is worsening.''

Nanna stood anxiously behind him. ''What is to be done?'' He shook his head. Pressing Deirdre's fingers to his face, he closed his eyes. A minute later Nanna touched him on the shoulder. ''Roman. There is something I must tell you, in case the Chataine—in case she—'' she could not say the word, but went on: ''You must promise me you will tell it to Galapos when the time is right.'' He raised his face to her. ''Not here,'' she said. ''In the outer room. Come.'' He followed her out and she closed the door.

When Deirdre at last opened her eyes, she saw nothing at first. The room was dark and cold. She was terribly thirsty and weak. She tried to move, but felt her limbs were weighted with lead. Then someone was standing over her. ''She's awake!'' a deep voice shouted. ''Bring water and gruel! Now!''

Water, yes. She tried to loosen her tongue. ''All is well, Chataine; you are going to be well. The fever has left you, as I prayed it would.'' Roman lifted her up and put a cup of cold water to her mouth. It tasted so good—though much of it spilled down her face and front. More, please. He refilled the cup and put it to her lips again. She focused on his face. He looked haggard. Good old Roman. She hugged him with what little strength she had. He enfolded her to him. Nanna rushed in and saw their embrace, but only cried, "Darling!" and ran to hug them both.

Weeks passed before Deirdre could even leave her chambers. Spring had come, and her betrothal fest would be soon. Yet it was clear that she was not yet strong enough to travel. She would have to wait until the fest the following spring. Karel dispatched a messenger to Corneus and his guests explaining her illness and giving deep—and sincere—regrets for her absence. But when the Chataine heard that the fest would take place without her this year (which was supposed to cruelly disappoint her), she breathed a sigh of gratitude. Her near encounter with death, at least, had gained her one more year of freedom.

11

The next months of her life Deirdre lived like a condemned prisoner out on leave. She savored every small pleasure and studied every natural beauty with new wonder. She practiced every kindness until even Nanna was abashed. She began sending provisions of her own to the villagers and restrained herself to obey her father.

As always, time with Roman was her greatest treasure. She gradually ceased laying demands on him and plying him with personal questions. He received full freedom from her to go where he wished and do what he needed without answering to her. Yet there was one sacrifice that still needed to be made. She avoided it, fought it, ignored it, but her irritatingly active conscience would not let her rest. So she rose from bed late one evening and summoned him to her receiving chamber. . . .

"Chataine?" Roman entered and bowed. Seeing her in her over-robe, he stayed close to the door.

"Roman," she began, pacing and rubbing her hands, "I have

152

not been fair with you. I have been selfish and demanding." She paused, but was annoyed to see that he did not disagree with her. She resumed, "I have decided to give you permission to marry any time you wish. You have waited long enough, and I thank you for your patience and indulgence." There. It was out.

He silently studied the wall beyond her. Then he cleared his throat. "Chataine, thank you for your gracious permission. I believe that I will not, however—not yet. The time is not right."

"Truly, Roman?" she exclaimed joyfully, clapping her hands. Then she stopped herself, feeling her reaction was somehow inappropriate.

"Yes, Chataine." He gave a tired smile. "Will that be all?"

"Yes, Roman," she beamed. "You may go." She slept sweetly that night.

And still they went riding. The green summer months were passed in excursions to the hills and even neighboring towns. And still they found their way to the willow trees to rest and talk. During these days Deirdre noticed a new peace and ease in Roman's manner, especially toward her. When she remarked about it, he smiled a little and said, "I believe I have finally learned to lay my burdens on God's shoulders. He has assured me that these things shall be resolved in His way."

She wanted to ask him if God had been talking to him again, but then thought, *Why do I want to ridicule him?* He cut his eyes toward her respectful silence and smiled again. She raised her eyebrows inquiringly. He said, "It is amazing to see the changes in you—how you have grown up right under my eyes. Yet you are still wonderfully a child." She could not tell him how much he was responsible for what he saw in her.

On one of these summer excursions they rode farther than usual, becoming hot and thirsty while yet miles from home. Unexpectedly, they came upon a little hut in a clearing in the forest. Deirdre sighed and dismounted. "At the least we can get water here."

Roman looked around uneasily. "I did not know there was a shelter here. I do not know who lives here. Chataine, stay beside me." He approached the door and started to call out, but immediately it creaked open and a young woman in grey silk appeared.

Deirdre startled, feeling a flash of jealousy. The woman was piercingly beautiful—blue-black hair falling loosely past her shoulders, and arresting grey eyes in a face modeled from the sirens of antiquity. *Why is a woman dressed as she is living in a hut?* she wondered.

The beauty never glanced at Deirdre, but gazed at Roman as if she had been waiting for him endless years. "You have done well to come, Roman the Warrior. I knew that you would come."

Roman stood uncertainly, evaluating her. "Who are you?"

"I am Varela, and I have many gifts for you, Warrior."

He was silent a moment, as if still trying to read her. "The only gift I desire of you is a cup of water for the Chataine and myself."

She laughed deliciously and reached out a hand to him. "I have much more to give than mere water." Her eyes took on a keen edge. "It has been given me to make you victorious in your battles to come, Warrior."

Roman gave a start as if waking from a trance. He stepped back in repulsion. "I have no need of your gifts, sorceress." To Deirdre he said, "Mount."

"What about some water?" she whispered.

The woman raised her voice: "You will not succeed without me!"

"My triumph has already been assured without you." He mounted. "In Christ the Conqueror."

Her face contorted and she shrieked, "A curse! I have a curse for you, then!" They spurred their horses, but she screamed after them: "I see death around you, Warrior! I see the death of thousands around you! I see death surround you!"

Deirdre shuddered. "What could she mean?"

"It has no meaning," he replied. "Do not let it trouble you." Nonetheless, they galloped rapidly away from the hut.

"Roman, I am thirsty!" she pleaded. At once they came upon a clear brook almost hidden in the forest floor.

"We will drink here," he said.

As they scooped up water, she watched him. "Then you will fight with Galapos," she observed.

"That is very likely. I do not need her to tell me that."

"Should you not at least hear her out?" she wondered. "I have heard that they are so often right—"

"But not always. And what truth they have is distorted to fit their purposes. You must learn, Chataine, to gauge truth by the source, because not everything that has the appearance of truth is really so."

"That sounds reasonable," she mused, "considering it came from you." He just shook his head.

It was the day following that she really began to notice Roman's chapel visits. She had known for years that he attended the little services there, but she had paid no attention. Her father did not go, nor the Counselor—as a matter of fact, she could not name any who went but him. Now, however, her desire to know him more fully drove her to the chapel doors.

It was a small, simple hall, with a dais at the front and behind that a rough wooden cross. There were perhaps fifty people inside, kneeling or sitting quietly on the benches. Deirdre was surprised to see that at least half of them were soldiers—yet not surprised, when she considered how respected Roman was among them. The rest were servants and a few lesser palace officials.

She picked out Roman quickly. Then her heart sank as she saw Angelina sitting close beside him. They were talking in earnest whispers. Deirdre hesitated, turned to leave, but changed her mind and sat on the last bench. Presently she saw Angelina rise abruptly and walk back to the door. When she saw the Chataine, she startled and then bowed stiffly to her before leaving. Roman had gone down on his knees. Deirdre stayed where she was. Soon, a man in a simple brown robe entered, walked to the dais, and nodded to those present.

"Brothers and sisters," he began, "hear the words of our Lord Jesus to His close followers the night before He was crucified. . . ."

(That is the one they worship, Deirdre recalled, and felt a little smug in her knowledge of the Way.)

The holy man read from a book of Scriptures: " 'Do not let your heart be troubled; you believe in God, believe also in me. In my Father's house are many places; if it were not so, I would have told you. I go to prepare a place for you. And if I go to prepare a place for you, I will come again, and receive you to me, that where I am, you may be there also. And you know where I go, and you know the way.' Thomas said to him. 'Lord, we don't know where you are going, so how can we know the way?' Jesus said to him, 'I am the way, the truth, and the life; no one comes to the Father but by me. If you had known me, you would also have known my Father, and from now on you know Him and have seen Him.' Philip said to him, 'Lord, show us the Father, and we will be satisfied.' Jesus answered, 'Have I been with you so long, and you still do not know me, Philip? Whoever has seen me *has* seen the Father, so how can you ask, "Show us the Father"? Don't you believe that I am in the Father, and the Father is in me?' "

(*"In" the father? The father "in" him?* Deirdre wondered. *That sounds absurd.*)

" 'The words I tell you are not from myself, but from the Father who lives in me—He does the miracles also. Believe me when I say that I am in the Father and the Father in me, if only because of the miracles. And I tell you that whoever believes in me shall do the things I have done, and even greater ones, because I am going to my Father. And whatever you shall ask in my name I will do it, that the Father may be glorified in the Son.' "

(*If that were true, all these people would be rulers instead of servants and soldiers.*)

" 'And I will ask the Father, and He will send you another Advocate, who will stay with you forever. He is the Spirit of truth, whom the world cannot receive because they cannot see Him or know Him; but you know Him, because He lives with you, and even in you. . . . Yet a little while, and the world will not see me any more, but you will see me, and because I live, you will live also. . . . If someone loves me, he will live by my words, and my Father will love him, and we will come to him and live with him. And the Advocate, which is the Holy Spirit, whom the Father will send in my name, will teach you all things, and bring everything I have said to your remembrance. Peace I leave with you, my peace I give to you, not the peace the world gives. So do not be discouraged or afraid.' ''

(At those words, Roman's rocklike stability impressed itself on Deirdre's mind.)

" 'I am the true vine, and my Father is the gardener. Every branch of mine that does not bear fruit, He cuts away, and every branch that bears fruit He prunes, that it may bear more fruit. . . . Live in me, and I will live in you. As the branch cannot bear fruit of itself unless it lives in the vine, so you cannot bear fruit unless you live in me. I am the vine, you are the branches, and whoever lives in me and I in him shall bear much fruit, for without me you can do nothing.' ''

(*"In" him, again!* Yet the analogy was clear enough to her. The branch withered and died when cut off from the tree. . . .)

" 'If you live in me, and my words live in you, whatever you ask of me shall be done for you. For my Father is glorified when you bear much fruit. As the Father has loved me, so I have loved you; live in my love. I have told you these things so that my joy may remain in you, and that your joy may be full. This is my commandment: Love each other as I have loved you. A man can have no greater love than to lay down his life for his friends. And you are my friends, if you do what I command you. . . . You have not chosen me, but I have chosen *you,* and given you a mission to bring forth fruit that will remain, and in so doing, whatever you shall ask the Father in my name, He will give it to you. This I command you, that you love each other.' ''

(*A command to love! As if it were hard. . . .*)

The leader finished reading and closed the book, then the people sang a song Deirdre did not know. When they ended, the leader knelt and the entire assembly followed suit. Deirdre awkwardly gathered up the folds of her skirt to get down on her knees.

The leader prayed, "Our Father, we rejoice in your Love that came among us as a man and brought us life. We kneel in awe at your mercy to set us free from the power of sin and death and raise us to the honor of serving your purposes. From the depths of your infinite wisdom you direct our ways to bring honor to your name and meaning to our once-futile lives. How astounding, Father, how unsearchable is your love! How boundless are your workings and how high your purposes! Lord of hosts, descend to hear us in the name of your only Son.

"Father, you know of the persecutions we face daily and the opposition to your worship here. We require your wisdom to go before us and your strength to sustain us. And Father . . . we pray for any unbelievers in our midst today. Draw them, as you have drawn us, to your fountain of life. Amen."

They repeated in unison, "Amen," and stood. The leader hesitated, then spoke again. "Brothers and sisters, many of you do not know of the latest trouble we have encountered. It seems that our number has grown so as to raise the displeasure of the Surchatain. He has now forbidden the use of this hall for our worship . . . nevertheless, we will make other arrangements. We will not forsake our gathering together." He raised his hand in a blessing. "For now, go in peace. Yet if any here have need of enlightenment or counsel, I am here to help." He stepped down from the dais. Roman rose heavily and walked to meet him.

Deirdre left the chapel most disturbed. Obviously, there were still matters private to Roman, and that depressed her. She could not understand either what comfort he found in these services. Why would her father forbid them? They were surely no threat to him. Yet, this God of Roman's seemed to demand devotion above the Surchatain, and she could imagine that anything which put the High Lord in second place would not be tolerated by her father. But— there was another contradiction. If this worship was something empty and useless, as her father claimed, or a delusion, as Rory had said, why would her father take such measures against it? He did not prevent other soldiers and servants from far baser activities.

At once, two memories presented themselves vividly to her mind's eye. One was of Roman, stamping out the sorcerer's patterns, saying, "They are dangerous. They bring ruin to a whole country if they influence the right people." The other was of Tremaine's rooms . . . the blackness . . . Roman's cry and the sudden light . . . Tremaine saying, "The rooms affect only those who claim God."

In a flash Deirdre stood on the brink of a chasm and glimpsed a great war raging on a scale that boggled her. These antagonists fought not for such petty spoil as boundaries and trade, but for lives—human lives—millions of little lights dotting the great plain. Each represented a sphere of dominion, a conquest—a spectacular victory or horrifying defeat. *No!* She buried her face in her hands, running from the chapel. She would have none of this war. Therefore, she made no further attempt to attend services, wherever they might have been held.

The summer melted quietly into golden autumn. How Deirdre loved the autumn—the trees bursting out in brilliant red and orange and yellow, the warm afternoons and cool nights . . . the abundant harvests and the aroma of produce drying in the kitchen for the winter store.

She and Roman sat on the high bluff overlooking the golden fields, watching the harvest in progress. He began rubbing his brow in the way that signaled pain, so she reached over to pull back on his shoulders and rest his head on her knees. As she massaged his face and forehead, he closed his eyes. "You remind me of autumn," she said suddenly. He opened one eye. "You are brown and warm, full of color and life. Yet you can be cool, too."

He considered this for a moment in silence. "You are spring," he said quietly. "Bright and delicate and beautiful . . . budding with promise . . ." She grinned and slipped her arms around his neck to hug him. His hand stole up to squeeze hers.

Suddenly winter was upon them again. Fortunately, it was a mild winter compared to the preceding one. For the first time ever, she coaxed Roman into ice skating with her. Always before, he had contented himself to watch her from the shore. She finally discovered why: he could not skate! Or had never learned. "Roman, I could have taught you," she said.

He shook his head. "I was too proud to be your pupil." But today he strapped on blades and stepped gingerly onto the ice. He promptly fell flat. Deirdre bit her lip to keep from laughing and helped him up. After the first few wobbly minutes, he skated remarkably well—stopping, turning, even making circles. But when she tried to skate with him, their feet got tangled up and they went down in a heap together. They were laughing, and then suddenly they were holding each other close. For a heartbeat he held her, then let go and scrambled to his feet. "This lesson has ended," he said.

They had the most fun riding in the sleigh. Deirdre would bundle up in her fur-lined cloak and heap furs in the sleigh, then she and Roman would set off to explore a strange new world of crystal and white.

One day he interrupted her lessons to take her sleigh riding. "How dare you?" she protested happily, throwing aside her books.

"I want you to go with me now, because there is someone I want you to meet."

"Yes? Who?"

"You will see." He took the armload of furs and they stole out of the palace to the waiting sleigh. "Deirdre," he said sternly, "please do not announce at dinner that I took you away from your lessons to go with me."

"I may, and I may not," she teased. "Who are we going to see?"

"You will see." He clucked Lady Grey to a trot, and Deirdre sang inwardly as she sat close beside him, watching the silver trees glide past. If she looked carefully, she might spot a snow rabbit or silver fox among the trees.

Roman guided the sleigh beyond the far side of the village. There sat one lone hut, removed from the others. Smoke billowed up from its center chimney. He jumped lightly from the sleigh and assisted her out. Then he drew out a basket from the sleigh that was filled with dried fruit, beef, and fresh bread. "Brother Avelon!" he called out. The door opened and a thin man in a brown robe motioned them in. Deirdre shyly stepped into the hut and looked around. It was so small and crude, she felt uneasy in her furs.

"Roman, thank you, son," he said, taking the basket. "I am grateful to God for your kind heart."

"It is a small kindness, Brother Avelon. I would like for you to meet the Chataine Deirdre. Deirdre, this is the holy man who taught my mother."

"Oh!" she said, her jaw dropping. "I am honored to meet you! But—do you live here? In this?" In her concern she somehow lost her tact.

Both Roman and Brother Avelon smiled ruefully. "As of late, Chataine, yes," the holy man answered. "My health no longer allows me to travel on my circuit preaching the Word."

"You must come live in the palace, then," she insisted. Roman gave a look that said "I told you" to the holy man.

But Avelon shook his head. "I cannot, Chataine, though you are gracious to offer it. I have not endeared myself to your father." Deirdre then remembered he was the one who had posed as a minstrel and sung a song which angered her father.

"Well—what can we do to help you?"

"Roman does much, my child. Not without risk, of course. He has already come under criticism from the palace overseer for taking too much food out of the palace. Your silence on these matters spares him further censure."

"Certainly," she said wonderingly. "But—Father has always allowed charity to the villagers."

"He seems to have had a recent change of heart," Roman replied.

The holy man turned to Roman. "God is moving swiftly. I see so many of our prayers being answered, especially in you. As long as you are here, Roman, let us pray together for your father."

Roman startled. "Later, Brother—I must return Deirdre to the palace before she is missed. I will be back—" he hustled her out to the sleigh. Avelon watched them dash away with a troubled face.

"Roman, does he know your father?"

"They have never met. Brother Avelon knows only that he needs prayer."

"Do you pray for him?"

"Yes," he said defensively, and lowered his eyes.

It was spring, then, in a rush of green. The Fair came, and Deirdre and Roman spent a day shopping at their favorite booths. She picked up a jeweled bracelet. "May I buy something for Angelina?" she asked him.

He paused. "It is not necessary on my account, Chataine. She has married another."

"Oh, Roman—I am sorry." She could not tell from his face how he felt about it.

Galapos returned from the border that spring. Both Deirdre and Roman were waiting to meet him at the gate. When he saw Deirdre, his face registered wondering admiration. "I left you a little girl and come back to find you a beautiful young woman! How old I must be getting!" But no—except for a trifle more grey at the temples, he was unchanged. It was good to have him back and to hear his jocularity again. The three of them went riding together, and Deirdre and Roman informed him of all the palace news. He had heard of her illness, and had waited anxiously to hear of her recovery. "To be frank, Chataine, I did not have much hope for you," he said. "That disease is most often deadly."

"Oh, I could not have died. Roman was standing guard over me!" she grinned. Galapos laughed and hugged her. Roman shook his head, smiling. Deirdre loved seeing them together again. Galapos brought out such a light in Roman's eyes.

Later, Galapos and Roman stopped by the Counselor's chambers. They knocked, and the Counselor quickly opened the door. "Galapos." He grasped the Commander's hand warmly. "I heard you had returned."

"Yes, and I have some news for you, Counselor. May we come in?" The door opened wide, then was shut and bolted behind them.

Shortly thereafter, Caspar, Chatain of Calle Valley, arrived in Westford to visit Deirdre before her betrothal fest. She was irritated to see him given Roman's seat across from her at dinner; Roman was placed further down the table.

"Well, Caspar, how does it go in the valley?" Karel opened cordially.

"Quite well, Surchatain. We had a remarkable yield from the vineyards last year, thanks to careful planting and perfect weather."

"The wine from your valley is always excellent," observed Karel.

Caspar inclined his head. "I am honored it pleases you, for I have brought twenty casks of our best vintage as a small gift." His eyes rested on Deirdre. "This fest has been long in coming, but I feel it will be well worth the wait."

Deirdre raised her eyes. "Will Laska be there?"

"No, I regret that she will not be. She married Gastin last year. She sends you her love, by the way."

"Please give her mine," Deirdre said listlessly.

After dinner, Caspar took her hand and they stepped out onto a private balcony overlooking the garden. For once, Roman was not standing in the shadows. He did not guard her in her own palace. "Deirdre," Caspar began, "you know why I am here. I wish you to marry me." She was about to say something sarcastic like "Stand in line," but he stopped her. "I know I am not as pretty as Artemeus or as powerful as Rollet but, in time, you will see I am the best choice. I will love you, Deirdre."

She was silent a moment. "What will become of Lystra if I marry you?"

"Why, nothing evil. We will rule it together. Of course, we will pay taxes to Tremaine, and the troops at your outposts will be sent elsewhere, but Tremaine will let us be."

"Why?" she demanded. "Why does he need us—or anyone?"

"Well—he cannot rule the entire area himself. He needs governors—"

"Puppet rulers," she said contemptuously.

"I have heard a saying that it is better to be a live dog than a dead lion."

"What then will become of Father? And Commander Galapos?"

"I am sorry, Deirdre. They must be put away."

Her stomach churned. "You mean they will be executed," she said evenly.

"It is Tremaine's order. The present leaders must be set aside. We have no choice about that, my love."

"But—if Tremaine plans to do away with my father, why should he spare yours—or Savin?"

He shrugged a little uneasily. "Tremaine spares those useful to him. All he wants of Karel is his sea trade—and you. It is no secret that he despises your father." He added, "You are very fortunate that Tremaine decided to use you instead of kill you."

Deirdre turned away from him. "What about the other officers in the army? Will they all be executed too?"

"Tremaine says that any heads which rise above the others must be cut off." She closed her eyes. He asked, "Will you marry me, Deirdre?"

"Ask me after the fest," she replied, wishing fervently that the day would never come.

12

cant weeks after Caspar's visit, it was time for Nanna to make her usual bubbling preparations for the trip to Ooster. This time, however, the Chataine took little pleasure in the beautiful gowns that were laid out for her approval. She felt as if she were facing her own execution.

With relentless inevitability, the day arrived for the journey. Deirdre had requested that no soldiers accompany them this trip, and her father had agreed that Roman was sufficient. Departing at dawn, the two of them journeyed in silence toward the watershed at Ooster.

With each mile they covered, the Chataine's burden grew heavier and heavier. Finally she reined to a stop. . . .

"Roman, what am I going to do?" Deirdre cried. "If I marry one of Tremaine's allies, you will all die. If I do not, Tremaine will kill us all anyway!"

"Not necessarily," he quietly replied. "Chataine, we have not been idle since Tremaine threatened you. Galapos has been gathering men and weapons into the greatest army this country has ever seen. We are now ready to fight. So follow your own judgment."

Deirdre knew then what she would do.

Arriving at Ooster, she saw that the splendor of Corneus's preparations was unmatched, as usual. But Deirdre eyed them almost with hatred. As she watched several pranksters draping flower garlands on the stone lions which stood guard at the palace gates, a voice at her side said, "You have grown some since I saw you last." She turned her eyes to see Rollet.

"It happens, with time," she replied coldly, then nodded to Roman as he stepped up with her bags. She threaded her way through the crowd of chattering guests, aiming only to get to her room.

Artemeus stepped in front of her. "Hello, beautiful creature."

She paused long enough to say, "I am not the beast here," and lifted her skirts to start up the stairs. Artemeus looked dumbfounded.

On the stairs she encountered Caspar. He took her hand. "Deirdre, seeing you makes me want to sing," he said sincerely.

"Thank you."

He whispered yearningly, "How long will you keep me waiting?"

She looked down at the marble stairs. "A while," she murmured. Caspar squeezed her hand and continued down the stairs. Looking after him, she whispered, "Forever, Caspar." Then she directed a deliberate glance at Roman on the step below. He was frowning slightly, peering at her, trying to read her. She smiled, knowing how anxious he was to know her marriage choice. Their whole defense hung on it. She turned and resumed climbing.

Deirdre stayed in her room until dinner, dressing with determined slowness. Eventually she had to go down. At the foot of the stairs Corneus and Jason met up with her. Before she acknowledged them, she scanned the room for Roman, and saw him standing against the wall with a number of other chaperons. He nodded at her very slightly.

Corneus was saying, "Deirdre, my dear, I was not even sure that you had arrived yet! How lovely you look! Jason?"

"Yes, Deirdre. You will sit with me tonight." He took her arm, and she allowed herself to be escorted to the banquet hall between them. It was already filled with waiting guests. Corneus took his seat at the head of the table, Jason to his right and Deirdre beside Jason, and the dinner began. Roman took his place behind Deirdre's chair.

A platter of steaming mutton was set before her. Jason was saying, "Deirdre, you are one fortunate girl. I turned Musa away to court you." Deirdre imagined the mutton plate turned on top of his head and smiled. He returned her smile with a wink.

Artemeus, to her right, smiled genially at Jason and said, "Your father's table is legendary at these fests." Then he leaned toward Deirdre and whispered, "But Jason is an idiot."

Jason raised his nose toward him and said, "Certainly no one living on a rock can match it." Artemeus's smile vanished.

Caspar said, "The greenness of Calle Valley is both productive and beautiful. It can grow anything—"

"Including greenhorns," smirked Artemeus.

Caspar quietly replied, "Innocuous appearances are intended so as not to panic harmless morons." Jason laughed so suddenly he choked.

Deirdre stood abruptly. "Excuse me. I need fresh air." As three or four others also stood, she added icily, "*Alone.*"

She walked the breadth of the hall to the gates of Corneus's verdant garden. She paused to let Roman open the gates for her, then they stepped onto the pebble-lined path. For minutes they stood silently, enshrouded in fragrance and cooled by the gentle night wind. Here, in the garden, she felt eons away from ridiculous charades and pretty faces covering murderous hearts.

She touched a rose petal. These things were real. This was truly a rose, from its petals to its roots, and the generation it produced would be roses, and the generation after that roses. Long after Jason turned to dust and Artemeus grew old and feeble, roses would grow up hedges and walls. These things were reliable, trustworthy, *eternal*—

"Did you speak to me?" she asked Roman with a start.

"Not aloud," he answered quietly.

She was searching his eyes when Rollet approached the gates and called, "Deirdre?" Stiffly, she returned to the fest.

The following day she remained detached and withdrawn

167

throughout the amusements, hardly speaking and showing no interest in the men around her. Strangely, the more withdrawn she became, the more interest she drew. Perhaps it was because she was a challenge, or an enigma, that one young man after another joined the siege to break down her ennui. They irritated her with their fawning and chafed her spirit raw in their attempts to arouse her interest.

After the noon meal she slipped away, intending to sneak up to her room. She had made it beyond the great double doors when two bony fingers jabbed into her sides. She gasped and spun around. "Otto!"

A large-boned blond man laughed and demanded, "Where are you running off to, pretty thing?"

"I am going up to my room to rest," she said through gritted teeth.

"Not when I came across a continent to see you." He grasped her hand to drag her away from the stairs. At that, Roman began advancing with a dangerous face.

But another fellow grabbed Otto. Roman paused. "Maybe she does not want to see *you!* Deirdre, I brought you some little silver bells for your mare's bridle."

"Take those bells and hang them on your ear, Morin!" growled Otto.

Morin shoved Otto. "That insult just earned you a pugil lesson!"

"To the courtyard, then!" agreed Otto. They stalked out together, expecting Deirdre to follow and watch them fight over her. But with a breath of relief, she leaped up the stairs. Glancing back at Roman, she could have sworn he had returned to his place laughing.

Deirdre fought down a strong desire to feign illness, and attended dinner that night. In between the onion soup and the roast chicken, the talk at the table turned to what women found interesting in men. Thoughts of Roman sprang into Deirdre's mind. He stood behind her chair, and she felt his presence like a warm fire at her back.

One girl said she liked a man with dark eyes. Someone said, "Oh-oh, that means you, Jason," and everyone laughed. Another girl said she preferred strong, muscular men. Another said she was attracted to men with beards. Then someone asked, "Deirdre, what do you like in a man?" They fell silent, waiting.

She put her cloth to her mouth. The fire burned warmly at her back. "It is good for a man to be strong," she said. "A strong man can do so many things. But a man who is both strong and gentle is wonderful. A man must be intelligent, of course, but if he is also humble, that makes him all the more appealing . . . a man who is strong enough to live a disciplined life, but who is tender with the faults of others . . . a man who is honest above all, but kind . . . a man with courage, who will sacrifice his life for someone else, yet who also has the kind of courage to stay with the same task year in and year out, even if it is boring or tiring or painful, simply because it is his duty . . . a man with the courage of faithfulness. I love all these things about a man." There was a momentary silence.

"You sound as if you are describing someone you know, my dear," observed Corneus.

"I am."

"The man you love," a girl said.

"Yes," Deirdre answered.

"Who is it?" "Are you going to marry him?" several asked at once.

Deirdre swallowed. "I cannot say who it is—I will not force his hand. But if he asked me I would marry him."

The conversation turned to other things and Deirdre said no more. As she rose from the table she looked at Roman, and the expression of love in his eyes made her catch her breath. But someone spoke in her ear and pulled her away. She had no chance to speak with him alone that evening. He was only her chaperon—one of many there. He did not share her suite nor eat with her at the banquet table. Now, when she desired his presence more than she ever had, he melted into the background, distant, obscured.

The day after, the men continued to harass her, leaving her no moment alone, until she locked herself up in her room again. Before the fest, Corneus came to her door and knocked. "Deirdre, my dear, are you well?"

She opened it slowly. "No, uncle, not really. I have been weak ever since my illness, you know."

"Well, we will get you some medicines so you will be able to come downstairs for the fest. You are coming down, are you not?" It was somehow a command.

169

"Yes, I will be down directly, uncle," she sighed.

Looking over the vast hall from the top of the stairway, Deirdre had an unsettling sense of déjà vu. Of course she had seen it before—two years ago at her coming out. Every year they went through the same silly pantomime of falling in love. She looked down on the couples dancing below her. She did not care at all to dance. Then she saw Roman standing below, face upraised to her. She gathered her dress and descended the stairs. Someone approached her. Veering aside, she walked straight up to Roman. "Dance with me."

"But, Chataine—"

"Dance with me, Roman."

He took her hand and led her out onto the floor. And they danced. Holding her waist, he guided her easily around the room. Perfectly in rhythm, they held each other bound in a wordless gaze. Deirdre felt a soaring inside that should have lifted her straight off the floor. "Roman, let's leave here—tonight!"

"No, Chataine. It is too dangerous traveling the road to Westford at night."

"Not to Westford . . . somewhere else—anywhere else!"

He looked at her for a long moment, then lowered his eyes. "I cannot leave," he whispered. "There is too much at stake . . ." Artemeus then cut in with a grin. Roman relinquished her hand and resumed his position near the wall.

Artemeus was talking to her—"and wouldn't our children be beautiful?" he finished. Deirdre tore her gaze from Roman to look at him with a hopeless sigh.

"What is wrong with you?" he demanded.

"I have never been more right," she answered, drawing away from him. She left the fest without a backward glance and shut herself up in her room again.

Early in the morning Roman was waiting for her with their mounts. She mumbled goodbye to her uncle and they departed at a fast gallop. Miles down the road, she suddenly reined in her horse. "Roman!" He careened to a stop. "Don't you understand?" she shouted. "I love you! I love you!" He trotted to her side, took her face in his hands, and kissed her with a yearning born in tears and blood.

At length he said, "Deirdre, I have loved you ever."

"You understand, then, that I will not have anyone but you," she whispered.

"I understand." He drew away and inhaled deeply, setting his face like a flint toward Westford. She followed him in a euphoria of love.

When they arrived at Westford, they immediately went to the great hall for the evening meal. Galapos greeted them joyfully: "Chataine, sweetheart, you are home! Tell me, are you betrothed yet?" Deirdre inadvertently glanced toward Roman, then dropped her eyes and blushed. Galapos quickly jumped to another topic.

But then an uncommon chain of events began. A messenger arrived, and the Surchatain took his note and read it silently. "Deirdre," he said. Her stomach twisted. "This is from the Chatain Artemeus, son of Savin. He offers his country to you in marriage."

"No," she responded quietly. Karel nodded and waved the messenger out again. Moments later, another messenger arrived. He carried a proposal from Caspar. "No," she said. Then, in sequence, came proposals from Morin, Carlin, and Otto. Deirdre turned them all down.

The table became strangely quiet. Roman sat staring at his plate and Galapos stared at Roman. Deirdre sat with her hands folded in her lap, not even pretending to eat. Another messenger arrived. Karel took his letter and then sat back, beaming. "Deirdre, here it is—a proposal from Rollet. What do you say?"

"No," she choked out.

He startled. "No? No?" He began to boil. "What do you want? Six proposals—seven including Gastin—whom will you have?"

Galapos laughed, "She's merely stacking them up to select from!" But he and the Counselor exchanged uneasy glances. In the midst of that turmoil one more messenger arrived. Karel seized his letter angrily.

He opened it. "Jason? Will you have Jason, Deirdre?"

"No," she said, but he did not react immediately. He seemed to be reading more.

He laid the note aside and turned full toward her. "Who is it?"

She blanched. "What?"

171

"Corneus said he hoped the man that you described—the one whom you love—is Jason. Obviously it is not. So who is it that you will marry?" Deirdre bit her lip and said nothing. "Answer me!" Silence. Karel rose from his seat. "Deirdre, you will answer or I—"

"High Lord," interrupted Roman, "it is I."

There was shocked silence around the table. All eyes fastened on Roman. Then Deirdre stammered, "Father—he lies! He—"

"He never lies," said the Surchatain calmly, walking over to face Roman, who stood. "He does not know how to lie. Soldier, have you made love to my daughter?"

"No, High Lord."

"Have you touched her? Kissed her?"

"Yes," Roman answered. Galapos put his head in his hands.

"You know the penalty you have incurred."

"Yes, High Lord."

"Guards," Karel turned. "Take him—"

"No!" Deirdre shouted, bounding from her chair. "No!" She kicked the chair over backwards and faced her father. "You will not do this again. You will not punish him on account of me again. You won't!"

"Take your seat, daughter."

"No! Father, I swear, if you execute him, I will kill myself! You will have no heir! I swear it!"

"Deirdre, no!" Roman cried in dismay.

"Guards! Take him to the prison. Escort her to her chambers and post a guard at her door. Counselor, to my chambers!" There was swift movement on every side as his orders were executed. Roman moved to walk between two guards who would not lay hands on him. As his eyes met hers over the table, she saw them pleading, commanding: *Don't—don't.*

Within his chambers, Karel slumped into a chair. "What do I do *now?*" he spat.

The Counselor stroked his beard nervously. "Well, High Lord, you yourself decreed the punishment for such an offense: death by torture."

"But what if Deirdre makes good her threat?"

Eudymon waved his concern aside. "An impetuous outcry from an angry child. Roman must be punished to the extent of your

172

commands. You are the Surchatain. He has wronged you grievously."

Karel shook his head slowly, musing, "But he has saved her many times. He has been so reliable—why did he have to do this, now, when she was so close to marrying?" His voice took on authority again. "No, Counselor, I will be merciful, for both their sakes." Eudymon relaxed visibly. "He will only be hanged," decreed the Surchatain. "In the morning. And send a messenger to Rollet accepting his proposal. Ask him to come immediately for the wedding. You are dismissed, Counselor."

Deirdre sat still as stone in her darkened room, waiting for some word as to Roman's fate. She had begged the guard at the door to allow her to go to him in prison. He had refused, though kindly. So she sat. And waited. Nanna quietly entered. Deirdre looked up expectantly. "Dear," Nanna began, "you must not—"

"Just tell me what will happen to him."

"I do not know, dear. No one will tell me anything. Just rest for now, Chataine. I am sure your father will be lenient with him."

"Leave me alone now."

"Dear, your father has ordered me—"

"Leave me alone," Deirdre repeated. Nanna slipped quietly into her own room.

Deirdre closed her eyes and prayed to the God she had never known, begging for the life of her beloved Roman. When she could no longer think to pray, she watched the shadows slip by into darkness until she fell asleep.

At dawn she awoke with a start. The guard was banging at her door. "Chataine! The Surchatain summons you to an open audience!" She stumbled fearfully out of the room. An open audience could only bode ill.

The audience hall was crowded, even this early. As soon as Deirdre had taken her place before the dais, the Counselor stepped up and announced: "The High Lord and reigning Superiority of the independent state of Lystra, the gracious and beneficent Surchatain Karel." *Liar,* Deirdre seethed. The audience bowed on their knees while Karel entered and took his seat.

He glanced at Deirdre and waved at the guards: "Bring out the prisoner." Roman, his hands bound behind his back, was led out between two guards to stand in judgment before the dais. Her heart almost burst at this humiliation of him who was blameless.

The Surchatain read a statement: "You, Roman, for the crime of indecency with the Chataine Deirdre, are sentenced to hang by the neck until you are dead. Have you anything to say in your defense?"

"No, Surchatain," he replied. Deirdre felt nauseous.

"Guards—to the courtyard." Karel stood and the people kneeled. Roman was led out of the hall.

Karel, Galapos, and Eudymon escorted Deirdre to a balcony overlooking the courtyard. Deirdre grasped the railing to steady herself when she saw a monstrous scaffold standing in the center of the grounds. A noose hung swaying in the wind above the trap door in the platform. Close around the structure stood many soldiers, rigid. The crowd from the audience hall milled in behind the soldiers to watch the execution.

Roman appeared between the guards on the grounds below the balcony. Deirdre heard Karel say, "Have you any last requests?"

"Yes, High Lord. I wish the Chataine to view my body after I am dead, and to receive my bequest to her." Deirdre sank to her knees, horrified.

"It shall be done," said the Surchatain. He motioned again, and a soldier stepped up and covered Roman's head with a black hood. He was then led to the back of the scaffold by the soldier. Disappearing momentarily behind it, they ascended the steps and reappeared on the platform.

The noose was fitted around Roman's neck. Deirdre opened her mouth to cry his name but, as in her nightmare, no sound came. The soldier left the platform. The Surchatain raised his hand, and dropped it. The trap door sprang open with a terrible creak and bang. His body jerked for only a moment, then swung lifelessly. Deirdre gazed in shock. All else was still. Finally, the Surchatain gave a signal and the body was taken down. A soldier began to lead her from the balcony.

"No!" she pleaded, coming to herself. "Oh, no, no." She collapsed in tears and would not move.

"Will you deny him his last request?" the soldier asked. Sobbing, she shakily rose and followed him.

He took her into the courtyard and around to the back of the platform, where he lifted the curtain that shut off the little room within. Roman's body lay on the ground, covered with a blanket. Soldiers were preparing to place it in a wooden casket and nail down the lid. One of them uncovered his face, but she could not look. She could not bear to see him dead. "Chataine, look!" the soldier hissed. She shook her head. He forced her to look down on the body.

It was not Roman. In her confusion and grief, she would have cried out, but the soldier clapped a hand over her mouth. "He wanted you to know so you would not do yourself harm," he said. Then he gave her Roman's gold medallion. "And he wished you to hold this until he returned for it."

"Where—how—" she stammered.

"He has gone into hiding for now," he whispered, then added, "You are not the only one who cares for him."

"Who is that poor man?" she asked, turning to the dead man again. His form was quite similar to Roman's.

"A condemned prisoner. He had confessed to the murder of a kitchen maid, Hana, years ago."

The soldiers put the body in the coffin, and were lifting the lid to cover it when the Counselor could be heard just outside: "I will view the body for you, High Lord."

"Stop him!" gasped Deirdre, but it was too late. He had stepped inside. He looked down on the dead man, then backed out through the flap and said loudly, "He is quite dead, High Lord." When he came inside again, Deirdre gaped at him in bewilderment. Strange—there was something familiar in his face . . .

"In spite of what you may think, Chataine," he said quietly, "I would wish Roman no harm. He is my son."

Deirdre's head reeled. "Come," said the Counselor, "let us allow these men to quickly dispose of the body. We will talk in my chambers." As they approached the balcony, the Counselor said, "High Lord, I will put the Chataine under a protective watch so that no harm comes to her before the wedding." The Surchatain nodded.

Deirdre held back a thousand questions until they were safely in the Counselor's chambers.

"This is yours, then," she said as she held out the medallion to him.

"Yes, I gave it to him; but no, he gave it to you—as rightly he should. He told me many times of his love for you, and how he feared it would only betray him to his death."

Deirdre steadied herself. "Did you plan the switch, then?"

"I and others, obviously, but I will take the responsibility if it is found out. No matter. I believe I have finally redeemed myself in the eyes of my son."

"The counsel I have heard you give Father has always been against him," Deirdre observed carefully.

"I must tell you how that came about. When I first became your father's counselor, I quickly discovered he is one of those men who believe themselves too wise to need a counselor. However, it is good form for a ruler to have one. So every counsel I gave him, he would ponder and then take another course. I believe he has never really trusted me. I soon found that if I played the devil's advocate—if I suggested extreme or hasty moves, he would consider and then choose the wiser route. Your father has made some wise decisions with my help."

"You mean you deliberately gave false counsel?"

"No. I merely encouraged him to think along certain lines. It is a tricky business—and sometimes ricochets. But when I ascertained that there was a plot against your life, that is essentially how I persuaded him to assign you a guardian."

"You suggested Roman?"

"Oh, no, then he surely would have rejected him. I merely pointed out all the qualifications a guardian must have, then I made certain he saw Roman display each of those characteristics. Your father selected him himself."

"Why did you want Roman selected?"

"An advancement for my son—you understand. And also because he truly is the best."

"But becoming my guardian prevented his advancement under Galapos," Deirdre protested in confusion. "Or—is that what you wanted?"

He shrugged. "A trade-off, Chataine. He could not have it both ways."

She considered this silently, knowing what Roman had really wanted. "Does Roman know how you give backward counsel? Does he understand what you are trying to do?"

"Yes, of course. But he does not appreciate it. He says it is deceptive at best, and may actually weigh against him more than help him. He claims your father does not trust me because of that practice. I maintain I began it because he did not ever heed my counsels."

She recalled Roman's bitterness associated with his father. "Why did you desert him?"

"What? When?"

"Why did you stop sending money when his mother died?"

"I did not. I continued to send money for months afterward, not knowing she had died. But the idiot messenger I sent was intercepted by her neighbors, who told him they were seeing to the boy's needs. I found when I came to see them that this was not so."

"Did you love her?"

"Of course I did."

"Why did you not marry her?" Deirdre was relentless.

The Counselor sighed. "Roman has never forgiven me for that, either. My dear, a man in my position, to marry a prostitute—it would have ruined me. I did the best I could for them. I just never could be—the father to Roman I wanted to be."

"Is that why you dislike Galapos? Because Roman loves him as a father?"

"Your blade is very sharp, Chataine," he said ruefully. Then, "Perhaps. I searched the whole province for Roman, but found no trace of him. I thought he was dead. Then I came to the palace and, lo and behold, he was in Galapos's care. Roman saw me, too, and hated me. It was years before he would even speak to me. Even so he has never acknowledged me as his father, though I have done what I could for him here."

"You killed the assassin," she said, suddenly remembering. "But why did you lie about it?"

"How would I explain to the Surchatain that I killed the man he most wanted to get his hands on? Should I have said, 'High Lord,

177

he was about to kill my son'? That was not in the least important to him. He cared only to know who was trying to kill his heir and rob his throne!''

"I was beginning to think you were in alliance with Tremaine,'' she said thoughtfully.

"No, Chataine. I know who Tremaine's spies are in the palace, and keep them filled with what knowledge I wish them to have. Speaking of whom—your father has sent for Rollet to come and marry you posthaste. He should be here within three days.'' Their eyes met in understanding.

"Goodbye, Counselor.''

"Goodbye, Chataine. May your guardian find you safe.''

Deirdre was escorted back to her chambers by a palace guard. She listened at the door. There was one guard stationed behind it. No matter—she would never get through the palace unseen anyway. Deirdre slipped Roman's medallion around her neck, then waited quietly through long hours until nightfall.

As always, Nanna attended her at bedtime. The nursemaid, having witnessed the execution, was pale and subdued as she hovered around Deirdre's bed. "There, dear, is that all right? More covers? No? Very well.'' She patted the quilts with a trembling hand. "You know, dear, I remember the night you were born, in this very bed . . . yes, the joy on your mother's face to see you . . . how lovingly she held you and nursed you that night . . .'' The memory clouded the woman's eyes with tears.

But Deirdre stared at her wide-eyed. "Nanna, you always told me my mother died in bearing me—that the physician could not save her—remember?''

The woman started and blanched. "Oh yes, of course—silly old me—''

Deirdre sat up. "How did my mother really die?'' she demanded.

The nursemaid had the appearance of a trapped animal. "She—she fell down the stairs when you were but weeks old.''

"If that is true, then why did you not tell me that? Why did you tell me she died in childbirth?''

"Oh, Chataine!'' Nanna cried. "May you never know the burden I have borne for you!'' She fled the room.

For some minutes Deirdre sat upright in bed breathing hard. She shook her head to clear it and quietly got up. No time to pump Nanna now. Some day, perhaps, if she ever returned. She selected some old, dark riding clothes and dressed with shaky hands. Fastening her cloak with one hand, she opened the window. The ground was at least forty feet below, but there was an ivy-covered trellis that ran from the ground to her window and beyond. She reached for the trellis, thinking, *If Roman could see me doing this, he would be furious.* . . . The thought of him caused a sudden ache in her, but she pushed it aside and swung out of the window on to the trellis. *Careful, now.* Step by step she found footholds and descended closer to the ground.

At one point the trellis ripped partially away from the wall, but she held steady and finally found herself breathless on the ground. Softly she ran to the stables, where Lady Grey whinnied at seeing her. Deirdre saddled and bridled her quickly, remembering ironically how Roman had insisted that one day she might need to know how to do just this. She led the mare toward the rear gate. Hiding in the shadows, she watched for the guard. He was nowhere that she could see. She took a deep breath and made for the gate.

"Halt! and be recognized!" A heavy hand forcefully spun her around, and she was staring up into the stern face of a soldier. "Chataine Deirdre!" He released her and fell back a step.

"Please, please let me go!" she begged. "I am betrothed to only Roman!" *He will not understand that,* she thought. But he blinked once, then deliberately turned his back. Deirdre rode out of the gate at a run. She found the familiar market road in the moonlight and paused. *Where to go? Where to go now? If only I knew the way to the outpost—surely Galapos returned there today. But I dare not risk getting lost in the forest. Hycliff? I know of no one there to hide me. Only one place that remains* . . . Grimly, she spurred her horse toward Ooster, and the home of her Uncle Corneus.

13

Deirdre rode impelled by panic all through the night. Before the distance was half covered, she was trembling with exhaustion, but feared the sinister shadows too much to sleep in the forest. How she wished Roman were with her! As she dismounted to rest Lady Grey, she nearly persuaded herself that any moment he would come galloping around the bend to her. But no—he was not there and would not be coming. She mounted again and urged her horse to a tired gallop.

As the hours wore on, she slipped into a daze, then began to see images of things not there. At one point she was alarmed to spot troops approaching her from ahead. But it was only a clump of trees. Later, she thought she descried Roman riding beyond her in the forest. But it was only a stag.

At length, shaken and weary, she arrived at her uncle's before daybreak. The guards let her in and Corneus came down to see her. . . .

"Deirdre, my dear, whatever has happened?"

"Oh, uncle, help me!" she pleaded. "I have refused Rollet and Tremaine is going to attack us!"

"There, my dear, you are safe here. No need for alarm! I have already conferred with Galapos, and we will fight with him against Tremaine. For now, you must rest." He summoned servants who took her to guest chambers, where she collapsed immediately.

After watching her go upstairs, Corneus turned to his wife, Bedelia. "Have your servants unpack your wedding gown. And summon Jason. She will marry him tomorrow."

Deirdre did not awaken until the following morning. After she had been served breakfast in the sleeping room, a maid brought up clothes to her—specifically, a spectacular wedding gown and veil, heavy with lace and pearls. The Chataine was informed that Surchatain Corneus wished her to wear it. She refused. Shortly, Corneus himself came up to see her.

"My dear," he said, "you cannot be married without a proper gown."

"I am not getting married, uncle," she said uneasily.

"Yes, you are, dear. To Jason, of course. Or shall I simply send you back home?"

"You would not!"

"I would hate to, of course—Jason wants you very much. And the marriage would solidify our two small provinces into one large one. I do not wish to force you, Deirdre, but if you choose to be stubborn, I will." He turned to leave. "Do not delay us, Chataine." Deirdre sat thinking, then rushed to the window. No escape there. There was sixty feet of smooth wall from ground to window. She moved away from it to the washbasin, sighing hopelessly.

Those in the hall below turned to look as she descended the stairs in the magnificent gown. "It is too tight on her," muttered Bedelia.

"My dear, you are a vision!" Corneus praised. He shifted his eyes. "Jason?" The young man stepped forward and took her hands.

"Thank you for accepting me, Deirdre. We will be the greatest rulers the Continent has ever known!" Deirdre looked at Corneus and bit her lip.

"Our carriage awaits!" Corneus said heartily, but Deirdre planted her feet like a mule.

"No. I never ride in a carriage. They make me ill. You must let me ride my mare or I will not go at all."

Bedelia uttered, "You are not riding a horse in that dress!"

"There, Bedelia, we will allow her this—we do not want her becoming ill on the way, do we?" Corneus said consolingly, with a warning look at Deirdre. He addressed a guard: "Have our horses—and the Chataine's mare—dressed out in the finest regalia and sent to the front immediately. With an outfit of soldiers. We want the Chataine well protected." The guard departed in haste.

In minutes Deirdre, Jason, Corneus, Bedelia, and Colin were all mounted and riding up the thoroughfare toward the cathedral of Ooster. On the road, they passed groups of citizens who had heard of the wedding—though Corneus had kept Deirdre's identity a secret—and who had turned out to watch. Many of them crowded close to get a good look at the Chataine, but the soldiers surrounding her kicked them away.

There was one old man they had difficulty with, however—a filthy beggar who was reeling drunkenly in the middle of the road. As the party approached, he brazenly greeted them with fragments of a drunken song: "A man an' 'is luv 'ad a *turrible* spat—"

The party was upon him now, and the soldiers pushed him aside, but he just seemed to bounce from one place to another until he was somehow beside the Chataine's horse. Then instantly he sprang up behind her on Lady Grey and kicked in his heels with a shout. The horse bolted, crashing through the soldiers ahead, trailing fragments of ribbons and bells. The soldiers sprang after them. Deirdre's horse veered crazily onto a side road that led out of Ooster and the race was on.

They came upon a stretch of road that fell away from the shoulders in a steep, grassy embankment. "Get ready to jump," her abductor said in her ear, and she gasped, "Jump?" The grass passing them was a blur. They rounded a curve and he said, "Now!"

They half leaped, half fell down the embankment, and the horse continued on. The man's shock of white hair flew off as they rolled to the bottom, then they scrambled for cover in a nearby grove. Deirdre threw her arms around his neck.

"Not yet," he whispered, and hustled her to a horse tied nearby. They mounted again and plunged into the forest. Riding in front of him, she hugged his arms with joy.

"How did you know where to find me?"

"The soldiers got word to me of your escape," Roman replied. "Then Corneus announced to all and sundry of Jason's marriage. I knew it had to be you." They galloped steadily until they reached the little town of Sittle, where Roman guided the horse straight up to a dingy inn. A weathered sign fixed to the doorpost read "Notary Within." The couple dismounted and found their way to a back room of the inn. There, an elderly man was sleeping behind a portly desk. Roman gently shook him awake. "Old man—we want to be married. Quickly."

"Eh? What? Married?" The notary squinted in disbelief at Deirdre, disheveled in her magnificent gown, and at Roman, disheveled in his beggar's rags. "Are you certain, Lady?" he asked her.

"Yes, yes, and please hurry!"

"Well!" he harumphed, then began searching around for his ledger, and his quill and ink, muttering, "These young people today . . . in such a hurry . . . no sense of decency . . ."

"We do not have much time, old man," Roman reminded him threateningly.

"Everything is here, sonny. Names?"

"Roman of Westford and Deirdre, Chataine of Lystra," answered Roman. The old man looked askance at them but wrote the names in his book.

"Now, Roman of Westford, do you swear to take this woman as your only wife, to provide for her needs and protect her from harm until the day that you die?"

"Yes."

"And Deirdre, Chataine of Lystra, do you swear to accept this man as your husband, to be faithful to him alone until the day that you die?"

"Yes!"

He wrote it all down, then handed them a paper. "That will be two silver pieces," he said. Deirdre and Roman stared at each other. Neither had any money.

"Do you still have the medallion?" Roman asked.

"Yes, but I am not surrendering that. Will you take payment in pearls?" she asked, as she began ripping several out of her dress.

The notary took them eagerly, then began, "Now, would you

two be interested in our best bridal suite . . . ?'' but they were already out of the door.

"Where are we going now?" she sang as he lifted her onto the horse.

"To Outpost One. Galapos is there."

They arrived within a few hours. The soldiers greeted them cheering and whistling, and Galapos himself opened the gate for them. "Chataine!" He hugged her tightly.

As he led them to an inner room of the fortress, Deirdre exulted, "Galapos, we did it—we are married!" She proudly produced the paper as proof.

"Is that so? A celebration then!—" he was just warming up when he caught Roman's eye: "—a little later tonight," he finished, excusing himself from the room with a wink.

Deirdre frowned and turned to Roman, but the question died on her lips when she saw the look on his face. "Deirdre," he whispered, taking her hands. He faltered, kissing her fingertips as he searched for the words. "Deirdre . . . you will never know how I have longed for this day—how I suffered believing it would never be. I swear to you, Deirdre, that I will never again allow you to be parted from me! But you, now that it is done—are there no regrets? Do you truly want me as your husband?"

"Roman! Yes—no—how could I love anyone but you?"

Tears welled up in his eyes. "Come then, my love." He opened his arms and she fell in his crushing embrace.

"Tremaine, I assure you we will find her immediately," Karel said anxiously. "She cannot have gone far, and we have soldiers combing the forests and towns for her."

Tremaine appeared unconvinced. "Two days have passed since she escaped you—time enough to get much farther than you think. Especially with that guardian of hers."

"Roman is dead. He was executed," her father answered.

"What kind of a game are you playing with me, Karel? One of my own scouts spotted him on the border with Galapos on our way here!"

Karel whirled on his Counselor "You said he was dead!"

"He is," Eudymon replied calmly. "Obviously, good Tremaine's soldier was mistaken."

Tremaine narrowed his eyes at them both. "I do not like deceptions, Karel. Your Chataine has disappeared and your Commander has been gathering his army. You will see me again, and I promise you I will not be quite so cordial. Goodbye, Karel. Counselor." Tremaine stalked out, and the Surchatain angrily faced his Counselor.

"What is Galapos doing?"

"High Lord, I gave Galapos the same report I attempted to give you—that Tremaine promised Deirdre to lay waste our province if she did not marry into his alliance. Galapos's actions after receiving that information are his own."

A shadow crossed Karel's face. "I see you are the one playing games, Counselor. Tremaine wants to unite with us, not attack us. We shall find Deirdre and our provinces *will* be united. You are dismissed, Counselor." The Surchatain turned his back, then wheeled: "And I hope, for your sake, that Roman is indeed dead. Dismissed!"

Deirdre and Roman lay very close. She caressed his chest as she listened to his rhythmic breathing. "Roman," she whispered.

"Umm." He stirred and put his arm around her.

"I spoke with your father—at some length."

"Oh, he told you," he said mildly.

"Yes, he told me many things. He really loves you, Roman."

"He was not around when I really needed him."

"But surely he told you that he did not know she had died—"

"He would have known if he had married her," he said tightly.

She paused. "He wants your forgiveness," she said quietly. "He wants you to forgive him." Roman made no reply.

Then came a knock on the door—rather, a pounding. Galapos's voice boomed through the door: "Fall out, soldier! To the dining hall! And bring that hussy you have hidden in that room!"

Deirdre giggled and Roman sat up, reaching for the uniform which lay folded nearby. "I suspect we are in for the celebration he promised," he said grimly.

185

Deirdre picked up the gown off of the floor. "I am so glad this lovely dress was not wasted." She smiled up at him as he dressed.

He glanced at her over his shoulder, then again quickly. "Do not look at me like that, or I will have to disobey my Commander," he murmured.

Deirdre laughed gleefully, falling back on the cot. Then she sat up again. "Oh, Roman—you brought it!" she cried, seeing him don the leather shortcoat.

"It was the one thing I asked them to take from my room."

"Not even your medal?" she exclaimed.

"Not even the medal."

"Then you must take this." She began to remove the medallion from around her neck.

"No," he said quickly, raising a hand. "Please leave it on. I—like the way it looks on you."

When they finally arrived at the dining hall, the soldiers crowding it stood, clapping and cheering. Galapos, at a head table, pretended to awake from a deep slumber and motioned them forward. Then he raised his hands for quiet from the soldiers, who sat expectantly.

"Now lads," Galapos began pompously, "I have invited you all here for a double celebration. All of you already know this man is an outlaw, having escaped the Surchatain's gallows by cunning and deceit—*whose*, I won't say" (a ripple passed through the soldiers). "Well, I wish to formally announce that since this man was not good enough to be hanged, I have selected him as my Second in command." The soldiers stood again, laughing and applauding, and Deirdre threw her arms around Roman.

But Galapos held up his hands again. "Wait—there is more. It seems that this rogue repented of the heinous crime for which he was sentenced, and determined to make amends by marrying the lady. Now fellows—what do you think of a Chataine who would marry a common soldier?" The response of the men was thunderous as they stomped and clapped and shouted. Deirdre hid her blushing face in Roman's shortcoat, and the men laughed harder. Roman hugged her, tears of laughter streaming down his face.

Galapos raised his goblet, and a multitude of goblets came up. "A toast," he declared. "Deirdre and Roman, may your lives be full and joyful together. May you reign over Lystra in peace and prosperity. May you set your firstborn on the throne and know the love of your children's children."

"To the Chataine! To the Second!" the soldiers shouted and drank the goblets down. Deirdre wept openly and Roman drew in shaky breaths. She left him briefly to embrace the Commander. "I love you, Galapos!"

"Fie! You fickle woman!" he chastened amid deafening laughter. She saw his bright blue eyes were very wet.

They feasted on cabbage, beans, bread and ale from the modest store of the outpost's supplies, and received toasts and congratulations from the soldiers far into the night. When they finally returned to bed, she did not know it. Roman carried her in his arms.

When she awakened the following morning, he was gone. She found a note on the small table: "My love. I am with Galapos drawing battle plans. There is a soldier outside your door who will bring you breakfast or whatever you need. Also, when you are ready, he will bring you to me." She smiled. How like him. Stretching, she reached for the dress, then made a face. This was Bedelia's, and she did not want to wear it anymore. Her eyes widened in inspiration, and she sprang to the door, opening it a crack. "Soldier?"

"Chataine." He faced her and saluted.

"Will you kindly bring me a uniform?"

"Chataine, the Second is already dressed and with the Commander—"

"Not for him. For me."

He sputtered, "Chataine—I do not believe we have one that would fit you!"

"Then bring the smallest you can find."

"As you wish, Chataine." He hurried away.

When he returned, he shoved clothes in through the crack of the door to her. "Thank you." She pulled on the trousers and tied them with a rope. The coat was hopelessly large, but the shirt she could wear. She rolled up the sleeves and trouser legs and slipped on her little embroidered shoes to complete the ensemble. She opened the door and the soldier, turning toward her, contorted his face so as not to smile. Deirdre handed him Bedelia's dress. "You may find enough pearls on this to pay for the uniform." He took the dress, sputtering thanks. "Now, please take me to Roman."

In the Commander's room, Roman and Galapos were drawing their plans over a large map. "Our scouts have reported no movement of troops as yet," Galapos was saying, "but it can only be a matter of days. And when Tremaine comes, I expect it will be through Falcon Pass. Going around the Fastnesses would take too much time, and he is an impatient man. Besides which, he does not need stealth. So you and I, my boy, will bear the brunt of the attack. It is likely, however, that Outposts Two and Three will be hit simultaneously by a combination of Tremaine's and Savin's forces. Therefore, we have pulled men from Hycliff to fight there. Now, Corneus's troops should assist Outpost Four in keeping Merce busy—" At that point there was a knock, and Deirdre entered.

Roman raised his face eagerly to her, then coughed to cover a laugh. He kissed her while Galapos concealed a grin behind his hand. "I had expected you to sleep later," Roman murmured, brushing a strand of hair from her face.

"How could I?" she demanded eagerly. "I had to be with you. Good morning, Commander."

"Chataine," he nodded, his eyes twinkling. "Would you like to see our plans for the gaudy?"

"Yes." She moved toward the map.

"As I was saying," Galapos continued, "Corneus's troops will be divided between our outpost, his border defense, and Outpost Four. Now—" There was another knock on the door, and a messenger appeared. "It is from Corneus," Galapos said, and read it silently. Then he bowed his head.

"What is it?" Roman asked uneasily.

"He knows Deirdre is here, and he very much resents your taking her. He says that if you do not send her back straightway, he will withdraw his troops from our defense."

"That's madness!" Roman exploded. "If we are defeated, his province is next. He must know that!"

"Nonetheless, that is his threat. If Deirdre is not sent back to Jason today, he will withhold his soldiers at his own borders. Roman," Galapos's face was somber, "we do not have a prayer without his troops. Tremaine will surround and garrote us."

Roman turned to the window and bowed his head. In the seconds that he was silent, Deirdre stood immobile. "Return her to Jason," he whispered.

"Roman!" she cried in pain and disbelief.

He wheeled to face her. "I will come get you again, Deirdre. I swear it!" But he had just sworn never to leave her at all. The memory of that rash vow closed his eyes. Deirdre, shaking in bitter tears, was led from the room by Corneus's messenger. Galapos came over and put his hand on Roman's shoulder.

"She will be safer there for now, my boy," the Commander said softly. "And when we are done here, we will both go and get her."

Roman pressed his face to the stone and let the tears come.

Deirdre arrived once again at Corneus's gates, this time towed by the messenger. She shuffled up the steps to face a hostile family. Bedelia bristled, "Where is my dress?"

"Torn in shreds, by now," Deirdre answered listlessly.

Corneus took her hand in an iron grip. "We will send another up to your room. Go wash for the ceremony."

"You are too late," she asserted defiantly. "I am already Roman's wife."

Jason croaked, "Your guardian?"

"Yes. Only now he is Galapos's Second."

Jason let out a string of obscenities, but she saw Colin give a little smile of admiration. Corneus slapped Jason's face with his open hand. "Control yourself!" To Deirdre: "Where did you marry?" She would not answer. "Well, as Surchatain of Seir, I invalidate your marriage on the grounds that you were already betrothed to Jason." Deirdre opened her mouth to contradict him, but he commanded, "To your room and ready yourself! We will ride in the carriage to the cathedral. Guard—escort her upstairs!"

The wedding ceremony was private, with only Corneus, Bedelia, and Colin observing as the priest gave Jason and Deirdre their vows. Deirdre refused to repeat them and, when asked if she would take Jason as her husband, she firmly replied, "No." The priest continued the ceremony as if nothing were amiss. The wedding party exited to the cheers of the people gathered outside and returned to the palace.

As soon as she and Jason were alone, Deirdre turned on him and said, "You will not touch me. I am Roman's wife."

"He gave you up to me," Jason replied. "He sent you away. Why should you want to be faithful to him?"

"Because I love him—and I have sworn to."

"He broke his vow to you," Jason observed.

Deirdre's eyes steamed. "No. He has never been false. He will make it good. I know it." Jason uttered a satirical laugh, but let her be.

Deirdre refused to touch the dinner set before her that evening. She could think only of how she might escape back to Roman. Jason was sullen and withdrawn, and Bedelia glared at her with undisguised hatred. Corneus must have seen Deirdre's thoughts, for from that point on she was guarded by two soldiers every moment she was out of her room. Once or twice Jason attempted to gain her favor, but she spurned him so vehemently he soon gave up and left her alone altogether.

The day after Deirdre's departure from the outpost, Galapos received a communiqué from Karel. His brows knitted as he read it. "He wants to know why I believe Tremaine is going to attack us. And he asks whether or not it is true that you are here," he told Roman. "I wonder if someone has exposed our little ruse—in which case I fear for the Counselor. Well. I will refer the Surchatain to his good Counselor for information on Tremaine, and send him a surprised denial concerning you. Is there any message you wish to send to the Counselor?" Roman slowly shook his head. Galapos wrote several lines, then turned to the messenger. "Here is my reply. And you never saw this man here, soldier!"

The messenger saluted. "Yes, Commander!"

For days the defenders at the outposts sat waiting for word of Tremaine's advance. Each day the scouts returned with no sighting of movement. Messengers between outposts carried the same report: no movement. Corneus's scouts also reported no sign of Merce's troops. Corneus's troops, still stationed at his borders, would be sent to the outposts once the assault had begun.

The days stretched into weeks. The tension of waiting in readiness soon began to tell on the soldiers. Quarrels became common and fights erupted repeatedly. Roman was doubly affected by the waiting, for he had no way of knowing Deirdre's state. Corneus absolutely prohibited messages between them. Supplies, too, had to be constantly renewed, for the outposts never knew when their supply lines would be shut off by the attack.

At the palace Westford, each day that passed with no hint of a threat from Tremaine helped to confirm the Surchatain's suspicions that Eudymon was working against him. Therefore, Karel assigned a spy to monitor the Counselor's movements and intercept his messages. The Surchatain even began to suspect Eudymon of assisting in Deirdre's disappearance. There had been not a word of her anywhere.

And how Nanna suffered because of it! She had cried for days after the Chataine's escape. She had accosted every returning soldier for news of her whereabouts. As weeks passed with no word, she slipped into the meaningless compulsion of continually straightening Deirdre's rooms and brushing out her clothes. "She will want to wear this when she returns," she would say to herself. Or, "How she loves that doll! I will clean it up and put it on her bed for her."

And Nanna cursed herself for failing to tell the Chataine what Regina had made her promise to tell. She had told Roman—but he was dead. Then the old nurse began to reason, "She loved him. She loved Roman. But her father had him killed, and that is why she ran away. The Surchatain killed the man my little girl loved . . ." And she began to brood over other knowledge she had never made known . . . dark memories which came to haunt her each day the Chataine was gone.

The weeks of waiting stretched into months. Deirdre remained a prisoner in Corneus's palace. Corneus and Colin had ridden out to the border to watch for Tremaine, but Jason stayed behind to run the affairs of the state and act as Deirdre's husband.

She, meanwhile, roamed the palace, always accompanied by soldiers. Looking over the empty halls, she remembered her betrothal fest, just months before . . . how she and Roman had danced . . . the memories of him kept her steady.

She still had his medallion, and for the first time she studied it closely. It was engraved only on one side. There were words she did not understand—*ecce homo.* And there was a drawing of a man wearing a spiked wreath. This was the Christ, she assumed. *Christ, can you help him now?* she thought. He had sworn to return for her. He was always as good as his word. He *would* come for her—if he could.

At this point another thought presented itself to her. Roman had once said something about how he believed he had a heavenly guardian who protected him. Could that be true? Could such a guardian defend him from Tremaine and all his army? Roman had even hinted that she, too, had a guardian . . . but that was impossible. She was not a believer as he was. Deirdre despairingly rejected the whole line of thought.

Wandering into the library, she looked over rows and rows of pompous leather volumes. They were mostly books on philosophy, on the nature of the universe and the nature of man. Books on trade and atlases of trade routes. Books with detailed drawings of great buildings on the Continent. Books that taught geometry and languages and law. "Are there no books that will teach me to endure being a prisoner?" she moaned. "God, if you are there, give me some help. Give me a reason to live through this." She turned from the shelves and looked up through the window at a piece of purple sky. She moved to stand at the window. The setting sun streaked the sky with colored fire. How she loved the sky. How she wished to soar into that beckoning expanse . .

Her eye was attracted by movement, and she looked down on servants working below. A farrier was beating out a horseshoe on an anvil. The clang, clang of his hammer rang up to her window. A goatherd led his flock toward their pen for the night, rapping the feed bucket and calling their names. Two girls hurried in with bushels from the early harvest. She felt something stir within. *So close to life, how can I give up?*

There was a rustle at her back and the guard with her said,

"Chataine, you are summoned downstairs for dinner." She straightened and silently followed him out.

Over time, Deirdre began to suspect, then be certain of, a change in herself. She was pregnant. But this knowledge which should have made her sing for joy only brought her dread. Jason would know it was not his child, and how he would react she could not guess. So she kept it to herself as long as she could. . . .

At the outpost, the months of waiting finally wore the men's fighting edge to bluntness. Roman sat in the dining hall, watching without seeing as a group of soldiers rolled the dice. He was thinking of Deirdre—always thinking of Deirdre. He relived every moment of their one night together. Those eyes looking to him . . . the feel of her lips, her skin . . .

He inhaled and sat back. He must not allow those memories. It would madden him to think of her, not having her now, not knowing if he would ever see her again. He set himself again to cleaning his sword, which already shone brightly. The soldiers nearby roared at a lucky toss. Another soldier passed by with parchment and charcoal in hand. Noting Roman's sword and buckler, he made a notation on his paper. "What are you doing?" asked Roman.

"Taking stock of our weapons for the Commander, sir," he replied.

"Pilar has already done that," Roman said testily. "Besides which, these are my personal arms. They do not go in the armory."

"Only doing what the Commander ordered."

"It is a waste of time."

"Well, sir, how do you suggest I spend all this time?" the soldier asked in sarcasm.

Aggravated, Roman stood, but one of the men playing dice suddenly shouted, "Cheat! These dice are shaved!" He grabbed a fellow by the throat and began shaking him. Several others fell on him at once.

Roman threw himself in their midst, tearing them apart and ordering, "Stop! Now!" They desisted, glaring, and Roman swore. "Will you kill each other before Tremaine has the chance?"

The first cursed and spat, "Where is this ghost Tremaine? What makes you so sure he is going to attack us? I say somebody should tell him we're holed up waiting for him so he'll know to come!"

There was a moment of tense silence, and then Galapos's voice behind them all said, "Good thought, Dero. Will you carry the invitation to him?" Dero reddened and mumbled something. Galapos continued, "Have faith, my boy. I promise he'll not disappoint us. Meanwhile, I suggest that you and your fellows should check to see that all the horses have been reshod. We won't have time for it later."

"Commander." Dero saluted and the soldiers filed out quietly, each saluting him.

"To my chambers, Roman," Galapos requested.

As they walked the narrow corridors, Roman pressed, "Galapos—what is he waiting for?"

"Well, he is either playing the waiting game with us, or—heaven forbid—building up his own troops. Either way, each day that passes wears us down further," Galapos replied, opening the door.

"Then why do we not attack first?"

"We cannot, my boy, not yet. Our troops are too spread out and we do not know yet where his concentration is. We have to wait until our scouts can locate his troops—or until he shows his hand."

"Do you still believe he will come through Falcon Pass?"

"Yes. When he does move, he'll waste no time." The Commander paused to close the door behind them. "Roman, I am a realist. I believe in facing the truth. The odds are against us . . . you realize we may not finish out our days as old men dreaming by the fire." Roman stared into the empty grate.

At that moment a messenger came from the Surchatain with a routine inquiry as to conditions at the border. Galapos wrote out a reply, then asked, "Roman, do you have any message for the Counselor?" Roman still stood gazing at the fireplace. "Roman?"

"Tell him . . . tell him I forgive him."

The message was written. Galapos handed two letters to the messenger. "This is for the Surchatain. And this one is for the Counselor's eyes only. Understood?"

"Yes, Commander." The messenger saluted and departed.

Roman turned. "Galapos, I have something to tell you. About Deirdre." The Commander cocked his head, listening. Roman took a deep breath. "She is not the Surchatain's daughter. She is yours."

Galapos stood motionless. "You are sure of this?"

"Yes," Roman sighed. "Her nursemaid told me that Regina confessed it on her deathbed."

"But—how could she know for certain?"

"It seems that Karel knew you two had been lovers, so when he married her he held off lying with her to be certain she was not pregnant. . . . But she *was* pregnant . . . and Deirdre was the child."

Galapos covered his face with one hand. "All these years, he knew and I did not. All these years, what was Deirdre to him?" He suddenly raised his face. "Does she know?"

"No." Roman's whole body drooped.

"She will, my boy, when we go after her. Call your troops together, Roman; we are going to drill. These men are getting fat and lazy."

That hour scouts returned with the word: Tremaine's troops were moving through Falcon Pass.

14

With definite word that Tremaine was on the move, Galapos agreed to attack. Informed by scouts that the Selecans had made camp for the night on the outpost side of the Pass, he made plans for his men to ride out before daybreak and strike while the enemy were sleeping. He sent a messenger to Corneus advising him of Tremaine's advance and requesting troops to aid them in the assault. Then they waited for the hour to leave the outpost. . . .

A scout roused Roman from uneasy sleep. "The Commander summons," he whispered. Roman sat up immediately, reaching for his shirt. He strapped on a stiff leather jerkin and belted his sword on his hip. He fastened on leather shin guards and arm guards, then pulled a helmet down over his forehead. He took up a buckler, pausing. *I need to pray. I haven't time. Lord, spare my life today.* He hastened out to meet Galapos.

The Commander was overseeing the organization of the troops in the deep blue darkness of a night half gone. Seeing Roman, he stopped in midsentence to address him: "No armor, my boy?" He himself was dressed in mail.

"No Galapos. I found I am a better fighter without all that weight."

"You had better be, then." He continued his instructions, and Roman watched two thousand men gather silently into units. When all was ready, Galapos gave the command to move.

After only a short ride they could see the watchfires of the invading Selecan army burning in the distance. Now came a critical phase of the attack. Roman and five other soldiers dismounted; they had to quietly dispose of the sentry guards to insure surprise—the only element they had in their favor. The six soldiers split up and crept silently across the plain, watching for the guards.

Roman spotted his target shortly. He inched up closer and closer, freezing when the man turned his way. Then he sprang from the darkness and silenced the guard with a blow. He continued on—there would be more sentries. But as he crept ever nearer to the campfires, no more guards came into sight. That disturbed him. Finally he was almost on top of their camp—still no more guards. Troubled, he made his way back to his troops and reported to Galapos. As the other scouts returned, they gave the same report of few or no sentries. Galapos nodded grimly. He spread his troops to form a half moon facing the enemy's encampment, and then they waited for the arrival of Corneus's troops.

And they waited. The time to attack came upon them, and still there was no sign of Corneus. "What do we do?" whispered Roman. "Return and wait for him?"

"No," Galapos replied. "We no longer have the luxury of waiting. We are on our own, my boy." With that, and without Corneus, Galapos gave the signal and his men attacked in a thunderous rush.

It was a total surprise. Hundreds of the Selecans were slain before they could even roll out of their blankets. Galapos's soldiers took full advantage of the surprise, tossing the enemy's weapons in watchfires and scattering their horses. Roman and Galapos spearheaded the attack together, driving their horses straight into a sleeping company. Galapos charged toward the officers' tents, and Roman scattered the campfires onto blanketed forms. An alarm sounded, and in seconds the invading forces came full to and responded to the attack.

At first, it appeared that Galapos might drive Tremaine's army back. Disjointed and uncoordinated, they were cut down as they fumbled to form ranks or find their weapons. Galapos's men responded eagerly to the easy kill. Soon, they were deeply advanced in the midst of the camp, fighting with flaming intensity.

Roman fought from his horse as long as he could, but when he was pulled down he held on to his sword and fought on foot. He cut into one man and then felt a stinging slash at his back. Wheeling, he answered it and dodged an attack from his side. He had not a second to pause in the battle. The instant he struck down one man, two appeared in his place—they seemed to spring up from the earth.

The battle intensified as the sun rose to their right. Roman leaped on a soldier about to spear Galapos. They rolled in the dust until Roman gained the advantage and plunged down his sword. At that moment he felt a crashing pain on the back of his head and he collapsed in the dirt.

He came to only a few moments later. Mercifully, he had been left for dead and the fighting had roared beyond him. Dizzy, he lay still for a moment to gain his bearings, then rose unsteadily to his knees and looked around. His stomach knotted at what he saw. Instead of his troops pushing the enemy back to the Pass, they were being absorbed into the middle of the Selecan ranks. They were fighting enemy troops at their front *and* rear. Roman steeled himself and seized a nearby sword to rejoin the battle.

But then he saw something else that froze his heart. Through the Pass appeared a regiment on horseback—more of Tremaine's troops. Roman watched in mounting horror as they came and came and still came out of the Pass—thousands more men riding furiously toward the battle. He shouted hoarsely, gesturing wildly toward the advancing troops.

Galapos spun to see the approaching legion and shouted retreat. Those of his men who were still mounted wheeled and spurred toward the rear. Others on foot sprang for riderless horses or doubled up with their fellow soldiers.

At once they found their retreat blocked by lines of Tremaine's soldiers. The Lystrans faltered in confusion and panic. Galapos shouted, "Drive! Drive!" and the men spurred fiercely, crashing right into the lines. This maneuver opened holes for their escape, but lost them many men.

Behind on foot, Roman yanked a Selecan from his saddle and swung up, then pulled a wounded fellow Lystran up behind him. He charged through a fast-closing hole just as Tremaine's fresh troops joined the lines.

The men rode back to the outpost as if the devil himself were giving chase—they slowed only to pick up their fellows on foot. As the last man slid safely into the fortress, the heavy gates crashed shut behind them.

That morning, as Deirdre dressed, she found she could no longer fasten her bodice. So she left it open and covered herself with a shawl, then studied the reflection in the looking glass. There was no hiding it any longer.

At breakfast Surchataine Bedelia observed, "My, you dress very sloppily as of late, Deirdre. Why would that be?" Her eyes pierced like knives. When Deirdre did not reply, the Surchataine commanded, "Open your shawl." She did not. Bedelia motioned to the guard.

"That is not necessary," Deirdre said hastily. "I am pregnant."

"Not by me," Jason said coolly.

"No. By my husband," Deirdre shot back.

The Surchataine gestured vigorously. "Your presence is an affront to me," she hissed at Deirdre. "You will remain in your room from now on out of my sight. Guards!" Deirdre was escorted back to her room, where she collapsed in a chair. It was so difficult to endure this imprisonment and hatred—and now she was further confined. *At least I will not have to face her again.*

But moments later Bedelia entered, her hands behind her back. Deirdre looked up, surprised. "You think now that you are pregnant, it will assure you a place in my husband's favor," Bedelia said. "Not so! For we do not need you at all anymore." Deirdre started to say she was not interested in a place under Corneus, but the Surchataine cut her off. "It may interest you to know of a little agreement Corneus has made with Tremaine as of late. My husband has agreed to fight with him instead, and he in turn will leave our province alone—even give us Lystra. We need only pay him taxes."

"You are a fool if you think Tremaine will stop with gathering taxes," Deirdre replied. She had learned much from her conversation with Caspar.

"You!" Bedelia hissed. "What have you done but spit on my son and try to usurp my place?"

Deirdre eyed her with interest. "Let me go, then. Let me go die with my husband and I will no longer be a threat to you."

Bedelia smiled, and her eyes glittered strangely. "Yes, I will do that. I will release you from the agony of waiting for Tremaine to come cut your heart out. I will do that!" And Bedelia raised the dagger she had held behind her back.

The Chataine leaped aside with a cry as the Surchataine rushed toward her. Bedelia hacked at the air, then spun on Deirdre, who grabbed her hand and wrenched the knife from her fingers. It clattered to the floor. Bedelia fell on her knees to retrieve it with both hands. Deirdre kicked her to the ground from behind, and waited breathlessly for her to rise and attack again.

She did not. She lay still on the floor. Cautiously, Deirdre rolled her over and saw the dagger plunged to the hilt in the Surchataine's midriff. Deirdre drew back in horror as Jason, alerted by the sounds of the struggle, entered with the two guards. He saw his mother on the floor and turned his dark eyes on Deirdre.

"You murdered her."

"No!" she gasped. "She attacked me—and we struggled—she fell on the knife—"

"I am not interested in how it happened," he said. "Nor do I care enough to kill you for it. Father will, though. It will be interesting to see what he does with you when he returns." He motioned to the guards, who lifted Bedelia's body to carry it out. He stopped them long enough to retrieve the dagger and throw it to Deirdre's feet. Then he left.

Deirdre fell across the bed, holding her stomach. "Roman," she moaned, "can you really come for me? Are you even alive now? Or will it be Tremaine after all? I cannot bear the waiting, not knowing, not knowing . . ." Then she remembered the curse the witch had placed on him, and she gave herself up to sobbing despair.

Roman surveyed his battered troops. Of the two thousand who had marched out that morning, seven hundred had returned. Of those, only six hundred could still stand and hold a sword. Roman himself had suffered injury enough to warrant withdrawal from the fighting, but he knew he would have no choice but to fight again. He looked over the wall toward the enemy. They had encircled the fortress two hundred yards out, and just sat—waiting, it seemed.

A soldier called him to Galapos. Roman found him standing over the large map, but not looking at it. His arm was wrapped in bandages and he limped as he moved toward Roman. "I am afraid, my boy, I have seriously underestimated Tremaine. I understand now why he kept us waiting so long and then posted so few guards at the camp. He was baiting us to come out and fight, so he would not have to waste time sieging the outpost. And like a fool, I rushed to his waiting arms. He has men to waste—thousands more than I had guessed. I have let you down rather badly, Roman."

"What happened to Corneus?" Roman's head was burning.

"I do not know. I suspect we have been betrayed."

Shortly afterward, a soldier arrived at the outpost, wounded and exhausted. He was taken immediately to Galapos. "Soldier! Where are you from?" he cried, seeing the insignia of Lystra.

"Outpost Two, Commander," the man panted.

"How did you get through Tremaine's lines?" Roman asked, giving him water.

"They did not hinder me. They let me come straight through."

The Commander asked quietly, "What news do you have?"

"Outpost Two has fallen, Commander," the soldier choked out. "We were attacked at daybreak, and held them off a good long while, but they brought in ramming equipment and fresh soldiers every hour—thousands, Commander! We were surrounded and overcome."

"How did you escape?" Galapos asked.

"I did not," he replied. "They spared me alone to come tell you of our defeat."

Galapos sighed and dismissed the soldier to rest. "Tremaine is not content merely to kill us. He wishes to torment us first. You'd best go get what rest you can, Roman. Tomorrow promises sufficient activity."

Roman turned to the door. He opened it to another Lystran messenger outside, poised to knock. This one carried a letter. Roman waited while Galapos read. Then the Commander sat down. "It is worse than I feared. This is an urgent summons for reinforcements from Outpost Four. Captain Basner reports that they were attacked at daybreak by an army of Merce's—and Corneus's—troops." Roman sucked in his breath and swore.

Galapos continued, "We are finished, Roman. We will make our last stand at Tremaine's convenience. Go rest now, my son, and pray if you have anything left in you." Roman numbly turned again to leave. "Roman." Galapos had one more thought. "You have been a good and faithful soldier. I have been proud to fight with you."

Roman stumbled from the room and found his way to his quarters. He put his hands on the rough bed. He and Deirdre had slept here together—was it years ago? *Deirdre! Chataine!*

He sank to his knees beside the bed and the words came rushing out: "Oh God! You have been with me all my life—protecting me, I know, enabling me, guarding me—why have you left me to die like this?" He steadied himself and went on: "I have done my best to serve you and be faithful. But now I do not understand what purpose you have in allowing Tremaine to slay us all and rule the Continent. He is evil and does not regard you, Lord—he cares only for his power. Christ Jesus! If I have found any favor with you, if only because of your goodness and mercy, for the sake of your name, save us from Tremaine! And oh, my God," he moaned, "protect my Chataine, as I have failed her in my vow." Then, wracked with pain and exhaustion, he fell on his bed and slept.

The Surchatain Karel summoned the Counselor to his chambers. "Well, Counselor, any word from the border? Still no sign of Tremaine's supposed attack, eh?"

The Counselor bowed. "Not yet, High Lord."

"Well, there is a message from Galapos that you seemed to have missed," the Surchatain went on brightly. "Shall I read it to you?" The Counselor was silent. "It says, 'R. sends his forgiveness.' Now Counselor, what do you make of that? Who could this 'R' be? Not Roman, surely, Counselor?" Karel was smiling fiercely.

"Of course not, High Lord," smiled Eudymon. "It is a soldier under Galapos—Rollo—from whom I mistakenly withheld pay. I sent it to him recently with my apologies. He was merely acknowledging my note."

"You are a clever liar, Counselor," said the Surchatain through gritted teeth. "But when I saw this, I did some inquiring on my own." He whirled. "Guard!" A nervous-looking Arin appeared from behind a curtain. "Tell the good Counselor what you have told me."

"Well, High Lord, at Roman's execution. . . . I saw that when they took him to the scaffold, they—they switched him with another man and the soldiers crowded in and hid him. Someone else was hanged in his place."

"Well, Counselor?" Karel cried triumphantly.

"You had better thank the powers that be that he is on the border with Galapos, because you are going to need every man alive when Tremaine strikes," answered Eudymon.

"You have deceived and betrayed me!"

"Deceived you, yes, but not betrayed you, High Lord. Your daughter is alive today because of my son."

"Your son?"

"Yes, my son. Roman is my son."

"Then you did help her! Where is she?" The Surchatain was white with fury.

"I do not know, High Lord, but I earnestly hope they are together."

"Where is she?" Karel screamed. Beyond control, he grabbed the Counselor's throat and shook him. "Where is she? Where is she?"

The Counselor could not have answered if he had tried. Karel squeezed tighter and tighter, until Eudymon stopped struggling and dropped lifeless to the floor.

Shaking, the Surchatain stepped back and wiped his brow, then called the guards to carry the body out. He followed them into the corridor toward the stairway.

Nanna met them at the head of the stairs. "What—?" she gasped as she saw the Counselor's body. Then her eyes filled with rage and she turned on the Surchatain. "You! You murderer! You were a murderer from the beginning! First Regina, and then Roman, and now your own Counselor!'' Karel stopped dead and gazed at her. "Oh yes," she laughed, "you thought no one knew. Well I knew! I saw you push her in anger—I saw her scream and fall. You are a murderer!'' With a scream she fell on him. The guards stood by and watched as they tumbled down the long stone stairway together.

The following morning at the outpost, Galapos evaluated their situation and called his soldiers together. "Men, Outposts Two and Four have fallen and we have had no word from Outpost Three. It seems our backs are to the wall, and I see no escape for us. But if you will lend me your swords one last time, we will give Tremaine nightmares of his last battle with Lystra. Are you with me?" The soldiers shouted at once and raised their weapons. "Very well, then," he continued, "attend to your wounds and rest up. We will answer when he charges."

So the men readied themselves and waited, but the charge did not come that day. The Selecan encampment could be clearly seen day and night just out of bowshot, but Tremaine's troops merely held themselves there and waited.

A messenger arrived on the day following, grey-faced and trembling. He fell breathless before Galapos and said, "Commander, Westford has fallen. The Surchatain is dead." Having given that message, he died. Galapos hung his head in despair. Roman stood like stone. At that instant they heard a trumpet blast outside. Tremaine had ridden up in armor close to the gates.

"Men of Lystra," he shouted. "You have heard by now that your Surchatain has fallen. I am your new ruler, and I am willing to give you your lives in exchange for a small present. Send out to me the heads of your Commander and his Second, and I will allow the rest of you to live in peace under my rule. I await your response!" He spurred his horse and rode back to the lines.

Galapos and Roman looked out over their ranks. The men seemed stunned at first. Then one by one they raised their faces toward the Commander's tower and shouted, "Hail, Commander! Hail, Second!" Roman breathed out relief and gratitude.

Then the waiting began once again. More of Tremaine's troops arrived continually at the lines, presumably fresh from victories at

204

the other outposts and Westford. Corneus's troops also appeared. Corneus himself rode up before the gates and shouted, "Galapos, my boy, how are you doing? Tell Roman his Chataine was safely married to Jason before she could waste herself grieving as a widow!" On hearing, Roman pounded his fists on the stone, then leaned on it and closed his eyes.

"I had her once," he murmured. "It was enough. I pray that Tremaine spares her."

One day followed on another, and the men at the outpost numbly waited. Each day Tremaine rode out and shouted, "Men of Lystra, have you an answer for me?" Each day the soldiers were quiet. Little by little, however, rumblings began among the men.

"Why shouldn't we live?" one man said.

"Have we pledged them our lives?" another asked. They were hushed up, but soon more and more began to grumble.

One week passed, and then two. Then one dawn Roman found Galapos staring in puzzlement out the tower window at the sea of soldiers surrounding them. "What is happening?" Roman asked.

Galapos knit his brows. "I don't know what he is doing. Giving some soldiers a rest, I suppose. He has drawn many of them away from the siege lines."

Roman nodded absently. "Why have twenty thousand to do what five thousand could do? . . . How long can we hold out, Galapos?"

"Longer than Tremaine's patience, my boy."

In that moment Tremaine rode up to again demand an answer. But today he shouted, "Men of Lystra, I am getting impatient. If you do not answer me today, we will attack and spare no one!" Some of the men looked around. A few even began shouting. But no one laid hands on Galapos or Roman.

At dusk, Roman said, "We should ride out to him. The men will not betray us. If we can spare their lives, we must."

Galapos shook his head. "It would gain us nothing. I know Tremaine's treachery—he will kill them all regardless."

None of the men slept that night, waiting for the morning. With the first weak light of dawn, the defenders gave mute farewells to each other and readied themselves for the last battle. A heavy fog which had rolled in during the night obscured the enemy lines around the fortress. But as Roman peered into the dense whiteness, he saw a shape slowly emerge from the mist. His last vestige of stubborn hope trickled away as he watched a battering ram being slowly positioned in front of the gates. It crashed once, twice, then on the third blow the gates buckled and men swarmed in.

"To the front!" cried Galapos. And the small band of defenders rose to the charge.

But something was unaccountably odd. Tremaine's soldiers seemed to be moving too slowly in their attack. Roman rushed on a soldier to fight. But the man stared at him blankly, then fell in a dead faint. Bewildered, Roman rushed to the next man. He fell before Roman could lift his sword. Incredulous, he spun around. Once they had penetrated the gates, the attackers seemed utterly spent. Galapos's men cut them down effortlessly, then looked to the shattered gates for the next onslaught.

It did not come. The men looked uncertainly to Galapos. "Another ruse to draw us out," he muttered.

"If it is, what of it?" cried Roman. "Will they not slay us eventually? Charge out!" he shouted. The defenders poured from the broken gates and halted in astonishment at the scene.

The fog was blowing away in wisps to reveal a deserted plain. Horses were standing idle, and the ground was littered with the prostrate bodies of a thousand or so men. "What the—" muttered Galapos.

Roman raised his eyes and saw makeshift tents afar off. He ran to a horse, calling the men after him. They pounded to attack the encampment.

They reached the lines and leaped from their horses, braced for battle. But not a soul answered. Roman stared across rows and rows of soldiers, thousands of them, lying on the ground. Some were in tents, but most by far were unsheltered. Most were dead; the remainder on the threshold. "This place looks like a damn infirmary," whispered a soldier at Roman's side.

Roman began shuffling through the rows while his men stood rooted in bewilderment. As far as could be seen, the bodies were laid out in death throes. Tremaine's whole army, reduced to nothing. The battle was won before they ever had a chance to make their last stand. He shook his head. It was impossible. It was inexplicable. Then he saw a water pot.

206

Not by might, nor by power, but by my Spirit. He gasped in the sudden realization of what had happened and fell to his knees, clutching the water pot. "God, you have done this! You answered my prayer and fought for us! Lord God, my strength and my Redeemer!" He was shouting and crying at once.

That seemed to awaken the men, and they leaped on each other, whooping and shouting. Galapos seized Roman's shoulders and hugged him till he gasped. Then the Commander cried, "But what *happened* to them?"

"This," said Roman, handing him the water pot.

"It is a water pot," said Galapos mildly.

"It is one of the villager's water pots," corrected Roman. "Tremaine's men must have been drawing water from the Village Branch ever since the fall of Westford." Galapos looked blank. "The disease, the villagers' disease!" said Roman. "God used it to answer my prayer."

Galapos stared. "What did you pray?"

"For God to save us from Tremaine!" Roman exclaimed. Galapos stood pondering the unthinkable. "Did your cunning save us, Galapos? Did my skill, or the courage of our men, deliver us from Tremaine?" The men gathered around them, listening. "God heard my prayer and sent this plague in answer. You may choose to ignore Him, as Tremaine did, but I will acknowledge this as deliverance!"

Their eyes locked, and Galapos's suddenly twinkled. "Your God is a mighty warrior, my boy." Roman smiled. His heart was still pounding with the thrill of the gift given him.

Word of Roman's prayer and the water pot spread like a blaze through the troops, and the soldiers who knew hymns began singing as they picked through the battlefield. Some others sang slightly altered versions of drinking songs.

Then someone shouted, "Hail Surchatain Galapos! Long live the Surchatain!" Others picked up the chant strongly.

But Galapos raised his hands for silence. "We must find Tremaine and Corneus first." Everyone began searching through the bodies, but only Galapos or Roman knew the fallen leaders by sight.

Roman, scanning the myriad of dead and dying, murmured, "Galapos . . . I will never again call another mortal High Lord—not even you. That title belongs to Another."

"Nor will I allow anyone to call me that," answered Galapos. "Dare I parade myself as a lord before such a God as yours?"

Then Roman startled in remembrance. "Deirdre! Galapos, we must go get her!"

"We will as soon as we are able. Send a messenger to her immediately."

Roman grabbed a soldier. "Ride to Ooster—find the Chataine Deirdre—tell her God has given us victory, and Galapos is the new Surchatain. Tell her we are coming for her very soon, and ward her till we arrive! Go!" The messenger bounded on a horse and galloped off. However, when he arrived in Ooster, he was intercepted by two of Corneus's men. They heard his message, then murdered him. They repeated his news to Jason at the palace.

At first he would not believe it. But one of the soldiers said, "Chatain, neither did we. So we checked at the sentry on the border, and he told us the Surchatain's last message was of a terrible plague among the soldiers. That report was sent two days ago. There has been no word since."

"Then Father too is dead!" he seethed, strangling on impotent fury. Then he added, "There is one last thing I can do for her."

He went to Deirdre's room and found her sitting by the window. She turned to face him. "I have news of the battle that may interest you," he said. "Roman and Galapos are dead. Tremaine is the victor and he is coming to kill you." Then he left her alone. Unseen by her, he went to the pinnacle of the palace and leaped to his death.

Deirdre sat immobile by the window. *It is over,* she thought. *He is dead, and I am soon to die.* "I will not permit Tremaine the satisfaction," she said, standing. She took Bedelia's dagger and raised it. As she did, a strong resistance rose in her. "What is the use?" she cried, shaking it off. "What hope is there?"

You have no hope because you have no faith.

Stunned, she held the knife in midair.

It was then that I opened her eyes to see me, and know that she was not alone. Her face blanched and she fell to the floor.

Roman searched feverishly through the fallen ranks, anxious to ride to Deirdre. He and Galapos looked through the tents first, assuming that the leaders' rank would assure them the most protection. But they were not there. They searched the front of the lines, but they were not there. Roman faced the sea of dead in exasperation. "Where are they?" Then a sickening thought struck him: "Oh Lord—has Tremaine escaped?"

He heard a soldier shout from the very rear of the ranks. "Commander! Second! We may have found something here!" Roman and Galapos ran over to meet him standing over a group of bodies.

Roman turned one face up. "It is Corneus. But Galapos—he has been run through!" The Surchatain's coat was split and bloodied.

Galapos turned up another. "Why, this is Savin—and he also has been slain by the sword."

Roman turned up the third. "This one also. But I do not know him."

Galapos looked. "That is Merce." They searched each other's eyes, trying to formulate an explanation. At the same time, they concluded, "Tremaine." Galapos growled, "He must have gathered all the troops here for his grand finale—he always had a weakness for overkill. But these three did not reckon the finale he had planned for them."

"Commander!" another soldier shouted. Roman and Galapos sprinted to his side. He pointed to a body lying prostrate among the soldiers. But this body wore a splendid golden robe.

"It is Tremaine," confirmed Roman. He stooped to touch him. "He is quite dead."

"Kam." Galapos turned to a soldier close by. "You head up the salvage and pyre. Roman, shall we be gone . . . ?" But his Second was already riding west. Galapos caught him on the road and they pounded to Ooster.

Arriving at the palace, they found it deserted and still. "Deirdre! Deirdre!" Roman called, but there was no answer. "I do not like this," he said fearfully. "Where is the messenger?" They split up and began a room-to-room search for the Chataine.

Roman prayed feverishly as he pounced from one empty room to the next: *Oh my God, after all this—would you take her from me now? Have mercy, Lord, she is yet unredeemed!* He threw open the door to her room and his heart stopped to see her sitting very still on the floor, facing the window. "Deirdre!" he rushed to her and lifted her bodily off the floor.

"Roman." She dropped the dagger and held his neck, holding him so tightly he almost choked.

"Are you well, Chataine?" Then he felt her protruding belly and his eyes took on a gleam. "Are you . . . ?"

"Yes," she whispered, "I have kept my vow to you, also." She suddenly searched his face. "Jason told me you were dead, and that Tremaine was coming to kill me! I—I was going to take my life . . . but he prevented me."

"Jason?" he frowned. "Where is he?"

"No, not Jason . . . someone else. I do not know who he was, but he just appeared—shining, clothed in white . . ." she trailed off and he studied her anxiously, fearing for her mind. "Roman, I believe you now," she said calmly. "I believe your story about the Christ. I want you to teach me in the faith." He gazed at her, and she added, "I love you so."

He kissed her deeply because he could not speak. Then as the tears ran down his rough face, he whispered, "I love you, Deirdre." They just held each other tightly for a few moments. Then he wiped his face and coughed. "I have been weeping like a woman ever since we got married."

"Oh," she said through her tears, "I have something of yours." She took off the medallion and hung it around his neck. "What do the words mean?"

"They say, 'Behold the Man.' "

"The Christ?"

"Yes."

For a moment she took in every line on Roman's precious face—every flaw, every scar, the broad nose, the scratchy beard, the deep brown eyes. "I have been seeing Him for years, and never knew it—His face in your face, His voice in your words. . . . It is true that He is living in you, isn't it?" He nodded. "I want to be like that, Roman. I want to be like you." He smiled, trembling a little.

"I have learned something else," she continued. "There is a great battle raging which I only wanted to avoid. But I found I could not, any more than I could avoid a war with Tremaine. I found I would be either victor or captive. . . . But tell me what happened at the outpost! How did you defeat Tremaine? And—" her voice lowered, "is there word of my father?"

"I am well, my dear," said Galapos as he entered the room. "And look here!" He drew up in joyful surprise. "My first grandchild will arrive soon! What more could I ask?" Deirdre frowned and smiled at the same time.

"Chataine," said Roman, grinning, "meet your father the Surchatain."

They continued at length with many questions and explanations and many embraces and tears, but for my purposes, this report on the charge you gave me is concluded. I am Penuel, guardian angel of Deirdre of Lystra, and I close for now, O Lord of Hosts.

(The story continues in *Stone of Help.*)

About the author:

ROBIN HARDY, a former editor of Christian books, sees *The Chataine's Guardian* as a parable of what God has been doing in her own and her family's lives. "When we had managed to work ourselves into a hopeless little corner, we sent up some feeble prayers which He answered in such a marvelous way as to leave us dumbfounded. After a series of these experiences, enlightened by Bible study, I learned that God is there, that He cares, and that He takes our prayers seriously. And as Paul says, He goes beyond them to do more than we ask or even think. His imagination for goodness toward us is unlimited. The book was a vehicle to communicate these things—besides being just a little bit fun!"

Robin now lives in Durant, Oklahoma with her husband, Steve, and daughter, Stephanie Ruth. She describes her life as "one of shameless pleasure—I spend my time doing just exactly what I want to do: playing with Stephanie and teaching her, gardening, sewing, reading, and writing (a sequel to *The Chataine's Guardian* is on its way)." She and Steve also team-teach a Sunday school class for young couples at the First Baptist Church in Durant.